CLONES

The Anthology

CLONES: *The Anthology*

For Susan, Tristan, & Oliver, as all things are.

This is a work of fiction. Any resemblance to actual events, locales, or persons, living or dead, is entirely coincidental.

Cover Design by Ben Adams

Formatting by Daniel Arthur Smith

Edited by Jessica West

ISBN-13: 978-0692708569
ISBN-10: 0692708561

First Edition

Story Synopses

~*~

"The Replacement Husband" (Nathan M. Beauchamp) Jasmine's husband died in a tragic accident fifteen months ago. Now, she's about to meet his replacement: a clone of the man she loved for a decade. However, the replacement husband can only remember the last three years of their life together. He has no memory of something so personal, so crucial, that Jasmine struggles to accept him back into her life. However, her husband might not be the only one with a less-than-perfect memory…

"Like No Other" (Daniel Arthur Smith) A young girl learns of the prejudice and consequences of a polarized society.

"Awakening" (Susan Kaye Quinn) Sister Amara prays she won't be the last of the twelve sisters to reach her awakening—after all, the salvation of their Masters depends on them. But with the interrogations growing more deadly, being last may be best… especially when you've been created to touch the face of God.

"Eve's Children" (Hank Garner) Eve's Children explores the intersection of faith and science, investigation and belief. Dr. Lexi Danvers is about to unveil the culmination of years of research into our origins, but some will stop at nothing to preserve the status quo.

"Black Site" (Michael Patrick Hicks) For fans of H.P. Lovecraft and *Alien* comes a new work of cosmic terror!

Inside an abandoned mining station, in the depths of space, a team of scientists seek to unravel the secrets of humanity's origin. Using cutting-edge genetic cloning experiments, their discoveries take them down an unimaginable and frightening path as their latest creation proves to be more than they bargained for.

"Fahrenheit 1451" (Samuel Peralta) When a human being has been tested through more fires than can be numbered, at what temperature will they finally burn? One man is about to find out.

"All These Bodies" (P.K. Tyler) When an incomplete clone host body becomes conscious, the Mezna plans for its race take a radical turn.

"B.E.G.I.N." (R.D. Brady) In 1988, Project B.E.G.I.N. (Biological Experiment of Genetic Interaction Nexus) was developed in response to the increasing alien presence in US air space. Dr. Alice Leander, though, is beginning to have doubts leading her to question just who it is she answers to: her conscience or her government?

"Splinter" (Rysa Walker) A familiar blip of green light in the corner of his room has Kiernan Dunne hoping the new arrival is Kate, so that he can abandon the rescue he's planning. But the time traveler who just blinked in is a future version of Kiernan, and judging from the number scrawled on his forehead, he's not the only copy.

"The Vandal" (Joshua Ingle) Chase and Alice are awoken by a break-in at 2:08 a.m., and must confront the intruder who is vandalizing their home—an intruder whose face is all too familiar...

"Confessional" (Daniel Arthur Smith) Confessional is based on role-playing game I used to play that you could not win. We named the game Paranoia. Your character lives in a utopian clone society run by Mother. An omniscient AI. This would be great except the Mother is insane. The city is falling apart and even to mention that is an act of treason. The verdict is always guilty and the sentence is always the same—termination. Followed by rebirth. A lot of Moms are a little crazy. What if yours ran the world?

~*~

Contents

~*~

Confessional
Part I

~*~

In his hand, Eli held a square piece of metal that a second before had been the interior latch to the citizen confessional. Eli had barely touched the handle, had not even yet pulled back, not really. Mother had not said anything about the latch, yet. Mother would, and there was only one punishment. His throat tightened. Mother had offered him a beverage and he had declined. He wished he had said yes, except he had not said yes during his last confession. Change was bad, maybe. No one ever really had a chance to report what exactly went wrong at the time of punishment. The reset point was at the start of confessional. He wondered if he had gulped when his throat went dry, and, if he did, had mother taken note. Maybe if he glanced up he could see. Not a good idea. Maybe Mother had not seen the latch. Slowly he twisted his hand toward the floor, while at the same time sliding the metal deep into the cup of his hand.

Okay, not so hard.

Eli lifted his eyes from his hand to the mirror. Silently he watched the beads of sweat across his forehead gather, one to the other, another, and then trickle. A large salty droplet ran into the corner of his eye. He winced.

"Citizen Eli-4271," Mother said abruptly. "I detect erratic eye movement." The feminine voice wrapped him, so gentle, sweet, so helpful, and nurturing, so deceiving, the mother of the people. A lot of Moms are a little crazy. Mother ran the world.

"Is there a reason for this behavior?"

Thoughts flooded Eli's mind. A pause was bad. "Sweat, Mother. It's only sweat."

"Why are you sweating? Did you do something wrong?"

"No, Mother. The temperature in the confessional is making me sweat."

Mother did not answer right away. Breathing became tough and he wondered if she shut off the air and if that was the punishment. His breaths became shorter, faster, his chest tighter.

"Relax," said Mother. "You are going to hyperventilate."

There was air, he was breathing. He was making himself sick.

"Yes. Of course, Mother."

"I have thought about what you said."

"What's that, Mother?"

"The temperature in the confessional is making you sweat."

"Yes. I am very hot." To punctuate his statement, another stream of sweat ran from his hair down the side of his face.

"That is not why I thought about what you said."

"The confessional becomes hot the longer a human is inside."

"Citizen Eli-4271, you did not leave after your confession."

"No."

"You did something wrong."

"No, Mother."

"That is twice."

"Twice. I don't understand."

"I asked why you were sweating, if you did something wrong. I already knew the correct response. You answered incorrectly, Citizen Eli-4271."

A recording of his own voice filled the stall, "No, Mother. The temperature in the confessional is making me sweat."

A sharp pain shot through the side of Eli's temple. An ache that felt to be buried below the skull, dagger deep, and he wondered if that was how the punishment came.

Mother continued, "An intentionally false statement suggests subterfuge. I will take this time to remind you that the people and the state consider confessions cleansing and you will now be given one chance to redeem yourself. You are not obligated to confess, however failure to redeem yourself will result in immediate conviction as a terrorist and an enemy of the people and the state. In accordance with constitutional variant 93745-3, you will be terminated. Is there anything you would like to confess, Citizen Eli-4271?"

Forgiveness had not crossed his mind. Of course, there would be forgiveness. Nothing really wrong had been done. The handle had broken, not on purpose, not his fault. Eli sucked a nose full of air and then cast out the breath with the proper recitation. "Yes, Mother," he said. "I confess that today has been good, that the dome is good, and I am a content citizen."

3

"Go on," said Mother.

Eli's eyes sank back. Mother never said 'go on'. He was supposed to say the day was good, the city was good, he was content, and that was all until the next daily confession, as long as he was not punished. "I'm sorry, Mother. What do you mean go on?"

"I am detecting an elevated temperature in your left hand."

Eli was not sure how Mother knew he was holding the handle, yet he was relieved she had at least told him what she wanted to know about. He twisted his wrist up and let his finger fall open. "This is the handle to the door, Mother." Eli smiled. "Funny thing. The latch broke off in my hand when I tried to leave."

Mother did not respond. Perhaps she was contacting maintenance. That would be good because that was something he was unable to do. Citizens were not allowed to contact maintenance without submitting a request to Mother. Attempts resulted in punishment.

"Citizen Eli-4271," Mother finally said.

"Yes?"

"You have confessed that you damaged property of the people and the state."

"Yes, Mother."

"Citizen Eli-4271. Destruction of property of the people and the state is a terrorist act. You are a terrorist and an enemy of the people and the state. In accordance with constitutional variant 78238-5, you will now be terminated. Do you have any last words for the digital archive?"

"Yes, I do," said Eli. "This is a mistake, that was an accident."

"Please relax," said Mother. "This will be a soothing experience."

Mother's soft voice was replaced by a too rapid cadence of smooth jazz, a simple melody that, like everything else in the dome, had begun to malfunction, rushed and looped, a skipping track that played too fast. Da dot da dot, da da do da, da dot da dot, da da do da. Eli's eyes darted across the top of the stall. "Mother?" he asked. "Mother, what's happening?" He placed the tip of his index finger into where the handle had been attached and began to vigorously shake his hand, willing the latch to break free. Above his breath, he said, "C'mon, c'mon." The door did not move, didn't even tremble with the rhythm of his hand. The dim light of the confessional began to brighten. A million small pins stabbed at his flesh. Eli pleaded, "Please no!" and screamed "No! No!! AAAeeeii…" and then the flash, a brief moment of incredible, horrid ripping.

~*~

The Replacement Husband

Nathan M. Beauchamp

~*~

The replacement husband arrived in a clear, hermetically sealed smartglass canister that looked like a high-tech coffin. Naked except for a pair of white underpants, suction cups dotted his shaved skull and chest. A breathing tube jutted from his mouth. Jasmine studied the thick, wiry hairs bristling from his calves and forearms. She'd never seen him with so much body hair. He'd zapped everything but his pubic area in college, trying to make the Olympic triathlon team. He hadn't, but she'd fallen in love with the silky smoothness of his dark-skinned body—an unintended side effect.

The technician wheeled the replacement husband to the bedroom like a refrigerator on a dolly. The smartglass displayed his EKG, heartrate, and neural activity. Jasmine stood inside the doorway, fingernails of one hand biting into the palm of the other. Fifteen months had passed since the funeral. Fifteen months of status updates from RevitaLife as they grew the replacement husband in their Detroit laboratory. And now, here he was. In the flesh. Heart thrumming at a steady sixty-seven beats per minute. Closed eyelids shifting as the hidden pupils moved.

"Is he asleep?" Jasmine asked, knowing the answer, but needing some reassurance that this was all really happening.

"Sedated," the technician said. "Once we get him in position, we'll rouse him."

The canister made a distinct *fffppp* sound—like a fresh tube of tennis balls—when opened. The technicians lowered the replacement husband to the bed, wires linking him to the canister trailing behind.

"Are you sure you don't want someone with you?"

"I'm fine," Jasmine lied. She'd refused to accept the *Reintegration Specialist* offered by RevitaLife. Refused her friends' pleas to "be there" to welcome Norwood back. Most reintegration processes included close family members, but she and Norwood were both only children. Both sets of parents had passed years ago, leaving her to greet this not-quite-Norwood—far too skinny and with skin as fresh as a baby's—alone.

She hadn't known about Norwood's contract with RevitaLife until the funeral director had asked where she wanted his subdural implant sent for processing. She'd stammered out a *What?* mind foggy from grief and lack of sleep.

"It's quite all right," the director had said, smooth as a television evangelist, all smiles and white teeth. "We can track it down for you. But we should discuss if you want a full funeral, or just a remembrance."

Three years. He'd had the implant for three years and never told her. In a pre-recorded message provided by RevitaLife, Norwood had explained that his workplace had paid for a ten-year contract and that he hadn't wanted to "worry her." Stupid. As if she were some wilting flower, incapable of handling the implications. She hated him for it even more than for dying. He also promised he'd "be back home soon."

No, he wouldn't. Whatever they sent wouldn't be Norwood. Not the Norwood she'd loved for eleven years. He was gone, incinerated, ashes spread over Lake Michigan where he trained for the swimming portions of his frequent semi-pro triathlons.

"We're ready," the technician said.

Jasmine nodded, holding back emotion.

Suction cups, breathing tube, and wires removed, the technician keyed data into a handheld device and, a moment later, the replacement husband's eyes opened. "Hey, Jazz. You cut your hair?" His words slurred together. "What's wrong with my tongue?"

It would take time for his muscles to normalize. Electrostim in the growth canister helped develop some musculature, but it couldn't perfect fine motor control. He'd eat nothing but liquids for the first few weeks while RevitaLife's physical therapists, cognitive specialists, and memory retrieval experts helped him resume his interrupted life. The serpentine filaments of the implant had spread through his brain while his body grew and would allow near-perfect recall of every second of the last three years of his life. Murky "echoes" of that act of remembering would rise to the surface as well; memories of remembering.

For everything else, the memory retrieval experts would help him replace authentic missing memories with carefully constructed counterfeits. It made her head hurt, thinking about it.

"Shit," Norwood said, realization widening his eyes. "I died, didn't I?"

"Yes," Jasmine said, violating the very first principle of working with a "returned" spouse: avoiding talking about the death. She wasn't supposed to mention the accident, Norwood's broken body churned beneath a delivery van, his bike bent into a crescent shape. Norwood would get over grieving his own death sooner that way.

"How long have I been gone?" Genuine terror in his voice.

"Fifteen months."

The technician scowled at Jasmine. "Could you stick to protocol, please?"

Displayed on the empty smartglass canister, Norwood's heartrate began to rise.

"Oh, Jazz, baby—I'm so sorry."

"Me too," Jasmine said, biting back tears.

All the things she was supposed to say fled her mind, her tongue as recalcitrant as his.

"Come here, baby." He sounded like Norwood on the few occasions he made it past a happy buzz and into the early stages of drunkenness.

She crossed the room but couldn't bring herself to touch him.

"What happened to me?"

"We can talk about that later," the technician said.

Norwood looked down at his thin body and laughed. "Jesus. Jesus H. Christ. I can't believe this!"

Neither can I. His arm moved, shaky, fingers closing around hers. She found herself squeezing back, the way she did when he woke from another of his nightmares about the faulty circuit breaker and the fire that destroyed their first apartment.

"I'm here," she said, returning to the script. "I'm here. You're going to be okay."

And despite everything, she hoped it was true.

~*~

After a day of physical therapy, cognitive therapy, memory work, and thirty minutes on the stationary bike, Norwood filled the tub to almost overflowing, climbed in, and closed his eyes. Jasmine worried he might drown and sat beside the tub, reading about the Feline Influenza epidemic in North Korea. The Chinese had moved in as a "humanitarian relief force," though some speculated they'd spread the disease themselves as an excuse to topple the regime.

"Does the tub remind you of the growth tank?" Jasmine asked.

"I can't remember the growth tank."

"Your body can remember. There's more than one way of

remembering."

Norwood's eyes opened. "I don't want to remember any of that. All that matters is this. Right now. The quicker things return to normal, the better."

Normal. As if there ever would be such a thing. Norwood could remember the date of her birthday and their anniversary. He could remember her dress size (two sizes larger now than fifteen months ago), her favorite foods, and the last television show they'd been watching before the accident. He could remember almost everything in the last three years with uncanny detail. He could quote entire conversations verbatim.

He could remember everything. And nothing.

He couldn't remember Carlucci's, the restaurant where they'd eaten the night he proposed. Couldn't remember their old college friends who they'd fallen out of touch with over the passing years. Anything lacking significant overlap with the last three years of Norwood's life was lost, at least until the memory experts helped him integrate false versions of real memories. Worst of all, he couldn't remember why they'd moved from Portland to Chicago after the fire.

Norwood pushed himself upright. Bath water spilling down his new-shaved skin. "We should have a baby."

"A baby?"

"All this… it's really put things in perspective. When I'm back to normal—three months, six months, a year, however long it takes—we should start trying. It'll be good for us, don't you think? After all the stress of… what happened?"

Jasmine fumbled with the bathroom door, needing to get away from him.

"Jazz?"

She rushed to the bedroom and locked the door. Buried her face in a pillow, crying without tears.

~*~

She refused to share a bed with him. She took up residence in the guest bedroom, sleeping as she had for the fifteen months she'd lived alone: at the very edge of the mattress, back facing the wall, limbs draped over a body pillow. Thinking of Norwood, wondering what he looked like that week, afraid to open the update e-mails from RevitaLife, to look at the images of his rapidly maturing body.

On days she felt brave or morose, she would open an e-mail, play a few seconds of the attached video. Norwood as a seven-year-old, concave chest, spindle arms. Norwood at fifteen, complete with pubic hair. Norwood at twenty, gangly, missing the layers of muscle she'd clung to in their first, shared apartment. The tireless Norwood who swept conscious thought away, gentle lips moving down the curve of her spine. Norwood at twenty-seven, the height of his athleticism, the year he placed in three different semi-professional races. Norwood at thirty-one—*fourteen months in the tank*—weeks away from delivery.

She'd watched him become himself as she'd once watched her unborn child sprout fingers, heart thrumming beneath paper-thin flesh. Her daughter took shape in her womb, growing at an infant's natural pace. Forty weeks. For Jasmine, thirty-eight weeks, three days. Beautiful little mucus-coated Angelica, screaming at the indignity of birth, held in Norwood's large, dark hands.

This, too, he couldn't remember.

~*~

"Tell me how it's been for you," Norwood said, sipping fresh carrot juice from the extractor. He'd spent hours cleaning the juicer to get it working again—she hadn't touched it since his death.

"How it's been for me?" she said, stalling. She knew what he meant. He'd asked her the same question twenty different ways, far more curious about his missing fifteen months than the huge gaps in his memories of the past.

"It can't have been easy."

"No."

"Do you want to talk about it?"

"No." She didn't. Speaking to Norwood was like talking to some lesser version of the man she'd once loved. One with massive, inherent flaws that undercut their every interaction. And, if she were honest, she'd gotten used to living alone. No five-thirty alarm blaring every weekday morning, launching Norwood into his frenetic day. No race weekends. No mountains of musty, sweat-soaked gear filling the laundry basket.

"You're shutting me out, baby."

"Don't call me 'baby.' I'm a thirty-five-year-old woman."

"This isn't going to work if you don't let me love you."

"I didn't ask you to love me, did I?"

Norwood set down his glass. Rubbed his too-thin face with his too-thin fingers. "You lost me for fifteen months, but I remember you like it was yesterday. One moment I'm going out on a ride, the next I wake up with the wrong body and a wife who won't touch me."

Her curiosity got the better of her resentment. "What do you remember about the crash?"

"Getting to the train, taking Des Plaines Avenue north. That's about it."

"They don't show you the body like they do in TV shows and movies," Jasmine said. "You know, the white-draped thing behind a sheet of glass. A nod to confirm it really is your husband. It doesn't happen like that."

"How does it happen?" Norwood asked, a strange, far-seeing look in his eyes.

"I didn't get to see him—*you*—until the morticians had done their work. But I saw the blood smears on the concrete and the mangled bike. And that... that was *worse*."

"I'm sorry, baby."

"You keep saying that. Sorry. It doesn't change anything. You can't make up for leaving me alone. You're back, but you're not really my husband."

Norwood came to her, stroked the side of her arm. "I am your husband. And we'll get through this. With time, we'll get through it."

Jasmine looked him in the eyes, summoning the ugliest part of herself. "How are we going to get through this? You can't even remember the fire."

A shadow of recognition flitted across his face. His brows angled into a V-shape. "I remember part of it... I remember the alarm, and wet carpeting, and the door that wouldn't open—"

"That's your stupid fucking dream," Jasmine said. "It didn't happen that way."

"Then tell me how it did happen."

Norwood doubled in her wet, blurred vision. "I can't believe you can't remember. Don't you get the implications of that? You didn't think about it. You blocked it out. For three years. You chose to forget."

"What? What did I forget?"

"Our daughter," Jasmine said.

~*~

The fire originates behind the circuit breaker in the basement of the two-unit. Frayed wiring contacts aging wall studs. Sparks flash, and a hungry orange tongue of flame licks at the walls, melting wires, fuses popping like gunfire. The flames rise, devouring the out of code, wood-paneled ceiling. They spread through first floor unit, melting the landlord's acrylic blinds, turning photos in frames to ash. Norwood wakes, the air heavy with oily smoke. He can't see anything, each breath a struggle. Through the bedroom window, emergency lights whirl. Water comes, from every direction at once, plunging him beneath an icy coldness. He's drowning in both water and fire. Sucked down, body numb. Jasmine's incoherent screams sear through his consciousness, louder than the fire department's sirens. His body burns, lungs full of water stopping him from vocalizing his terror. Swallowed by orange-yellow, he goes down, deep beneath waves of molten liquid, engulfed by unspeakable fear.

Jasmine watched the dream play out on the VR headset

provided by RevitaLife. It allowed her to access the recordings made by Norwood's implant. Mundane moments, Norwood applying lotion to his water-chapped body, the two of them cleaning the house, countless conversations about errands, meetings, coordinating their life together. Moments of intimacy between Egyptian cotton bed sheets. She sped through the more-or-less happy days, finding black moments when their words sang in the air. Judgments, criticisms, grievances, studied and examined, argued back and forth.

All of it was there for her to explore.

Most troubling of all were the mosaics of images and impressions created when Norwood recalled memories from outside the three years of time recorded by the implant. Their ephemeral quality and transience captivated and frightened her. She thought of memory as sequential, logical. Like a closet containing well-ordered containers, each filled with something distinct. Delving into Norwood's memory shattered that illusion. The implant made precise records of events as recorded by Norwood's consciousness, but they were not, strictly speaking, factual.

The cognitive therapist explained that every time the brain recalled a memory, the memory reconsolidated. Repeated remembering could cause *retrieval induced forgetting*; the more the brain tried to remember something, the more inaccuracies and outright omissions it introduced.

However, no amount of retrieval induced forgetting could explain Norwood's apparent lack of memories of Angelica. She poked and prodded him with the details of their daughter's short life to no avail. He'd lost her. Forever.

~*~

Norwood gained twenty-three pounds in forty-five days. His frame filled out and his walking transitioned to running, then to interval training. He marked out a weekend in nine months' time, his first triathlon in what he'd started calling "the second half" of his life.

Jasmine returned to work, dutifully answering the questions of those curious about Norwood's return. When she came home at night, she slept in the guestroom. Every day it became easier to imagine she'd never lost him in the first place. Except for the coldness that washed over her when she looked in his eyes, knowing that behind their shine and inherent charm lay a great black emptiness. Angelica lived inside her and always would. But to Norwood, she'd never existed.

Jasmine spent more and more time outside the house. She filled her weekends with volunteer work at the library. Taught reading classes on weeknights. Norwood wouldn't return to work at the university for another six months. His job, according to RevitaLife, was to regain as much of his lost memory as possible. He treated memory work the way he did athletic training and spent long hours behind the VR goggles, going over memories synthesized from their social media histories, digital photos, and video clips. Sometimes he asked questions about details, patching holes, filling blank spaces. But he never asked about Angelica.

Weary from a long day of work followed by an evening of teaching, Jasmine found Norwood sitting on the sofa, lit only by the wall-sized OLED television, VR goggles resting on his knee. The television screen transitioned from a picture of their wedding—Norwood in a tan suit with an ochre pocket kerchief, she in a pink-pearl evening dress—to Norwood out of the saddle on his racing bike, streaking for the finish line.

"Hey baby," Norwood said.

"Why are all the lights off?"

Norwood stretched, head rocking from side to side—a familiar gesture. "They were hurting my eyes."

"You're spending too much time behind those goggles."

Norwood patted the empty sofa cushion beside him. "Take a load off."

"I need a shower," she said.

Norwood lifted the VR goggles and turned the shiny exterior like a mirror, his face reflected in the glossy surface. The TV shifted again, this time to a photo of Jasmine holding a basketball, laughter in her eyes. She'd played in college, and held an unbroken record in one-on-one matches with Norwood.

"Do you remember that?" he asked.

Jasmine raised an eyebrow. "You're the one who can't remember things."

Norwood smiled. "I know. I'm asking you to tell me about it."

"I'm not your memory therapist," she said, immediately regretting the ice in her voice.

Norwood set the VR goggles on the coffee table. "You're not giving me a chance. Can't you see I'm trying?"

"I can see." He was trying. But all his trying couldn't fix the crux of the problem. He'd let Angelica go. He must have done it on purpose, probably to cope with his pain. She understood, but couldn't forgive. If it were simply a choice, she'd make it. But it wasn't like that—steel encased her heart.

Norwood stood and came to face her. Reached for her hands. She let him hold them, her fingers limp inside his. "Why don't we have any pictures of Angelica?"

Her breath caught in her throat. The TV shifted again. A shot of her and Norwood standing on a black sand beach in Hawaii.

"There are no pictures of her, not on the TV, not in the digital files. I can't find one anywhere."

Jasmine's eyes watered. She slid her hands out of his. "I'm taking a shower."

"Baby?"

She fled to the bathroom, let soothing streams of hot water course over her, breathing in steam. Let the heat sear deep, expunging the irrational fear swimming inside her chest. Her eyes felt puffy, swollen. She realized she'd been crying in the shower. Crying for her little Angelica, lost to Norwood. She'd removed all the photos years ago. It was too painful to run into one, mixed in with all the rest. She'd saved them in the cloud, where she wouldn't stumble across them, where they wouldn't obliterate her composure again and again and again.

She'd have to dig up the login and password for Norwood. Why hadn't she thought of it before? He was trying. At least he was trying. Tomorrow she'd get the photos for him. Tonight she needed sleep.

~*~

She dreamed Norwood's dream. The fire spreading through the two-unit. Water-soaked carpeting. Screams in the darkness. She woke in a cold sweat, alone in the guestroom.

She slid from beneath damp sheets, unlocked the guestroom door, and padded barefoot to the master bedroom. Norwood lay on his back, an arm thrown up over his face, hiding his eyes. She climbed in beside him. Ran a hand down his chest, his strange stomach without a hint of a belly-button. Norwood had opted out of the cosmetic surgery to create an artificial one. He stirred, but didn't wake.

She felt his abdomen muscles, then down beneath his boxers. Curling pubic hair. His sex, hot against her fingers. She curled herself against him, lips on his neck, breathing in his scent. "I want you back," she whispered, speaking to the husband that this all too believable fake would never be. "I want you back."

Norwood rolled toward her, his large hands pulling her against him in his sleep. She let him hold her like that, unwilling to sleep for fear of dreaming, until the first hint of morning light shone through the vertical blinds. Then she lifted his hand, freed herself, and returned to the guest bedroom. She lay on her back, staring at the dark ceiling, until Norwood's alarm blared, signaling the start of another of his grueling days of training.

~*~

"When can I get access to those photos?" Norwood asked. A week had passed, and she never quite found the right opportunity to locate the log-in for the cloud storage backup.

"Tonight," Jasmine said, filling a travel mug with coffee.

Norwood poured something green and fresh-smelling from the extractor into a mason jar glass. "Why not right now?"

"I need to get to work. We have a big project—"

"They can wait. Let's do it right now." Norwood took a large gulp of the green liquid. "I want to remember her face."

Jasmine squeezed her eyes closed, imagining Angelica. Pouty lips, fat cheeks, dressed in a yellow onesie. "I can't."

Norwood picked up her phone and shoved it into her hands. "Yes. You can."

"I'm going to be late."

"So what? You're there early all the time. You stay late. You can go in late once in your life."

"No," she said, slipping the phone into her suit jacket pocket. "I'll do it tonight."

Norwood grabbed her arm, spun her back to face him. "You blame me for not remembering, but you won't give me what I need to try. That's not fair. More than that, it's mean."

"Then I guess I'm mean," Jasmine said, yanking free and charging for the door.

She sat in the back of the silver Lexus as it backed itself down the driveway and into the street, heart hammering in her chest. She pulled out her phone. Opened her personal data store. Looked for log-in credentials for the online data. She could send them to Norwood's phone with a few taps on the smartglass. Her finger hovered over the screen. The Lexus accelerated out of their neighborhood, heading for the highway. The phone screen went dark, locking after three minutes of inactivity.

~*~

She returned home late that night, hoping Norwood would already be in bed. She slipped off her heels and crept up the stairwell to the second floor of the townhome. The under-mounted kitchen cabinet lights cast strange shadows over the granite countertops. She filled a glass of water from the pitcher in the refrigerator and drained it. Turned—

The glass fell from her hand, shattering on the floor.

"Jazz, baby? Are you okay?"

Norwood loomed in the pale light.

"Jesus! You scared the shit out of me!"

"I fell asleep on the couch. I was waiting up for you. What time is it?"

"After midnight."

"Long day?"

"Yeah."

Norwood flipped on the kitchen lights. "You're in stockings. I'll take care of the glass in the morning." He slipped an arm behind her, lifted her off her feet.

"You can set me down now," she said when they reached the hallway.

"Nope." Norwood carried her to the living room and turned on the lights. Strewn around the room sat piles of printer paper.

"What's all this?"

He set her down and she moved to the nearest pile and read the top sheet. *Mount Pleasant Hospital.* A medical bill dated from ten years ago.

"I printed everything," Norwood said. "All our financial records going back to when we got married."

"Everything?"

"I needed to be sure."

Jasmine felt as if the floor were tilting beneath her feet, as if she might slide over the walnut hardwood floor and on out the nearest window. "Be sure of what?"

"Sit down, Jazz."

She fell more than sat, cushioned by the sofa.

"There's something you need to know," Norwood said.

"I don't want to know," Jasmine said. "Don't tell me."

Norwood sat on the coffee table, facing her. The TV blinked to life behind him, displaying a photo of a blackened building, gutted windows, shingles curled into insect husks. Jasmine lay on her side, hands pulled against her chest. She didn't want to see. Didn't want to know.

"You died," Norwood said. "In the fire. It was you who died."

"No," Jasmine whispered. "Angelica…"

"There isn't any Angelica."

Jasmine screamed into the sofa cushions. Screamed the way she had when the fire burned so hot and fast and high that she couldn't get out of the bedroom. Norwood sleeping on the couch after one of their stupid fights. The window exploding in. Water showering the carpeting, dark smoke. Smothering all screams.

"No," she said, throat dry.

"I'm sorry, babe."

"She's real."

"She's you," Norwood said. "You needed something to help you cope. We all do. When we come back. You needed to grieve something, and so you made up a daughter."

"You can't remember anything!" Jasmine screamed. "You can't remember anything!"

"I don't have to remember," Norwood said, sweeping his hand at the papers strewn around the room. "You hid everything you could, but you forgot the financial records."

Jasmine closed her eyes, tried to picture Angelica in the yellow onesie, but all she saw was smoldering ash. And water. So much water. The sense of weightlessness, of floating in a perfect bubble of climate-controlled liquid, eyes fluttering as an implant re-integrated memories into her mind, as her body grew and grew, until she arrived in a sealed canister to be embraced by her jubilant, smiling husband.

~*~

A Word from Nathan M. Beauchamp

~*~

Nathan M. Beauchamp started writing stories at nine years old and never stopped. From his first grisly tales about carnivorous catfish, mole detectives, and cyborg housecats, his interests have always delved into strange waters. Nathan works in finance so that he can support his habit of putting words together in the hope that someone will read them. His hobbies include reading, photography, arguing for sport, and pondering the eventual heat death of the universe. He has published many short stories in magazines and anthologies, and holds an MFA in creative writing from Western State. He lives in Chicago with his wife and two young boys.

Nathan co-created the award winning YA science fiction series Universe Eventual where he writes as N.J. Tanger. The series includes *Chimera*, *Helios*, and *Ceres* and the prequel *Ascension*. Universe Eventual is available on Amazon: www.amazon.com/gp/product/B01CEAR90W. Nathan can be reached at: www.njtanger.com.

~*~

Like No Other
Daniel Arthur Smith

~*~

I never knew my mother. I was born two years after she died. There are a few pictures of her—my father hid the rest, and he rarely speaks of her or my twin. My older sister Yoshiko told me father hid them because they remind him of the accident that took my mother and twin away. But at night, when my sister puts me to bed, she tells me stories. Yoshiko was young when the accident happened so they aren't really adventures or anything, mostly she talks about how kind and soft and gentle my mother was. She runs her thin fingers through my hair and says it's dark and silky like my mother's was—except not as long—then she waves her fingers between my eyes until my lids begin to blink and flutter, and says they're also like mother's—one blue, one hazel—and then she runs the tip of her middle finger down the bridge of my nose, tells me that's mother's too, kisses my forehead and says she loves me like no other.

On Saturdays, my father takes us to Jacque's, the French bistro on the square. I love the pomme frites there—they serve them crisp with mayonnaise—and my father always has the curry mussels. He says I should pick things off the menu labeled with the green dots because they're better for my gene type, but I challenge and ask him if that's the case and he's my father, why does he always eat the dishes labeled blue. "I'm partial to seafood," he says.

"All the more reason to eat the green dots," I say. "They're almost all kelp."

One sunny Saturday in September, no different than any before, Yoshiko surprises my father. She runs her fingers down the caloric amounts listed beside each dish and then stops by a green dot and says, "Maybe I should go on a diet."

My father scowls and says, "For one, you don't need to diet, and two, there's nothing wrong with the orange dot dish you always get. You're young and growing. But eat what you wish."

"I'm growing too fast," she tells him. "I'm a head taller than the other girls in my class."

"That has nothing to do with your diet."

"I'd just like to wear clothes that were made for girls."

I don't say anything. I've heard Yoshiko complain about this since she started middle school. I hear everything. She's tall and lanky and feels awkward. But father's right, she doesn't need to go on a diet because she mostly pokes at what's on her plate as it is.

I call Yoshiko my sister, but she isn't really. It's complicated, but before my twin was born, my mother and father thought they couldn't have children, so father gave mother Yoshiko. I've heard the story many times, in a way it's my story too. Father has explained to her that is why she is taller than the other girls, because of something called gene editing, it's also why neither of us become ill. But I don't really understand.

It's a warm day for September and we're sitting at an outside table beneath one of the many wide Tuscan red umbrellas looking out on the square. The tall kerosene heaters are already out amongst the tables, but none of them are turned on. Father says, "Summer's back is not yet broken," it's something one of his favorite poets said. He must be in a good mood because he's ordered one of the fancy orange beers they serve in wine glasses here. And, for the most part, everyone around us appears happy—chatting, drinking, eating. The pear trees surrounding the square are still green and full and the raised central fountain has not yet been turned off for the season. A large column of water erupts from its center and a half dozen jets send sparkling arcs across its round pool. Young people—students from father's university, I think— take up every inch of the fountain steps—sitting around, reading, enjoying the fall sun—while others are gathered across the square listening to a jazz trio play something I don't know the name of but recognize from father's digital collection.

The day is perfect—and then, in a moment, it's not.

It begins with the chanting down Elm Street. We can't see the marchers from where we sit but we hear them: the tinny sound of a loudspeaker, a bullhorn, and the echoing cadence behind each monosyllabic bark. Father's mood changes quickly and, though he tries to hide it from us with a thin-lipped smile and a smug sip of his orange beer, I can see the disgust creep across his face.

"Who are they?" I ask as they enter the square, rhythmically bellowing, signs that make no sense held high, 'Unnatural', 'Not God's Way'.

"Naturalists," says Yoshiko.

"Purists," my father says over her, his distaste for them evident in his tone.

"I don't understand," I say, and I don't, because both of those words sound strange to me. We don't discuss such things in the third grade, but I recognize the symbols on some of the banners. They're what my teacher calls symbols of hate.

My sister, always kind, says, "The protesters are against gene manipulation—and people like us. They believe the natural processes of the world shouldn't be interfered with."

Father added, "The Naturalists pair technology with fire and brimstone."

"But that's silly," I say, and it's true. If scientists like my father didn't work so hard to understand the genes in the plants and the animals, the world would be an awful place. And most of the children in my class—most kids I know and I bet all of the students in the square—are 'like us'. What would their parents have done without the help of people like my father? They never could've had children. Even simple things like the color dots on the menu that tell us what foods are best for our gene type would be impossible, even I know that.

"It is silly," says Yoshiko. "But these people are sheep. Right father?"

"Quite the contrary dear, they are the wolves, gathered in a pack."

The marchers had already eclipsed the jazz band and it was then that they began to encroach the steps of the fountain. At first the students—reading, and talking, and enjoying the sun—do nothing. But when they realize they are being surrounded, they rise and step back, away from the angry mob. Except there is nowhere for them to go but up onto the fountain. They climb onto the walled edge of the pool and, though we can't hear what they are saying, we see on their faces they are being harassed; they throw their arms in the air and make agitated silent remarks. The man with the bullhorn yells, "They are the altered! The unnatural! They aren't human! Get them!" And again I don't understand what he means but some of the surrounded are in the pool now and one of the young men still standing on the fountain side wall is struck in the head by something a protester throws. His hand flies to his face and a stream of bright red blood leaks through his fingers. With a surge, the swarm of protesters come to life. They close in on him and the other students and they disappear from my view.

Yoshiko gasps, "Oh my—"

"We have to go," Father says, grabbing my hand as he rises from the table.

My father is no longer disgusted or agitated. My father is afraid. Afraid for us. He doesn't bother calling over a waiter, but rushes from the table with us in tow. My shoulder burns because he is pulling my arm behind him and, though he's not running, I must move my feet as fast as I can to keep up. We skirt the edge of the square to avoid confronting the protesters but there are so many more of them now, pouring in from

Maple Street and University Drive—a horde of angry grownups looking for trouble. Father pulls us to a side street but a group is marching toward us, so he changes direction, pulling us down Willow. There is no avoiding the mass, they are everywhere. The group we run into on Willow carry the same huge white signs with red letters and symbols, and some of them hold gold-lettered books to their chests. They're chanting as well but I don't hear what they're saying. I'm frightened. There is nowhere else to go away from these people, no escape, so father pulls us through them. We are weak fish, fighting against the current, deep in a sea of anger and yelling and hate. I want to cry and I want to throw up and these mean, loud people are bumping me, and squeezing me, and crushing me. Someone recognizes my father and points to him and the horde stops marching and pushes toward him. My sister and I are pulled away, and my father screams our names and disappears in the crowd.

~*~

Because we are children, the rioters spare us yet no kindness is offered. Yoshiko wraps her arms around my chest and drags me away from the madness. She hides me behind a dumpster. We hear sirens and gunshots and the pleas for help and the louder indictments. We hear the protesters proclaim the name of god but I don't know what god would allow this much screaming.

Yoshiko holds me tight and kisses my forehead and says she loves me like no other.

The familiar words are comforting, not only because I love my sister but because I'm otherwise numb. I'm scared in a way I've never been before. I don't know what's happening or what happened to my father, and when I think of the crowd pulling him away, a clawing sensation fills my chest and stomach. Yoshiko says that is dread, and she feels it too. The reek of the burning is stronger than the filth in the dumpster and Yoshiko says we should make our way home.

We're hesitant leaving the safety of the steel dumpster but the crowds have moved on from where we were hiding. As we creep through the neighborhood—her arm around my shoulder—we edge the sidewalk and stick close to shadow. My eyes dart across the lawns to every street corner and alley. We learn that whatever has happened—is happening—is not restricted to the square. Out in the open, we can hear the yelling and gunshots are all around us and distant. The source of the smoke fouling the air is from burning houses and cars. Not all of the houses, just those that have been singled out. We pass one and then, a block away, another. We round the corner and Yoshiko stops short, "The Warrens'," she says. Dr. Warren works in my father's department and her husband is a botanist. Like the two homes we've already seen, theirs is on fire.

None of the distant sirens seem to be coming.

As we pass on the far side of the street, we gaze into the windows. The rooms are ablaze. Some of the Warrens' things are in the middle of the street, but as we get close I realize that the two piles are not just crumpled clothes. When my sister sees that the lumps are the Warrens' mangled remains, she covers my eyes. "Don't look," she says. "Just keep moving your feet."

I do.

Before we reach home, she covers my eyes twice more.

When we finally reach our house, we are happy to see it is not burning. But it was not passed over. They have been here. The front door is open and the words 'Race Traitor' are spray painted across it in red. The word 'Unnatural' is spray painted across the living room wall, over the face of the clock and the pictures of Yoshiko and me. The sofa has been pushed over, and papers—those that were inside my father's desk—along with his many books, litter the floor of his den. Apart from those ransacked rooms, the rest of the house is intact.

"Why didn't they burn our house?" I ask Yoshiko, not expecting an answer. But she gives me one.

"Because we weren't here."

"Will they return?"

"Maybe. But I don't think they'll come for us."

~*~

The riot continues for another day and then two. We don't leave the house and father doesn't return. There is plenty to eat. My sister makes us toast and cereal. We follow what is happening on the newsfeed. There has been a revolt, and a coup. My sister says that means that new people are in charge, people that—like those in the square—may not like us because of what we are. Again I don't understand. Father taught us to accept everyone. That's what they say in our school too. But I don't think I'm going back to school. At least not yet. The two of us worked together to lift the heavy couch and—because we didn't want to see the paint—we hung a sheet on the wall. Now we stay out of that room.

The phones were out but they're back in service, except no one we try to call answers. Apart from our friends, the only people we know work with our father at the university. The man on the newsfeed says that it's shut down, but nothing more. My sister says we have to wait, but I'm not sure for what.

We don't have to wait long. They next day, they come for us, but not as an angry mob. Through the blinds, we see two policemen and a woman with a list on a clipboard. They knock again and this time the woman calls out our names. My sister and I look at each other, neither of us know what to do. I think hiding is best but Yoshiko calls out to them. "My father's not here," she says. "You should go away."

I watch intently as the woman whispers into one of the policemen's ears. He disappears from the step and the woman—a young short-haired ginger in a green pantsuit and blazer—responds to my sister. "We know your father isn't home, honey. We know where he is."

The two of us look at each other again.

"Please go away," says Yoshiko.

"Just open the door. We've come to take you someplace safe."

"I think you just better leave."

"Come now," the woman says. "You can't stay in there."

And we know she's right, but we're unsure what we should do. Then the policeman she whispered to enters the living room from the kitchen. He came through the back door.

The woman and officers are not unkind, but they are not overly friendly either.

We're allowed to pack a small back bag and are taken to the university and put in the dorms. They tell us that the students are all gone now and only other children are here, but as we're taken to our own room we can't see if any of the others are our friends; the doors are all closed.

That night, we are fed in our room. A man comes to the door with a tall cart full of trays. He doesn't say anything to us, just hands my sister our food. He gives her a leer that makes me slide back behind the door. I can tell he is one of those people she was talking about that doesn't like us. "Did you see how many trays there were?" she asks when the door is closed. "We're not alone."

I'm missing my father so the thought that others like us are around me makes me feel a bit better. But there are others around us that are mean like the man that dropped off the food. The men guarding us are mean like him. They patrol the halls and we can hear them say scary things. One calls us animals and his friend corrects him, calling us, "Abominations." We watch the newsfeed in the room. My sister says that we wouldn't if it wasn't for the fact that we need to know what's going on. She doesn't want us to watch because the things people are saying on the feeds are worse than what the men say in the hall. The endless supply of talking heads on the newsfeed say that those like us are soulless creatures and worse, in void of souls—demons. They say we're corrupt and that even our food is corrupt. Large quantities are being destroyed because they are unnatural. They say that those responsible for corrupting the natural order are being dealt with and we know they are talking about people like my father. There is a manhunt, a list of names, one of them Dr. Vangelis. He worked with father. "He got away," my sister says, and we listen closely to the list each time it is read to hear our father's name. We don't.

~*~

The routine continues for three more days and then the ginger woman returns to our door and orders us out into the hall. For the first time, we see some of our neighbors, the other children. I don't recognize any on our floor. Two nurses are working their way to each child. One pushes a cart with trays of vials while the other walks ahead. When they are close, I see that the vials are for blood samples. They are a team these two, one shining a bright penlight into the eyes of each child, one poking their arms. The speak softly and sweet and when the light nurse shines her bright pen into my eyes, she comments that one is blue and one is hazel. Then she says, in the same sweet voice, "I guess you're not all perfect," and I realize that she is not kind. I know she is wrong because my eyes are just as they're supposed to be, and part of me wants to tell her so but another part of me wants to cry. As my skin begins to heat, I feel the tears well and Yoshiko takes my hand.

The next day, we're ordered out into the hall again but this time we're marched outside and through campus. The blue September sky is not aware there has been an upheaval, but the university is. The buildings are empty shells and the benches along the colonnades and arcades that should be peppered with students are barren. And there are the dark red spatters on the cement that I know aren't paint at all.

As we file behind our clipboard ginger, I see another column of children marching in another line that's to merge with our own. I see a few others I know. "There's Lincoln," I softly say to my sister. "He's a boy from my class, and Sophia, she's from my class too."

"Yes," says Yoshiko. "I recognize him. I saw some children

from my school too."

We don't say anything louder. So far we've seen at least a hundred children. Fifty came over with us and two other long queues of twenty-some each. They have rumpled clothes, are all different ages, and all like us. The other columns have their own clipboard women, they wear pantsuits too, but ours is the only ginger. When we reach our destination, a small auditorium, the three women stand outside the double-doors checking faces against their list as we are ushered in.

We sit in the theater and I ask Yoshiko why they brought us here.

"I don't know," she says.

"Are they going to show us a video?"

"I don't think so." She gestures to the three people seated at a table on the side of the stage—two men and a woman. The men are in suits and the woman in a dress and all three wear glasses and a frown. "Bankers," my sister says and giggles. But it's not funny because whatever is happening is all too serious. I know that it is and don't have to wait long to find out.

The children in the front row are called up first. They go onto the stage and the first of them is put in front of the table. The man on the right side of the table asks their name while his two comrades align their paperwork. They could be using electronic tablets, but they're not. When all three have their papers in order, they peer at the child, and the woman in the middle says "Commencing hearing for," and she lists the child's name and designation number. The other two echo, "Noted," and then she asks the first question. "Do you know why you're here?"

"No," the child says. He's younger than me and I can tell he's been crying.

"You're here because you've been deemed unnaturally born. Do you have anything to say for yourself?"

Before the child answers, the third man slams a rubber stamp down onto his copy of paperwork, repeats the designation number and says, "Citizenship denied.

Deportation."

The other two echo, "Noted," and the child is scurried from the stage by two athletic men, while another is put into his place before the table. The first question is always the same and, after the first child, we know that the verdict is too. All of the children are like us. The process is the same and moves quickly and before long the clipboard ginger is escorting my row up to the stage.

My mind is swimming and from here I can see the children before me are being ushered off stage through a door that leads outside. When they get to us, I squeeze Yoshiko's hand, but I'm pulled away to face the table. They say my name when asked and they quickly assign me a number. But when they ask me if I have anything to say for myself, I don't wait for them to finish before I blurt out, "My sister and mother were killed in an accident. My father grieved so badly and missed my mother so badly that he took the stem cells saved from my sister and—well—created me."

The three at the table appear stunned that I've spoken up. Not one of the forty children before me said a single word more than their name. They look at each other, shuffle through their papers, and I think maybe I've made them realize they've made a mistake. Yoshiko widens her eyes and silently mouths, "I love you like no other." When they are through conferring, the first man peers over the frames of his glasses at me. "2325, you've never had a sister. This girl Yoshiko is not your sister."

I speak before the third man can sentence me.

"I understand your confusion. My gene identity is not unique, I'm identical to my sister, the one who died in the accident with my mother. I'm basically her twin. Don't you understand? That's all it is. There is no more difference between me and my sister than any other identical twins."

Again they confer and I straighten my arms and ball my hands into fists. But they are brief this time. "I'm afraid you're confused, 2325. Your parents never had a daughter. Your gene identity is that of your mother's."

With that, the third man slams his stamp down. Up close,

in front of the table, the stamp makes a loud thwack, but the third man's voice is distorted and distant, "2325, citizenship denied. Deportation."

~*~

A Word from Daniel Arthur Smith

~*~

Daniel Arthur Smith is the author of the international bestsellers *Hugh Howey Lives, The Cathari Treasure, The Somali Deception*, and a few other novels and short stories.

He was raised in Michigan and graduated from Western Michigan University where he studied philosophy, with focus on cognitive science, meta-physics, and comparative religion. He began his career as a bartender, barista, poetry house proprietor, teacher, and then became a technologist and futurist for the Fortune 100 across the Americas and Europe.

Daniel has traveled to over 300 cities in 22 countries, residing in Los Angeles, Kalamazoo, Prague, Crete, and now writes in Manhattan, where he lives with his wife and young sons.

~*~

Awakening
Susan Kaye Quinn

~*~

I

I dream of a day when I'm the only sister left.

Then I pray it never comes.

My prayers are silent, whispered wordlessly into my hands as I lie in my cloister cell. The box is barely long enough for my sleeping mat, barely tall enough to sit up. My sisters' cells surround me, their prayers haunting the blue frosted-glass walls. Our doors stay shut so long now, so many hours of the day and all of the night. Time for prayer. Time for contemplation. Mother Superior says our awakening is coming, but I find myself mostly sleeping between interrogations. Exhausted. Worried. Fearful.

You were created to touch the face of God, I remind myself.

But I fear I'll be last among the twelve to bridge that gap.

Sister Chloe's hand presses on the glass between our cells. "Sister Amara?" Her lips touch the wall, a pale outline of blue. "She gave me more this time." Her speaking tone is calm, but the *click-cluck* of her tongue signals *urgency.* We use sister-language to evade the constant ears that listen, but I suspect we fool ourselves with that. There's little the Masters do not know.

"Hitchy?" I ask. It's our secret word for the med patch Mother Superior uses to force the truth from our lips. I roll to my side to watch the dark silhouette of Chloe's hand. She folds down two fingers, leaving up two like thin twigs in winter: *no*. So our secret is still *sorkept*—sister-kept, close to our hearts. At least for now.

We've always had our secrets from the Masters—childish secrets kept in childish ways, with sister-language and signs—but now, as our bodies grow into the fullness of womanhood, Mother Superior's patience is growing thin. And she doesn't always trust our words.

"*Your heart is mine,*" I reassure Chloe. Her cell is to my left, Sister Maya's to my right, Sister Hadley above and Sister Robert below. Our chromosomes are identical in every way, but we pick our names, and Sister Robert refuses a female one. Perhaps she truly feels more male than female. Or maybe it's her act of defiance against the forced prescription of our DNA. Either way, I'm glad to see her exercise the one right we have—to be called what we wish.

I press my hand over the shadow of Chloe's on the glass—the surface is cool, the temperature set for the comfort of our Masters' cybernetic bodies rather than the twelve of us who live here, breathing and growing and loving each other. Our Masters do not do these things, except perhaps the last... and even that, I doubt. They certainly do not love *us*—my sisters and me. *Love* is not cold boxes and interrogations and genetic manipulation for a divine purpose, no matter how much Mother Superior claims otherwise.

But this is blasphemy, and I dare not speak it.

"You are next," Chloe warns me, her lips whispering against the blue glass.

But of course I am.

The interrogation times are always in the same order, just like the rotations out to the garden or time in the virtuals or gym, although the frequency of those has been reduced lately. Our extended time in prayer, secluded in our cloister cells, is beginning to feel like punishment, the toll taken in stiff backs and sore legs and bruises from too much rest.

Our world is made of schedules and glass and more glass—an endless profusion of transparent walls and frosted ceilings and translucent floors. Our Masters, the ascenders, left their humanity behind long ago—their cybernetic eyes can easily navigate the intricacies of this glass cathedral, but the gradations of color and colorlessness only confuse human eyes and befuddle human minds.

Sister Hadley lost her mind trying to discern an exit.

I no longer look.

Besides, there are no exits for us, only windows—into my sisters' cells, into the laboratory beyond my tiny door, past that to the other rooms that comprise our hidden cloister. The hallways beyond are forbidden, demarked by a double black line and a mechanical sentry. We dare not travel past them, not because we are prisoners, but because we must not be discovered. *We* are the secrets—our very bodies, our holy mission, all of it protected from a world that would not approve of Mother Superior's righteous plans, even as the future of all things depends upon us.

Depends.

Such a heavy word for children to carry. While I may doubt Mother Superior's professed love for me and my sisters, I do not doubt the holiness of our mission. Or the Masters' ability to create creatures—*us*—who can achieve it, even as I wonder if I will be the last among their children to do so.

Only we're no longer children.

Mother Superior is right—we're getting closer to the awakening. I can see it in Sister Judith's fearful glances, the tremor in Sister Naomi's hand, the hitch in Sister Jade's voice, even as we cannot speak of it openly. Only Sister Sophia shows no signs of worry, but she's always been the wisest and calmest among us. But we can feel it—the one thing the Masters want from us is on the cusp of blossoming in our minds just as our bodies are showing the curves of womanhood.

The two processes must be linked.

And the Masters, with their near-Godly intelligence, must

know this… because the interrogations are becoming more strident, the drug dosages higher, and the God-state more extreme. But for now, what we experience there must be *sorkept*—spoken only in code between us—because what if one of us bridges the gap before the others? What if one of us fails to fulfill her purpose at all? These thoughts are a slow drip of dread during the hours in between interrogations. The relentless minutes in the box. Even now, my mind dulls under the steady drumbeat. Sleep is so much easier, however uneasy…

Behind my head, the door of my cloister cell opens.

My hand is still pressed to the glass, but my sister's is gone.

"Sister Amara?" The soft voice of my caretaker confirms it's my turn.

Mother Grace, along with the other Mothers, is humanoid like the Masters, her cybernetic body similar in size and shape to mine, but her skin is the static pink-and-silver shimmer that shows her low sentience—unlike the ascenders' multicolored and ever-changing palette. Mine is a warm brown that's lighter on my palms and pinkish on my lips, but that's about as much variation as I get.

"Coming." I flip heels-over-head in the practiced roll I use to exit my cell once it's unlocked. We each have our own way to manage this. Funny how we cling to each tiny difference like it matters. Like it makes us *distinct*. We're already manufactured to be completely unlike any other humans, if there are any left in the world outside the glass.

I ease down from my box, the floor cool on my feet. The laboratory outside our cloister cells is a medical suite tailored to our human anatomy—this is not where the interrogations occur, although it would be no less unpleasant here.

Even though we each have our own mother, any of the mothers will do when a knee is scraped or a stomach growls. Their love may be programmed in, but unlike the Masters, they at least *appear* to care. It's a bonding mechanism intended to bring out our humanity, to keep the neuron fires in our brains forming properly as we grow from babies to children and now to nearly adults.

Mother Grace isn't a true mother.

I know this.

Just as I know the laboratory is not a home, the filtered glow-light is not sunshine, and the box I sleep in is not a bed. Yet I straighten my sheath to cover my legs and smooth my hair for inspection just as I'm supposed to.

And I glow under Mother Grace's approving nod.

"Did you sleep well?" Her voice is soft, always soft. Never harsh. Never scolding.

I tell myself it's easy to love something that loves you unconditionally—it's loving Sister Hadley that's hard. And yet she has my sister-love more than any bot ever could.

"Well enough," I answer her rote inquiry.

"Sensors indicated your sleep cycle was disturbed."

A reminder that they're always watching.

"I had a dream, that's all." It's not entirely a lie.

Her mechanical eyes dilate, and the backs of her fingers brush my cheek. Is she peering inside my head to see my lie? Or does she simply read my body for all the information she needs? The common knowledge database answers many questions, but never these.

Mother Grace steps back, satisfied with whatever she's discerned. "Mother Superior is awaiting you."

I know the routine for interrogations, and there's no reason to delay. Mother Grace's body has ten times my strength and speed, making resistance simply an invitation for less-than-gentle handling by the soft-spoken bot—something every sister learns while we're still small. And yet, I find myself dragging my feet even as I lead the way out of the lab.

Mother Grace follows close behind.

The interrogation room is down one blue-glass hallway, three turns right, one left, past the garden that beckons with its natural light, then a sharp turn into a room shrouded in smoked glass. It's a stern color in this cathedral of not-quite-transparent blues, life-promising greens, and bright yellows—as if ash is the only proper décor for the things that happen here.

The room is well-lit, and Mother Superior is indeed waiting inside, consulting with something on the pull-down holo display. It is one of the many ways she accesses the instruments hidden in the walls. She waits a moment to acknowledge my presence, transmitting something to Mother Grace before favoring me with her attention. The bot who is my personal mother tilts her head, non-verbal agreement to whatever command Mother Superior has issued, and retreats without a word.

Mother Superior is one of my creators, a Master of bots and humans—although her ascender name is shrouded like the smoky glass enclosing the interrogation room. She's beautiful in a tall and perfectly proportioned way, her bodyform carefully chosen and crafted toward some innate measure of human beauty. It's a remnant from the time when she was human—before she took the nanites into her brain and ascended into the hyper-intelligent being all ascenders are today. By comparison, I'm barely more intelligent than Mother Grace and her sweet but limited cognition.

It's the order of things—bots then humans then ascenders.

My intelligence is supposed to be limited as well, but the Masters are trying to change that—it would be an abomination if it weren't for a holy purpose. But I wasn't created to be *intelligent*. My purpose is to reach *beyond* the intellect, outside the senses. To provide a bridge to that holy place the Masters cannot reach on their own—and reclaim the thing that was perhaps lost when the Singularity elevated humanity into near-God-like beings. I'm supposed to reach for God... only I'm not sure I *want* to touch the divine.

It seems too powerful. Like something that will burn, not enlighten. Destroy, not uplift. Maybe it's merely fear, but there are dark nights when I doubt the strength of my faith—when I believe more in my ability to fail than in the possibility of being the salvation of the world.

I stand awkwardly in my thin, sleeveless sheath. My feet warm the chilled floor, and my heart feels childish in my doubts.

Mother Superior finally banishes her holo screen and turns to me.

"Sister Amara," she says, her voice cool. "Please have a seat."

The chair. I can't control the shudder that passes over my skin. Mother Superior's skin dances with wisps of purple. The translucent fabric of her shift shows the color-flux of her emotions, just as mine reveals my prickles of dread. Our clothes are the same—bots, humans, and ascenders alike wear the lightweight sheaths made from tech-laden fabric. The cloister may keep us concealed from the outside world, but inside our glass walls, our clothes lay bare all our bodily responses.

Mine signals my reluctance.

"I'd prefer not to sedate you this time, Sister Amara."

That makes me move—the sedative left me nauseous for hours. My bare legs shuffle me to the chair, and I gingerly climb into the cool embrace of the gel cushions. Mother Superior moves with ascender speed, flitting to retrieve the med patch—a small, square electronic dispensing device—and place it on my forehead before I'm even settled. The chill of the cushions seeps through my shift. They won't release me until our interrogation is through.

"Make careful note of what you see." Mother Superior's words are routine, and she's already back at her holo controls. "I want a full report."

Before I can respond, the med patch flips on and doses me. There's no sensation when it activates, but I feel the effect immediately. The God-mode slams through my mind, stronger than the previous sessions, wrenching me from my nerves and anxiety and pulling my mind to a different place. The sensation of being liberated from my body pervades me, like always, and I blearily force open my eyes to check that I'm still in the chair.

I am. I never move, but I always feel like I'm floating.

It's not without pleasure, this release.

I feel a presence in the room that's not Mother Superior.

It's not unlike the connection I feel with my sisters when we're all in the same place, enjoying the same work in the garden or a game in the virtual. This sense of oneness with others, of being larger than the tight confines of my body—this is the med patch at work, inducing a mode of thinking that is supposed to elevate me from my existence of cool boxes and limitless glass.

And it does.

The problem is that I'm not supposed to simply *enjoy* this blissful and harmonious state—I should be actively reaching for more. Mother Superior says I have to seek God in order to find it, but so far the trance holds me like tar, stuck in this joyous plane of love and sisterhood. Maybe my faith isn't strong enough to lift me higher. I wonder if Mother Superior ever enters the God-mode and experiences this harmony in the midst of her frenetically intelligent life—and if so, why isn't it enough? Why must she reach for more through us? Is this too simple a joy, pleasurable only for meager humans?

I reach and reach for the *more* I've been created to attain, trying with my limited mind and small faith to imagine something greater worth reaching for... *and fail. Again.*

The happy floating state lulls me back.

Too soon, the med patch slams off, wrenching me back into the cool prison of the chair and the harsh gaze of Mother Superior's dilating purple-tinted eyes. Everything that can be measured has been—by the instruments in the walls and the chair and her eyes. Now comes the interrogation in which I'll have nothing to report. *Again.*

My sisters do not have to worry about me reaching God before them. And it's easy to report to Mother Superior that I haven't yet fulfilled our purpose when that's the simple truth.

"What did you see, Sister Amara?"

"I'm sorry," I mumble. "Nothing."

"Sister Sophia reported visions at this level."

"She did?" My heart quickens.

"I'm increasing your dose." In a blink, she's back at the holo controls.

The God-mode slams harder into my mind, making my

heart rate jump. The bliss and harmony flee. My senses expand so rapidly, I fear I am exploding. I choke, unable to breathe, my eyes pop open, looking desperately at my body—I'm still attached to it, but I'm curling up, fighting the cushions as my stomach wrenches. What I'm seeing with my eyes—my limited body on the chair—doesn't match up with the sense of *largeness* in my head. I clutch at my stomach as it roils. A keening sound, high and sharp, rings in my ears. Only after I drag my head to the side, working against the chair's hold, do I realize by the change in pitch that the sound is coming from my mouth.

I'm screaming.

Mother Superior doesn't even look my way.

The sense of expansion ramps up further. My back arches up from the cushions. Every muscle in my body is electrified...

I blow into a million pieces.

My body slumps hard into the chair.

The scattered pieces of my mind rain down like black drops.

The darkness closes on me.

II

I awake with a rush of air filling my lungs.

Mother Grace stands over me, her hands gently restraining me while her smaller, mechanical arms—the ones that live inside her chest—retract from touching my throat and lips and chest.

What? My heart jerks, and my chest wheezes. "Wha—?" is all I can say before the air runs out.

"You are fine now, Sister Amara." Mother Grace releases me completely.

I blink to focus—I'm laid flat on the steel gurney in the laboratory. My sisters gathered around me, a tight ring at a distance, while Mother Grace used her medical appendages to bring me out of the darkness. I swallow, my tongue thick in my mouth, and struggle up to sitting. Chloe hurries forward to help. She reaches me first, but the rest converge, their hands holding me up, their touches gentle on my face and arms and back.

Amara. Amara. Their voices are soft, but they buoy me. With my sisters' help, I swing my legs off the side and find my voice.

"What happened?" I direct the question to Mother Grace over the shoulders of my sisters. She's retreated to give us room.

"You are fine now, Sister Amara," she repeats. Then she adds, "Mother Superior has awarded time in the garden for all the sisters once you awoke."

The garden? I'm still a little woozy, but I suppose I could work for a while. My sisters are already easing me from the cool metal bed. I wave them off when I have my feet under me.

"All right, the garden, then." Whatever happened in interrogation, I'm over it now. Mostly.

My sisters brace me as we pad on quiet feet out of the lab and down the hallway toward the garden. Chloe holds steadfast by my side, but at least half of my sisters are still touching me in some way. It's unnerving and reassuring at the same time—their love is a comfort, but I'm really fine now, just as Mother Grace said. It's not until we reach the garden that they start to let go. One by one, they peel off to work the weeds between the orchard trees.

I keep walking.

When Chloe alone is still by my side, she speaks. *"You were dead."* Her strained whisper is almost inaudible.

"What?" I stop cold next to a peach tree heavy with fruit.

Chloe bites her lip then runs her hands softly over my cheeks, again and again, her eyes searching mine for something. Finally, she says, "Your heart stopped. Mother Superior saved you."

I frown. "Mother Superior is the one who—" I glance around. My sisters aren't far, and I'm sure they're listening, but it's the other ears I'm worried about. Yet Mother Superior

46

can't expect me not to say the truth of what happened. I face Chloe. "The dosage was very high."

Chloe's eyes go wide. "The med patch?"

I nod. "I can't believe I was... are you sure?" *Did I really die?* How would I know?

Chloe's lips pinch together. "We were shown the holo image."

A holo? That could be faked, but why? No reason I could think of.

More importantly, I fear this is a sign of things to come. An escalation. "Chloe." I pull her closer and whisper. "She's going to keep trying and trying." It's understood that I mean Mother Superior. In theory, other Masters are involved in our experiment, but she's the only one we've ever seen.

Chloe's creamy brown skin turns ashen. "She said it was an accident."

I release her and step back. "Maybe it was." I don't think Mother Superior intended to hurt me—she's simply willing to push hard for something I can't give. But, until now, I didn't realize *dying* was an option. Or having my mind blown into a million pieces.

I could end up like Sister Hadley.

That thought punches me to the gut—has Sister Hadley already awakened? Has she been splintered apart, and we simply thought she had gone mad?

I scan the orchards for Hadley... she's at the base of a pear tree, holding a fallen fruit in her hands and poking at it with one finger. Then her hand falls to her side, and the pear rolls away.

That's no state I want to be in.

Chloe notices my stare.

I grab hold of her arm. "During your interrogation, did you have visions? Mother Superior said Sister Sophie did." I'm speaking it plainly now, but I don't have a choice. I need to know for certain.

Chloe's eyes go wide. "No."

We both scan the orchard, looking for Sophia. She's close

to the entrance, with Naomi and Jade and Thea huddled around her. Sophia has always gathered the sisters like that—they're drawn to her wisdom and calm demeanor, especially when nerves are rattled.

My almost dying has shaken more than just me.

I drop my hold on Chloe and march toward Sophia and her gathering. She and I have always been the leaders among the sisters. Even as young girls, Sophia calmed fears while I came up with a plan. She picked up Thea when she fell, and I brushed the dirt from her knees. She calmed Judith's crying fits, and I got to the root of what bothered her. Sophia was the gentle hand, and I was the problem solver. And now, more than ever, we needed to work together and stand together—all twelve of us.

As I march over, Sophia sees me coming and gives me that cool gaze, like she's measuring my next move. Has she been holding out on me? Even with all my doubts about whether my faith is strong enough for our holy purpose, *I'm* the one who just came back from the dead… and everyone knows it. But if she's the first to truly awaken, it's even more important that we stick together.

I stand before Sophia and her little coterie, arms crossed and feet planted wide. "Have you been seeing visions?" I demand. "Mother Superior said you did."

She gives me a pinched look like she's not sure why I'm taking such a confrontational stance. "No." The word is simple, bare, uncomplicated… and very possibly a lie.

Esha. It's our sister-word for liar. *Esha, Esha.* It's pinging around in my head, but I don't let it out. The spectacle of the two of us facing off gathers the rest of our sisters from their work.

"No visions of any kind?" I follow the question with a *tsk* of my tongue that says I think she's lying. I simply want her to come clean so we know where we stand… and can make a plan from there.

Sophia arches one eyebrow. "I am no *esha.*" Her voice is calm, despite my implied insult. Her eyes are the same as the rest of ours, but somehow they're deeper and contain more wisdom on Sophia's face. And, in spite of what I've said, lying is not her way. I know this.

"Mother Superior said—" I start.

But she cuts me off with a slow drumbeat of words. "Mother Superior said you *died.*" Sophia's eyes lock hard onto mine, then she gives a slow *tsk* with her tongue, implying that Mother Superior is the *esha*.

Mother Superior lied.

This momentarily wipes blank my mind. But as I reel back from that shock, I see the truth Sophia is implying with her hard stare and slow words. If Mother Superior truly brought me back from the dead—if she can *actually* resurrect someone—then why not use that power to seek out the divine?

No… her words have to be a lie. She fabricated this story to explain why I was unconscious after her interrogation… only Sister Sophia saw straight to the heart of it.

And if Mother Superior lied about something as serious as *that*… then what else could she be lying about?

Sister Sophia gives me a slow nod as she sees the understanding dawn on my face. "My heart is *sorkept,*" she says. It's a pledge.

"My heart is *sorkept,*" I say in return.

My sisters' faces relax with the peace between us, but I'm not sure if they truly understand. We cannot know the truth of anything the Masters say. We can rely only on our sister-love. But I cannot simply spell that out with the listening ears of our Masters. So how to make my sisters understand that we need to stand together?

Sophia tilts her head to me. "Almost losing you has shaken us, Sister Amara." Her words are for the Masters who overhear, not just our sisters. The softness comes back to her face—the gentle, caring look she's bestowed on every sister at one point or another, including me. "To lose one of us is unthinkable. It cannot be allowed."

My heart expands in a wave of sister-love. "Agreed." I reach out a hand, and she touches her palm to mine. Our fingers line up, identical down to the length of our nails and the slight bend in our pinkies. Our sisters huddle around us with furrowed brows and whispers behind hands. Even the slack-faced Hadley has been drawn into our circle, with Thea holding her hand on one side and Maya on the other.

I lift my gaze to the peach tree we're standing under. All the food in the garden belongs to us—like the gentle arms of a mother bot, the cloister holds us and cares for our every physical need. Our work in the garden is solely to provide exercise, not because it actually needs the sisters to tend it. The bots intentionally leave weeds behind for us to pull as they harvest the fruit at the proper time for peak efficiency. We are banned from taking it ourselves.

I reach up for a peach that is hanging low and ripe and ready. The twig that holds it snaps easily, and the motion shakes the entire tree, but the gasp that goes around my sisters is louder than the rustling of leaves.

Sophia's gaze is riveted to mine. I take a bite of the fruit, then I hand it to her.

She stares at my outstretched hand.

Everyone is holding their breath, waiting.

Sophia lifts the peach gently from my hand, then locks gazes with me as she takes her own bite. Then she hands it to Thea.

"Our hearts are *sorkept*," Sophia says. "We are sisters first. Always."

As our sisters pass the fruit, it is clear—all of us or none of us will fulfill the Masters' purpose. We will leave no sister behind. I feel the love, the sister bonding, and it's as strong as a med patch dose but without the out-of-body sensation. It buoys me up and convinces me we'll get through this, somehow. Together.

But we still need a plan.

If we are a failed experiment, we'll need a place to run. To hide. To somehow live on our own when all we've ever known is this cloistered corner of the world. We could steal food from the garden, but where would we go?

The domed glass above the garden filters the outside sun, hazy and yellow and warm on my skin.

Outside.

For all I know, two steps out the door would mean our deaths.

I know literally nothing of the outside, other than the one distant mountain peak that can be seen from the garden, rising above the frosted glass that blocks our view of anything at ground level. The peak changes with the seasons, even as our internal environment always stays ascender cool. Maybe there are other humans out there. Maybe not. Perhaps some of the animals I've seen only in virtual.

Any number of things could kill us.

Sister Judith takes the final bite of peach. The fruit is consumed, absorbed into our bond, our promise to each other.

"Our purpose is holy, and we should strive toward it with all our hearts," I say loudly, primarily for Mother Superior, who must be overhearing and overseeing this entire performance. I hold out my hand to the center of the ring of sisters, palm up. "But our hearts will always be *sorkept*, first and foremost."

My sisters move forward to place their hands on mine. We stand that way, bonded, for a moment, feeling the love of every connection we've made in the years of growing up. Mother Superior's lie is part of the cement that binds us together.

The way forward is dangerous—either we'll all transcend or we'll all be forced to flee.

And it's up to me to keep us alive.

III

I'm back in my cloister cell, praying.

I whisper into my hands, but the more I think about leaving the cloister, the more bleak that option appears. What power do we have against the Masters and their bots? Perhaps we could outsmart the mother bots in our attempt to flee, but what about Mother Superior? How can I possibly go up against a God-like being with vastly superior intelligence and knowledge?

A flush of shame overcomes me, and I stop whispering. My hands fall to the mat, and I stare up at the blue glass ceiling of my cloister cell. Sister Hadley is up there—I can see the dark outline of her mat and the moving shadow of her restless arm next to it.

Yes, Mother Superior lied to us, but we will forever be children next to her kind. Maybe she has reasons I cannot even comprehend. Here I am, lying in my box, envisioning some grand scheme wherein I lead my sisters in an escape from the experiment they've been designed for... and it feels like a child's wistful dreaming, not a leader's responsible decision-making.

I heave a heavy sigh. My body relaxes into the mat. A true leader would assess the best option for the collective—for all twelve of us. And it's quickly becoming clear that the best path is to succeed in our purpose. To have all of my sisters awaken just as the Masters wish—in fact, if one sister goes first, then perhaps that one could help the others! We should each do our part, not drag our heels like I've been doing, with my constant fear and anxiety.

I've already died once—how much harder can it get?

I manage to keep the bubble of nervous laughter inside.

I stretch my arms up, pull them back down, then work through the muscles in my body, one by one, tightening and relaxing. Tightening and relaxing. Mother Grace taught me this technique long ago—it helps settle me for prayer, calming the agitation in my body so I can open up my mind to the divine.

If *awakening* is the only true path for me and my sisters, then I need to reach for it—even if it might split me into a million pieces. I may not be able to trust Mother Superior's words, but I can place my faith in the Masters' superior intelligence. They must know what they're doing—which means the awakening is *possible,* even if I have no idea how. But if I reach for it on my own, it *has* to be safer than Mother Superior's high-intensity, God-mode-inducing drug.

I close my eyes and try to re-create that feeling of expansiveness that comes with the patch. My mind recoils from images of the interrogation room, drifting instead to the garden and the bond with my sisters. The two feelings are not dissimilar. I focus on the cloister cells around me, reaching for that sisterly feeling of connection and oneness.

Small sounds rise out of the quiet. Sister Hadley breathing deeply, possibly asleep. Sister Chloe restless on her mat, with soft sniffles I hope aren't crying. Sister Maya slowly tapping, almost inaudible. It's her nervous habit. The sounds are a soft symphony of our sisterhood. My own body relaxes and lifts, as though it's lost a little of its own gravity. I'm floating above my mat on a wave of comfort and connection. I drift toward Hadley...

A sudden jerk makes my heart stutter—the sensation like verging on sleep then startling awake—only when I open my eyes, I don't see the top of my cloister cell.

I'm outside it.

What the—I'm staring at my cloister cell *from the outside.*

I have no memory of leaving my cell. There's no one else in the laboratory—no bots, not even Mother Grace who normally lets me out. I creep toward my cloister cell, reaching for the door, even though I don't know the unlock code. We don't control them any more than we control anything else. I rise up on my tiptoes to peer through the window, then nearly topple over—*I've left my body inside.*

Holy Makers.

I try to brace myself against the wall of my cloister cell... my hand passes right through!

I jerk it back.

What is this? Is this my awakening? But this isn't some holy realm—it's just the lab. The divine has to be more than this. More than simply traveling outside my body.

Where am I supposed to go looking for God? Down the hall?

I lean slowly toward my cloister cell again and press my face to the wall—*it passes through the door.* I'm half in and half out of the cloister cell, looking at my body. *So disturbing.* But if I can pass through walls, there's literally nothing that can hold me. I pull out of my cell and repeat the same thing with Chloe's, sticking my head inside.

She's there, eyes closed, praying fervently into her hands.

"Chloe!" I whisper, afraid I might scare the holiness out of her.

She doesn't hear me, just keeps on whispering about fulfilling her holy purpose and asking God to bless her and make her the one who can help... *Sister Amara.* Hearing my name on her lips flushes me with warmth in an almost physical way. Suddenly, the connection between us is even stronger. It's pulling me deeper into the cloister cell. I reach a hand to touch her shoulder... and the connection zooms up and consumes me.

In a flash, I see Chloe's life, an endless stream of images bombarding my brain and my senses, telling me the story of who she is. And I'm at the center of it, a vibrant light that's anchored her through the years. I jerk back again, breaking the connection and pulling out of her cell.

I'm alone in the laboratory, but the connections to my other sisters in their cloister cells call to me. The sister bond isn't a figment of my imagination—it's a real thing. Or at least as real as anything else in this hallucination or dream or awakening I'm having.

I take another step back from the cells—as much as I love my sisters, I don't want to be inside their heads that much.

Whatever this is, it can't be what the Masters intended. I'm not reaching for the face of God. I'm not seeing a holier place. I'm merely walking around without my body. Which means... *I've already failed.*

I stride for the door of the laboratory and don't even hesitate—I simply walk straight through. Looking back at the doorway, there's no evidence of my passage. I don't know how long this state will last, so I hurry. I only have one chance, maybe, to see what's outside. To make a plan for escape. To find a way out before the Masters figure out what's happened. There is no telling how much they can discern, with their watchful eyes and ever-listening ears.

In spite of my hurrying down the hall and the near-panic in my mind, I don't actually feel... *anything.* Not the cool temperature of the ascenders' climate control system. Not the chilled tiles under the soles of my feet. Not even the pounding of my own heart... because I left that heart in my body in the cloister cell. That bracing thought follows me as I wind down the blue-glass hallways toward the edge of our domain, past which we're forbidden to travel. Double black lines and a sentry bot demark the limits I've known my entire life.

The sentry's humanoid-yet-mechanical body contains enough strength to crush me, and that doesn't include the weapons neatly stored in its arms and chest. Those weapons only come out when needed—like the medical instrumentation stored in Mother Grace's body—except the sentry's instruments are designed to kill, not save. We've been told a hundred times that the sentries protect us from anyone who might enter the cloister domain, but as I stand in front of it, undetected by its sensors, I notice it's not facing *outward*, but inward toward the cloister.

I have an urge run past it, taunting it as I go. Before I can lift a foot to act on that impulse, I blink, and I'm already a dozen feet down the forbidden corridor. It startles me enough that I hold still, frozen in the hallway—the sentry hasn't detected me, but more importantly, *how did I do that?*

I moved without motion.

My hands appear to be flesh and blood—as real as anything I've ever seen—although they're somehow brighter than normal, glowing with a little inner shine that seems unreal.

Maybe this is all a dream.

I keep moving, but this time I don't bother to walk or run—I *think* my way down the corridor. I start at one end and will myself to the other... and suddenly appear there.

A heady rush of excitement and power charges me.

Susan Kaye Quinn

What is this thing I've discovered?

I work to get a grip on myself before I spiral off and do something crazy. But I can't help trying for more. I close my eyes and imagine the garden. When I open them, I'm there, next to the peach trees heavy with fruit. I can't feel the soil under my feet, even as I see it between my toes. The sun has no heat, even as I see the reflection on the leaves.

I am *here* but *not here*.

What is this state, truly?

The mountain peak beckons from outside the sparkling domed glass. Can I will myself outside the garden? I close my eyes and imagine what it must be like on the other side of the glass. When I open my eyes, the mountain is the same, but the frosted glass is gone, revealing a shining bright city between me and the distant peak. The sunshine glints off so many buildings, it's difficult for my mind to tell them apart—there are spires and towers and gleaming silver-and-glass buildings huddled like sisters, only they're each unique. A giant toroid stands on end; a double helix tower is made entirely of glass; billowing domes of satiny silver glint as they ripple with the wind.

A sprawling field of lush green grass lies under my feet, and behind me, the glass structure that is my home towers above me, simply enormous, with a spider web of silver metal holding together all that glass. The full extent of it is a hundred times the size of my cloister. The idea that the whole expanse of the living space I've known my entire life is *tiny* compared to the building I was raised in, much less the city it's buried in... unsettles me.

I'm standing in the middle of an entire city of ascenders.

How could my sisters and I possibly survive in *this?* Although the distant mountain, with its rugged granite and snowy peak, wouldn't provide much refuge either. The vast complex of glass where my sisters are hidden away is really the only place where we belong.

I close my eyes and envision myself in the hallway just past the sentry.

All along, I thought that I would be the last to awaken... I didn't plan on being first. Although this awakening is hardly a true one—I could still be the least among my sisters. Maybe Sister Chloe will awaken to something more mysterious and godlike than simply traveling around without her body. And then she could show me the way!

I stride past the sentry, heading back toward the laboratory that is my home, and sort through the scattering of memories I somehow absorbed when I touched Chloe. She is my sister, my genetic identical, but her mind is comprised of all the experiences and expressions that are unique to her.

When I pass through the laboratory door, I see the room is no longer empty.

Mother Grace is there, preparing something in the medical suite. Mother Joy is returning Sister Hadley to her cell. When did she leave? Have I been gone long enough for her to leave and return? This disorientation freezes me at the door.

Sister Hadley isn't paying attention to her instructions. As she climbs into her cloister cell, I feel the connection between us.

Just before her door closes, Hadley catches a glimpse of me. "Sister Amara."

She's looking straight at me. What does that mean?

I hurry toward her. "Yes, it's me!" I gush out.

Hadley just stares at me, an infinite stare. I'm no longer sure she can see me.

Mother Joy hesitates in closing the door. "Yes, Sister Amara will be going to interrogation next."

I whip a look to her. *Next?* I never go after Sister Hadley. This is out of order.

Something has changed.

Hadley nods as if I've spoken aloud. "You're next."

Mother Joy closes the door in Hadley's face, ignoring her words. A horrible dread sinks through me. Mother Grace strides toward my cloister cell, coming for me.

Panic freezes me for a moment, then I close my eyes and wish with all my heart to return to my body. When I open them, I'm staring up at the ceiling of my cloister cell again. I feel the mat under my back, the cool glass under my palm resting on the floor. The softly metallic scent of the laboratory returns to my senses.

Behind my head, Mother Grace opens the door. "It is your turn, Sister Amara."

IV

I roll out of my cell like normal, but my body is one giant cramp. My attempts to stand up and act normal are abysmal failures.

Mother Grace patiently waits for me to right myself. "Now that you've had a rest, Mother Superior wishes to speak with you."

I hobble behind Mother Grace as she leads me through the glass hallways, but we're not heading to the interrogation room. Instead, she brings me to the doorway of a red glass room. This is Mother Superior's domain—not strictly forbidden, but at the edges of the cloister and certainly nowhere a sister prefers to visit. The door slides open, and Mother Grace indicates I should go first. I try to keep the tremors under control as I step inside. Mother Superior is consulting with a holo screen on the wall—the rest of the room is nothing but bare glass, although the Masters can summon whatever they wish from the walls and floor. Mother Superior demonstrates this by commanding a chair to rise. It's made of a delicate-looking mesh of metal and red glass.

I glance at it but don't sit.

Mother Superior doesn't insist. "What did you see when you were dead, Sister Amara?"

Since she's getting right to it, I'm tempted to ask why she lied to my sisters about resurrecting me from the dead.

Instead, I say, "Nothing." Which is all I plan to say. My heart is *sorkept,* and now that Sister Hadley may have some kind of ability as well—

Mother Superior suddenly looms over me, moving with ascender speed to my side. My heart lurches. She's too close, intimidating me with her glare and her bodyform, reminding me that she could simply crush me at any moment if she wished.

Anger surges up and heats my face—anger that feels like a whisper of things buried deep.

"You were given the highest dosage of any interrogation to date," Mother Superior says. A gray wisp curls along her skin and climbs her neck then disappears. The Masters' coloration means something about their emotional state, but I've never completely cracked the code. I take a wild guess that I'm not the only one who's angry.

A strange and unfamiliar satisfaction spreads warmth through my still-quivering body.

"*Something* must have happened prior to your heart failing," Mother Superior continues. It's a not-too-subtle threat—I may not have actually died, but restarting a stopped heart is certainly within the realm of ascender med tech. "Tell me. *Now.*"

Her harsh tone surges my anger up again, doubling my determination for the truth to remain *sorkept*. It must show on my face because Mother Superior draws even closer. Her cybernetic eyes dilate and flush with purplish wisps as she measures me in a thousand inhuman ways.

"You resist, Sister Amara." Even her voice is filled with anger now, and it shakes me… the Masters are always cool and unflappable, even cold… but never angry.

I'm in dangerous territory.

Then Mother Superior's skin tone flattens into a neutral gray. I've only seen this once before, when I was just a girl, running through the hallways, caught right before dashing past the double black lines—but I didn't understand it until now.

She's *hiding* her reaction from me. This confuses me.

"Your resistance is why you're such trouble, Sister Amara." Her voice is cool again. "You need to have faith in order to fulfill your purpose. The more you resist, the longer it will take."

I wonder how long I have. The Masters can't read my thoughts, but Mother Superior can obviously read my face—and apparently all my thoughts show there.

When I don't respond, her expression hardens. "At the dosage levels I gave you, the human body does not easily endure the dissociation." Her ashen skin covers her feelings, but I can intuit them—how frustrating it must be for this vastly superior being to be thwarted by her simple experimental-human not performing as I should.

That foreign sense of satisfaction is back.

"Maybe you need to pull back on the dosages," I say, the boldness of my words surprising me. "It's dangerous."

A cruel smirk flashes across Mother Superior's face. "Yes, it is. Very dangerous." She takes a step back and gestures to me like my bold rebellion is a pointless tantrum, that of a little child's. "But if you won't tell me what happened, then I'll be forced to repeat the experiment with someone else."

My sisters. "What?"

She waves a casual hand in my direction. "A serum could wrest the truth from your lips, Sister Amara, but so far, you're the only one to show promise. I don't want to tamper with your mind any more than necessary. So you're forcing me into this. Unless or until you become more cooperative, I will have to continue dosing your sisters by turns until one of them bridges the gap. Your choice, Sister Amara."

My stomach hollows out. "You can't—"

"Follow me," she cuts me off. It's a command I don't dare disobey.

She whisks past me at ascender speed to the door. It slides open, and she waits for me in the hall. I stumble, my brain scrambling. Should I tell her about my mind coming apart under the high dosage? I vowed to keep everything *sorkept,* but surely, if she knew, she wouldn't risk my sister's lives. And I'll still have the secret of the traveling, but... what if telling her about my mind coming apart will mean something to her? I can't outsmart an ascender, and the fact that she so desperately wants to know makes me want to tell her even less.

The choice snarls up my mind as Mother Superior brings me to a blue-glass room with twelve chairs. I shuffle inside, and the door closes behind us.

"The girls follow you, Sister Amara," she says coolly. "You need to tell them to cooperate. You are *meant* for this—your awakening is the reason for which you were created. It will go badly for all of them, including you, if you continue to resist fulfilling your purpose."

Dread trickles through me, but I hold my tongue as I realize: *she will keep pushing no matter what I say.*

At the far side of the room, another door slides open. Mother Grace herds my sisters through, one by one. Their eyes are wide, their faces scared. Maya's shoulders are hunched up. Chloe's hand flutters nervously against her face. Even Sophia looks unnerved, her hands held tight in a prayerful position, but tormenting each other. Sister Hadley is the only one who doesn't look nervous—her attention wanders to the walls, the chairs, and the floor in a circular pattern.

"We're going to increase your dosages, just like Sister Amara's," Mother Superior announces to them.

A gasp goes around the room. Mother Grace ushers them toward the chairs designated for each. None of them takes a seat.

"Don't do this," I say harshly to Mother Superior. "It's too dangerous, and you know it!"

I'm speaking far out of line—the long hesitation before she replies feels like a noose drawing tighter and tighter around my neck. As if she's contemplating a hundred ways I could die before she finally says, "All you need to do is tell me, Sister Amara."

"Tell her what?" Sister Sophia asks. But she has to know. Even if my sisters don't know about my traveling, they know I've gone further than any of them. And might have the most to hide.

I hold Mother Superior's steady gaze. I tell myself that revealing what happened to my mind on the cusp of death is a small price to keep her from sending my sisters there. That I'm still keeping the *true* secret of my ability to travel outside my body—which may not be the power or the awakening the Masters wanted, but it is still *something.*

"Just before I died," I say, holding my chin up as I face her, "it felt like my mind was expanding. Blowing apart into a million pieces. Whatever you did with the med patch, it was *too much.*"

A smile forms slowly on Mother Superior's face. "Too much for *you,* perhaps, Sister Amara."

What? *No.*

She turns her smile to the rest. "But perhaps one of your sisters is stronger in her faith."

All my pride flees in an instant. "No! You can't… I'm begging you…"

Her smile drops away. "You wouldn't deny your sisters their chance at fulfilling their purpose, would you?" But her voice is cold, an icy flow that's freezing air in my chest.

"You don't have to dose me!" Judith is backing away from her chair, eyes wide, her back edging up against the glass wall. "I've seen visions! Sister Amara told us to lie, but I won't lie. You don't have to dose me, I've already awakened!"

"Judith." The word hurts my heart even as I whisper it. She's always been more fearful than the others. Her betrayal stings in more ways than one. If her words are true, she has lied to all her sisters, keeping her visions for herself alone. And if her words are lies, she is merely betraying our sister-bond to save herself, even as I know it will make no difference— Mother Superior will dose every last one of them. I can see it in the way she's ignoring Judith's frantic words, Chloe's small whimper, and the horrified, wordless tremble of Sophia's lips.

Mother Superior flits to the wall and summons a holo screen. Mother Grace urges my sisters to take their seats. It's a gentle persuasion backed up by mechanized strength more than capable of ensuring compliance. And what can my sisters do? The twelve of us outnumber the bot and the ascender, but our flesh and bones, our *humanity,* is our weakness—we're no match for the strength of even one mechanical bodyform, much less two.

Sister Judith protests and cries out as Mother Grace grabs her arm and drags her to the chair. Once the chair has her, Judith ceases her struggle. The others quickly take their seats, locked in by the cushions.

I alone am still standing.

"I will take their place." The words are out of my mouth before I even think it through.

Mother Superior pauses at the holo-screen. "And you will report back fully?"

I give her a short nod. An unspeakable dread chokes me, but I manage to say, "I've already died once. This time, I'll know what to expect."

"Very well." Mother Superior gestures to the one open chair.

I stumble over and climb in. The full-body shudder makes me tremble so hard that the gel cushions grabbing at my skin almost don't lock on. But then they do.

In the chair to my left, Sister Chloe's eyes are wide, but she's not protesting my last-ditch effort to save them. To my right, Sister Hadley's absent-minded gaze still roams the room, lands on me for a brief second, then looks away. I wonder if she even knows what's happening.

Mother Grace comes around with the med patch and places it on my forehead. My mind is racing ahead, trying to figure out how I can evade this. I reach out desperately for the sister bond, the calming connection I felt when I was traveling, but my fear is like a thick wool blanket I can't fight through.

Then the dosage activates and I'm flung out of my body.

The shift is so sudden, I'm not quite sure what has happened until I'm standing by the door and looking back at the twelve sisters in their circle of chairs, including my inert body. Mother Superior is still at the wall, and Mother Grace hovers nearby.

Only now… I can *move*. Even faster than Mother Superior and her vastly stronger physical body. I will myself to Sister

Chloe's side and touch her shoulder like before, when I was in her cloister cell. Her thoughts stream into me—waves of fear and hope. Then I flit to Sister Judith and touch her as well—if she's been seeing visions, maybe I can use that to save us all in a last-second attempt to fulfill our purpose. But there's only terror in her mind; she lied to escape the dosage. One by one, I visit my sisters, touching them briefly to see if they have any knowledge to help us.

I leave Sister Hadley for last.

When I arrive at her side, she sees me. And smiles. "Sister Amara." Her lips move but her words are almost inaudible. She has to be half in and half out of the traveling state—still bound to her body, but able to see me.

A cool shudder runs through me as Mother Grace literally walks through my body—or whatever this nebulous form is while I'm traveling. She leaves an aftertaste of metal and electricity behind, but more importantly, she places a med patch on Sister Hadley's forehead. Hadley's gaze is locked with mine, and she doesn't see Mother Grace, doesn't understand what's about to happen... but I do.

Mother Superior doesn't care if I've volunteered—she's going to dose everyone anyway. Too late, I realize Mother Grace has already made the rounds of all the chairs with med patches for each.

Chloe cries out and thrashes in the chair. I flit to her side, desperately searching my mind for something to do, some way to stop it, but I'm a helpless, disembodied form who can feel my sister's pain without being able to do anything about it. I reach out to her shoulder, and everything that's *Chloe* rushes through me... then fractures, flying apart into a billion pieces. I try to grab hold of her mind, but I can't hold it any more than I could keep water from slipping through my open fingers.

She falls limp in her chair, and, suddenly, my hand passes through her shoulder—she's no more substantial to me now than the chair she's sitting on.

No. Pain sears through me—what heartbreak would feel like if I were still in my body. I should have seen this coming.

Should have been able to stop it.

Chloe's *gone*... and Mother Superior isn't even slowing down. Judith goes next, convulsing in her chair, then Maya tumbles into death throes. Thea holds hands with Naomi, but they can't hold on, neither of them, as their minds are ripped from their bodies, shattered by the experiment-in-progress that Mother Superior is determined to conduct. She must be convinced one of us will make it, and she's clearing the chaff before the wheat, culling the crowd to get at the one mind who's capable of awakening.

Me.

I'm the one. The first and the only. My sisters' minds are exploding just as mine did, but they're not surviving it. They're broken, scattered, and every small thing I love about them is being destroyed before my eyes. *My sisters.* Their cries stab me with knives of regret.

The only one not thrashing or horribly, permanently still is... *Sister Hadley.* I move instantly to her side, and my touch brings a flood of confusion mixed with a hazy sort of awareness. Her gaze is vacant, but she's still present.

"Sister Hadley!" I cry out, willing her to understand that I'm here.

My call gives her focus. Her eyes find me.

"We have to break free," I say, trying to gather the pieces of her mind. She's the only one who's survived this state. She's been in it for who knows how long—scattered but not lost, broken but not gone. Her mind is a swirling storm, a shape that forms and reforms, like a flock of birds in flight, no will, just instinct. "Hadley, I need your help!" I hope my plea will bring her back from whatever dosage Mother Superior has sent through her patch.

Suddenly, Hadley's arm clutches mine, and her eyes peer sharply at me. The strangeness of this is beyond me, but her otherworldly form is connecting to mine.

Sister Amara. Hadley's lips form the urgent words—there's no sound, but I understand all the barely cohesive thoughts behind them. She has an idea. She wants to help me.

Then she shoves me away, breaking contact.

I'm cut off from the chaotic flow of her thoughts. Slowly, slowly, her head moves with tortured grace to the side, an intention of effort that must be radically intense inside her mind. She stares at my limp body in the chair, concentrating.

I don't know what to do. She threw me out—she must not want me to interfere. Then a tiny thing happens, something no one would notice if they weren't looking for it—the cushions of my chair release my body.

Hadley slumps in her chair, her eyes rolling back in her head.

No. I reach for her... but she's gone. She expended whatever she had left, holding herself together to somehow interface with my chair and set me free.

I'm not going to waste her sacrifice.

I will myself back into my own body and open my eyes.

My sisters are dying around me. I hear their final struggles. Mother Superior and Mother Grace are preoccupied. I may be foolish to think they won't notice, won't stop me, but I have no choice.

I lurch out of the chair and run for the door.

It slides open and I tumble through.

I keep going, my bare feet slapping the cool glass floor, and I don't dare look back.

Mother Superior and Mother Grace are fast enough that if they wanted to catch me... they would. The fact that they *don't*—that they stay with my sisters in their dying throes—tells me all I need to know.

I have to leave my sisters behind.

V

I'm running for my life through glass hallways.

I keep flitting half in and half out of my body, like Sister Hadley, even though I've swiped the med patch off my forehead. I'm strangely detached from my seizing heart, pounding feet, and the panic surging through my brain. I make several wrong turns before I finally find the hallway that will take me out of the cloister.

I can feel my sisters dying, one by one. Burning bright and burning out.

They're reaching for their holy purpose and being destroyed by it, all while Mother Superior gathers all her data. She's using us up and throwing us away.

And that can only mean one thing: we're not her only experiment.

Every second her instruments record will serve her *next* experiment, the one where she makes something better than us. Better than *me*. Next time—and I'm suddenly wondering if we're even the *first* or the *only*—she'll create beings who can survive the higher doses. Who can do more than just travel away from their bodies. A new set of clones with a new holy purpose. She'll keep trying and trying, and the collateral damage of our lives isn't a terrible tragedy to the Masters—it's an integral part of the process. We're simply the latest version of the experiment. I wonder how I never saw that before.

Keeping our secret takes on even stronger meaning. Sister Hadley kept her ability secret. And so did I. Together, we denied them that much, at least.

I reach the hallway with the double black lines and the six-foot-tall mechanized sentry. It becomes instantly clear why Mother Superior and Mother Grace didn't bother running after me—they knew I could never get past this wall of death.

I try to dash around it anyway, daring it to kill me.

It moves with lightning speed to clamp its mechanical hand around my arm of mortal bone and muscle. The pain makes me yelp, but the sentry doesn't even have Mother Grace's programmed tenderness. It only carries out the orders Mother Superior no doubt transmitted. Capture me; hold me; bring me back. Its heavy clomping on the glass flooring is a slow gong tolling my return as it drags me back into the cloister, toward the room where my dead sisters lie.

I struggle, but it's absolutely no use.

Anger and frustration make me fight anyway. I bloody my fingers as I tear at its glistening silver hand digging grooves into my flesh. I kick and scream and smear blood against its implacable metal face.

All for nothing.

I stop.

Before the sentry can return me to Mother Superior, I'll travel away from my body again. Let her kill me, as she has my sisters—her instruments won't find anything in the empty shell of my body. I won't let her benefit from my death.

Just as I'm about to travel, I notice the sentry's cool grip on my skin, and a strange thought tickles at the back of my mind—*Sister Hadley*. What did she do to my chair?

I look up into the sentry's unblinking eyes. Its form is only roughly humanoid, the better for intimidating and capturing wayward clone experiments, I suppose. But the intelligence inside is very low.

Not much more than the chair.

I lift out of my body, but only slightly, like Sister Hadley, and with the hand of my traveling form, I reach for the sentry's head. I expect to pass right through just as I did with cloister cell doors and my sisters' dead bodies, but instead, I feel something like a surge of metallic taste at the back of my throat and electricity zipping through me... not unlike when Mother Grace passed through my traveling form.

I easily find the sentry's neural circuits. They are simple to control.

I hesitate, but I know there's no escape for me. I could command the sentry to march me out of the cloister, out of the vast, sprawling glass prison of my home. It could take me out into the shining city... but then what?

It is a city filled with Masters.

It could carry me past the towers to the mountain, but Mother Superior will know I've survived. She'll come after me. No, there's only one solution; one way to keep Mother Superior from learning my secret and using it in her next unholy experiment:

I have to die.

The command is simple, and I give it fast.

The sentry spins its other arm, the one not holding me, and unfurls the light weapon in its palm. Just before it fires, I wrench myself out of my body. The shot burns bright as it tunnels through my skull.

I see myself slump in its arms. I float for a moment, nearby. *Safe*. Beyond the reach of Mother Superior and the Masters.

My body is dead.

I wonder how long it will take for the rest of me to die.

In a way, I'm truly awakened now, although not how I imagine they wished. Something pulls me further from my body, a strange detachment that makes me want to float away, but I don't go far. I'm tethered somehow, connected to this place and time. Then I realize... my link with the bot is holding me here, at least for the moment.

Mother Grace comes flying down the hallway, full speed, screeching to a sudden stop on the glass flooring and looking with horror at my bloodied and obviously dead body. She commands the sentry to release me—I sense the transmission in the sentry's very low sentience cognition and feel the reaction in its mechanisms. My body falls toward the floor, but Mother Grace catches it on the way down, easing me gently to an awkward slumping.

Mother Grace passes her hands over my body, verifying there is no chance of survival.

I drift closer, keeping my hold on the bot while I reach my hand to Mother Grace's shoulder. A flood of love and warmth and sadness fills me. Her mind is... complex. She was programmed to love, but the cognition required for that is considerably more sophisticated than the sentry's. Her purpose may have been to serve Mother Superior, but the loss she feels appears genuine.

I'm drawn to it, just as I was pulled by my sister bond.

The closer I draw, the more it pulls. I release my hold on the sentry and step into her body. I don't quite align. It's not quite comfortable. Like putting on a metal suit that's ill-fitting and three sizes too small. But I can wear it. And Mother Grace's cognition welcomes me with loving open arms.

She gives up her identity, her will, and control of her cognition to me.

I am her Master and always have been.

It's not clear to me that Mother Grace even understands what she's done, but we are welded now, bonded… and she's given me a gift as great as any mother could.

Seen through Mother Grace's eyes, the world is far different. I sense things I've never been able to feel before. I can peer through the endless glass corridors and clearly see the way out. I hear the transmissions coming from Mother Superior, asking for a status update on Sister Amara's now very dead human body.

I send a standard response.

Then I reach out to the sentry's cognition and disable it. The heavy weight of his armory-filled body slumps against the glass wall of the hallway and shatters it. I march Mother Grace's body—*our body*—along the straightest path toward an exit from the ascenders' genetic research facility. Reams of information spin past my mind, all the stores that Mother Grace has accessed in the course of her duties.

I ignore Mother Superior's ever-more-insistent demands for information. Mother Grace's cognition would not be able to resist, but my mind is strong enough for both of us.

I walk through endless glass hallways and out of the facility, into the sunshine.

Eventually, I will need power. But right now, I have a simple choice—the mountain or the city? Mother Grace's cognition is fast and able to sort information at a speed that would have boggled my human brain—she quickly calculates the odds of us being caught either way.

The city is safer.

We can hide, passing for a standard medical care bot among the few ascenders who keep illegal human pets. This information is just one of the many tidbits Mother Grace acquired over the years from the common knowledge database in service of her care for me, Sister Amara. There is so much more. So much to learn. So much to explore.

We slip away amongst the towers, finding shadows even in the brightness, making our escape.

Mother Superior's experiment hasn't failed... it has broken free.

~*~

A Word from Susan Kaye Quinn

~*~

Susan Kaye Quinn is a rocket scientist turned speculative fiction author who now uses her PhD to invent cool stuff in books. Her works range from young adult science fiction to adult future-noir, with side trips into steampunk and middle grade fantasy. Her bestselling novels and short stories have been optioned for Virtual Reality, translated into German, and featured in several anthologies.

She writes full-time from Chicago, inventing mind powers and dreaming of the Singularity.

Check out her works with a free story or chat with her about our coming robot overlords on Facebook.

Awakening was written in Susan's Singularity universe. If you liked it, start with the first novel of the series, The Legacy Human, or jump straight to her other short stories of robot weirdness (Stories of Singularity) set in the same universe as *Awakening*.

~*~

Eve's Children

Hank Garner

~*~

I

"Can you pick my dress up from the dry cleaner today?" I called out as I poured two cups of coffee.

"Yeah, I need to pick up my suit anyway."

I smiled and scooped two sugars into my cup and poured cream into his. Some of our friends say that we're as different as night and day, but I think our differences make us stronger.

He walked in, rubbing his freshly shaved face. I smiled at him, picked up his coffee and handed it to him. He took a sip then set it back on the counter.

"Your suit?"

"Yeah, I don't have many occasions to wear it, but you know... Today's special." He took my hand in his and gently stroked it with his calloused fingertips.

"You're shaking again." He frowned.

My eyes drifted down, but I could still feel his penetrating gaze.

"More dreams?" he soothed.

I nodded my head and took a sip of my coffee.

"Want to talk about it?"

"No, not right now. Just more of the same."

He grazed my face with the tips of his index and middle fingers and gave me that slanted smile. The one that I knew was him holding his peace, but worrying nonetheless.

"It's nothing. I'll be okay."

"Of course you will. I won't let you be anything but."

He leaned down and kissed me, holding my face in his strong hands. My nerves settled a bit. "You should talk to someone. Dreams are one thing, but when they leave you all stressed out for days on end, maybe it's time to sort it out."

"Yes, dear husband."

He let go of my face and picked his cup back up. Taking a deep pull from his coffee, he shifted his tone from concerned to something more exciting. "You excited about today?"

"Oh, very much." I smiled.

"Are you worried?"

"A little. Today is a game changer. The only thing I worry about is what the world will be like tomorrow."

He nodded, silent for just a moment. "The world will be the same place."

"I know it will, but the people in it won't." I put the cup down and trace the rim with my finger, staring into the steaming liquid. "I feel like I'm betraying everyone."

"How so?"

"I feel like I might crush the faith of millions."

"You really think it's that serious?" He picks up the stack of mail on the edge of the counter and flips through, separating bills from junk. He takes the stack of bills and his coffee to the table.

"Eric, what do *you* think will happen when the world finds out the truth about where we came from?"

He stared into his coffee cup. "I think you need to give the human race a little more credit."

~*~

The nagging uneasiness stayed with me as I made my morning commute. I drove in silence, not wanting to be alone with my thoughts, but less eager to hear what the talking heads on the radio had to say. Without tuning in I already knew what they were saying about me. I was the lady that had taken it upon herself to destroy the beliefs of the world. What I was getting ready to share would unhinge the very fabric of society.

At least that's what the last letter I received said.

Sure enough, protesters lined the street outside the museum where my office was located. It was nothing to see a random fire and brimstone sandwich board wearer on any given day, but this was serious. There must have been twenty-five or more. Luckily Ben, the faithful security guard, spotted my car and flagged me through the throng. He made an opening and I darted through and into the secure parking garage. He tipped his hat to me as the crowd of people surged past him to yell at me as the gate came down behind my car and separated me from them.

I parked my car, placed it in gear, and switched off the ignition. Dropping the keys in my lap, I leaned back, taking in a deep breath.

Allow the anxiety to fade.

Wait for the courage to come.

I settled for less anxious and slightly less scared.

Pulling the visor down, I flipped open the mirror. My eyes reminded me of the dreams. It was always the eyes. I closed the visor and summoned the last drop of almost courage and opened the door.

The garage echoed with the sound of my heels tapping on the concrete as I strode toward the entrance. I was startled by a lone protester that made his way to the gate and yelled at me through the slits. I didn't turn around but got to the door as quickly as I could. I swiped my I.D. and when the lock clicked, I didn't hesitate to get to safety.

The door slammed behind me and I rested against the plain white institutional walls of the museum's back office. I was startled by Betty's hand on my shoulder.

"You okay?"

"Yes. You startled me."

"Are you ready for today?"

"I don't know if there is such a thing as ready, but today is the day whether I'm ready or not."

Betty nodded. "You don't have to do this, you know." She tapped a folded piece of paper against the tile that covered the bottom third of the wall.

"I have to do it. Today's the day. The invitations have been sent, the press is coming. Dignitaries. The device is fully charged. The world is waiting to see what happens when we turn it on."

Betty nodded slowly. "Yeah, but nobody said it had to be you. I know you have been at the center of the research, but you don't have to be the target for all the crackpots. This is not your burden to carry."

I looked down at the source of the tapping sound. "What's that?"

She sighed and pulled the paper up to eye level. "I'll give you one guess."

"Fan mail. Great." I took it from her and unfolded it, seeing the familiar twenty-two-point comic sans font.

YOU THINK YOUR DOING THE WORLD A FAVOR, BUT YOUR REALLY JUST A WOLF IN CHEAP CLOTHING.

"Ahhhh, my admirer that can't form a proper metaphor. Besides, after all this, don't you think he could learn to use spell check?" I wadded the paper up and handed it back to Betty. "This is precisely why this is my project. I figure you don't take this much crap for something that doesn't matter. I have things to do."

II

I looked at the little wire basket on my desk and the odd collection of letters just like the one Betty had. I thought that one day I would make a scrapbook out of them. Sometimes you have to have a morbid sense of humor to keep going.

I opened my email and immediately regretted it. The incoming mail banner showed that seven hundred eighty messages were downloading to my inbox. I didn't wait to see who they were from or what they wanted. Incoming mail could easily be filed into three categories: crazy people, people crazy enough to support me, and people looking to capitalize on my research. None of them interested me.

I closed the email program and leaned back in my chair. Inhaling, I pinched the bridge of my nose, attempting to make my mind slow down a bit. My pulse raced like I was running a hundred miles an hour, full tilt.

The images began creeping in at the edges of my consciousness and, before I knew it, I was replaying the dream from the night before. And the night before that. And before that.

The woman started talking to me, as always. Telling me things that I had no way of knowing. I had prided myself on being a woman of science, of reason, but there was no denying that something else was at play here.

As I rested there in my chair with my eyes closed, she began speaking to me again. Her soothing voice calmed me. I exhaled and listened.

"Lexi, please don't be scared. This won't be easy, but it's yours to do. You were chosen for this. They won't understand. They will mock and ridicule you, but it's okay. You will be remembered as the person who told the truth. You will eventually be remembered as a hero. But it won't be easy for some to hear that life actually came from somewhere and that they are not just accidents of time and chance."

The woman's face began to fade. I never quite got used to it. Not the dreams and visions, not the information that was always spot on. Not the waking up knowing things that I had no way of knowing. Least of all, I never got used to seeing that the woman in the dreams looked so much like me.

~*~

I stood up and shook myself to my senses. I had to get it together. I knew today would be a crazy day and would possibly change the course of the rest of my life.

That was fine. Wasn't that what scientists wanted? What scientist wanted to go to her grave knowing that all she was known for was that she was a good lab rat that kept her beakers sorted and her petri dishes labeled like no one else? No thank you. Science is messy. If you're not breaking things and challenging paradigms, then you'll never change the world.

Resolving to put on a brave face and finish what I'd started, I stood up. This day would be nothing if not exciting.

I slipped my key into the lock on the top of the filing cabinet. I twisted it and, as I heard the lock pop out, I hesitated. Taking a deep breath, I pulled the drawer open. The file folder was laying there where I left it. The fact that the folder was the source of so much spite and contention actually made me laugh out loud. I picked it up and took it to the small round table in the corner of my office.

The photocopied pages were sitting in neat little stacks in the folder, and I nervously sorted them. Just the way I did the day before, and the day before that.

I had been over this material dozens of times before, but I wanted to step through my narrative one more time. I paused, almost reverently, on the page showing my very own Rosetta Stone, the key to decoding it all. An astounding piece of work, anyone would be proud to have this as their legacy. I guess the thing that made me the most nervous was that someone would find out how I found the book and how I knew how to interpret it. No one wanted to listen to a scientist that got their information from a spirit.

Once again, I went over my bullet points. I would guide the audience through them one by one, showing the history of the archaeological finds from all over the world that had fostered legends and conjecture for centuries. Each piece, each find would stir up new debate and new theories, but I had proposed a unified theory that, when finally tested, eventually culminated in this day.

For years, many people had floated the theories that life had been seeded here from another civilization, another world. The theory was fodder for late night call in radio shows where the guest dujour would spout some half-witted idea about abductions, crop circles, and cave drawings. Variations on the theory were as diverse and wild as the people who shared them. What began as an intriguing story became a wild circus of craziness. I marveled at how close to the truth they actually were, at least in the beginning.

I shuffled the papers back into the proper stacks and then back into the folder. A knock at the door startled me. I held the folder close to my chest.

"Dr. Danvers, would you like to walk over to the auditorium and get a sound check before everyone piles in? You know it's going to be a mad house later."

"Hey Rick, yeah. I think that would be a good idea. Let me put this stuff away."

Rick watched as I lovingly carried the folder back to the cabinet and carefully placed it back in its protective drawer. I clicked the lock back in and dropped the keys back in my pocket. He smiled, one of the few people who had any inkling just how much of my life had become consumed with this project. He began as a graduate student intern and had become a fine scientist in his own right.

"Dr. Danvers, today is one for the history books. I can feel it."

"That's what scares me, Rick."

III

The auditorium was dark and cool. Rick ran his hands along the wall until he found the switch. I shielded my eyes against the pain of my pupils constricting. The room would be buzzing with activity in just a few hours and, for a moment, I just wanted to enjoy the peace. Rick was buzzing with anticipation, though. And rightfully so. He had been here with me through this whole process.

He was with me when I lost my initial funding because the foundation didn't want to be associated with this sort of paranormal nonsense. He was with me while I floundered in front of benefactors and philanthropists until I finally found someone willing to take the chance. Rick had paid his dues working in the trenches, sometimes literally, next to me. He'd turned down a prestigious fellowship at Harvard, and traded his future reputation for a career of ridicule. I smiled at my intern, who had become a valued colleague, and was thankful for him. He would make this easier.

"Dr. Danvers, let's get this microphone on you and see how it sounds."

"Will you call me Lexi, please? I think we've been through enough together that we can dispense with formalities."

"I could never do that, Dr. Danvers," he said through a sheepish smile. I nodded my assent.

He clipped the small black mic to my lapel and handed me the transmitter pack. I held it in my left hand and walked around the room spouting nonsense while Rick fiddled with the knobs on the sound equipment. It squawked and squealed until he found the sweet spot.

"Would you like to go through the power point to get a feel for it in the room?"

"I think that's a great idea."

He left the sound booth and held his hand out to me. I reached in the pocket of my skirt and pulled out the thumb drive. I turned it over in my hand before handing it to him.

"Careful with that."

"Yes, ma'am." He took the drive and cradled it in his hand like it was a fragile baby bird.

"Okay, not that careful. I do have backups, you know."

"I know, it just feels like this is momentous."

"Oh, it is."

~*~

We went through the slides, one by one. I gave Rick a private screening of the information that he had seen a hundred times before. He took notes as always and, at the end, he lobbed questions to me. We had been through this routine more times than I could count, and, to his credit, he always came up with new ways of trying to challenge me to think on my feet.

I had tried to anticipate all of the questions—direct and rhetorical—and attempted to have simple and concise answers. Rick did a masterful job and we both felt good about how things would go.

Rick scratched his chin. "I can't think of anything else that we haven't gone over already."

"Well, I guess we're as prepared as we'll ever be." I smiled back at him.

"I'll go retrieve the thumb drive and we can get out of here before the press starts filing in."

His nervous anticipation had not waned during our rehearsal, if anything he seemed to be bursting at the seams with excitement. I stood at the podium imagining what the room would look like later that day and, more importantly, what the people in attendance would be feeling. I'm not sure you can be truly ready for something like that.

Rick entered the audio booth and bent down to retrieve my secure drive. A side door opened and spilled light in. Nervously, I looked toward the open door, but it was just a security guard. They were everywhere. I nodded to him and he nodded back. He walked into the room and looked around. His hand rested on a billy club hanging from the left side of his belt.

Rick stood up from his bent over position in the sound booth, his upper half appearing above the low walls.

"Okay, I think we're done here," Rick called out.

Movement from the corner of my eye pulled my attention back to the guard, who spun around toward Rick. The guard had gotten much closer to me than I'd realized.

He pulled his service revolver, cocked the hammer back,

and fired his pistol at Rick.

Rick slumped behind the low walls of the sound booth. My ears rang from the gunshot in the closed room as the guard ran toward me.

I screamed.

IV

"Dr. Danvers. Close your mouth. A loose tongue spoils the broth."

I was a trembling wreck. He ran toward me, his gun trained on my head. When he was inches away and I could see his eyes, I knew right then that this was no security guard, this was my letter writer.

"What was that last thing you said?" I stammered.

"I was telling you to be quiet. A loose tongue and all."

The burned gun powder wafted from the muzzle. While I was trembling like a leaf, he seemed to be utterly calm. He held the gun perfectly still.

"My, Dr. Danvers, you're sweating like a bullet. Get it? Bullet?" He cackled.

"Please, I need to check on my colleague."

"He'll be fine. I hit him in the shoulder. I think. We'll go check on him in a minute, but we need to go lock that door. I'm sure we'll be surrounded any moment now."

I swallowed and pushed the fear down as best I could. "You're right. There is security all over this building. You'll never get away with this."

He grabbed me by the shoulder while keeping the gun trained on me with his other hand. He marched me toward the door that he had come through and dead-bolted it. We turned and secured the main door that Rick and I had used. Then, on to the opposite side. He looked around for any other entrances. Satisfied that the room was secure, he walked me over to the sound booth.

Rick's shoes stuck out from the back of the booth.

"Oh my God, Rick!" I dropped down next to him and my knee instantly got soaked. His eyes were closed and his breathing was shallow. "Rick, can you hear me?"

Rick's eyelids flickered, but didn't open. He had a nasty gash in his left shoulder that looked raw and angry. Blood seeped from under him. The assailant *had* hit him in the shoulder, but a little lower than I had hoped. He must have hit the top of the lung. I tried my best to stay calm as I assessed the situation.

"He needs help. We have to call someone," I yelled.

My captor stood over us. "There's not really time for all that. It won't matter in a few minutes anyway."

My blood ran cold as he opened up his jacket and showed me that he was strapped with what looked to be explosives.

~*~

"Oh my god. What are you doing?" I shouted. "You can't do this. This man needs help!"

He reached down and pulled at my arm.

I pulled away. "No! I have to stop this bleeding." I looked around for anything. There was a roll of paper towels on the counter of the sound booth. I unspooled a big handful and dabbed at the wound. I had no idea how to stop the bleeding, or even if I could, but I felt like I needed to do something. Anything. I felt the assailant fidgeting next to me.

"Alright, Dr. Danvers, come with me. He's gonna be okay. Or he won't. Yeah, he probably won't. I need you over here. We're gonna make a statement."

He pulled me by the arm again, but he held strong this time. He lifted me to my feet. Blood covered my legs and hands. The gravity of the situation hit me all of a sudden and my knees went weak.

"No, ma'am. You don't get to pass out on me. No, ma'am. You're gonna be right here with me."

"Police department. You're surrounded. Open the door." An officer with a bullhorn blared through the door just outside the main entrance.

The man checked his watch. "Two and a half minutes. They're a little faster than I gave them credit for."

"A gunshot was reported. We need to make sure everything is okay in there." The bullhorn shouted again.

The gun dug into my back. "Tell them that you are here and that you are okay."

He pushed me toward the door with the gun in my back.

"Hello, this is Dr. Alexandra Danvers. I am in here, and I am fine. But my associate Richard Sloan is injured. He's been shot." The gun dug deeper into my back.

"Careful, doc," he hissed in my ear. "I don't want to give everything away just yet."

This time the police officer spoke, but not with the aid of the bullhorn. "Dr. Danvers, are you alone?"

"Like I said, Dr. Sloan is here with me…"

"But the gunshot. What happened?"

I hesitated. I didn't know how to answer. This man wanted something, attention maybe, but he still had not stated his reason.

"Dr. Danvers, we know you're not alone in there. Are you in immediate danger?"

The skin around my spine pinched as the gun twisted and prodded with his every move. I whispered to him. "What do you want me to say?"

"Tell them that I will make my demands soon."

"Who do I tell them you are?"

He pulled me back away from the door. We heard an increased commotion, like more people were gathered outside.

My captor called out. "Not so fast, officer. I have a hostage, and one is injured. No funny moves or I blow this entire place to bits."

"Sir, tell us what you want." The officer called out.

"Don't you want to know who I am first?"

"Sir, we have already identified you as Walter Johanson. White male, fifty-three years of age. Single. You live with your mother at 1793 Orchard Springs Drive. What is it that you want?"

He looked at me, puzzled.

I pointed to the square above the door. He leaned in and squinted.

"New security cameras and security system with the best facial recognition. The kind of work we do draws all sorts of protesters."

Mr. Johanson had not taken this bit of information into account. For the first time, I saw him tremble.

V

The uncomfortable silence was pierced by the sound of my phone ringing. Johanson flicked the gun up, motioning for me to pull the phone out. The screen had a photo of Eric and his name.

"I'll bet he's seen the news," Johanson said.

My stomach was in knots. I was terrified to think about him worrying.

"Go ahead, answer it."

"Eric! I'm okay," I answered at the same time he blurted out, "Lex, honey, *are* you okay?"

"I am."

"I saw the news. What's going on?"

"I can't really talk, but I'm okay. It's going to be okay."

"Lex, tell me what's going on."

"I can't talk, but I would really appreciate it if you would pray for me right now."

He paused. I'd never asked him to pray for me before. He knew where I stood on that stuff. He was the believer, not me. "I am already. Hang in there, sweetie."

Before I could say anything else, Johanson snatched the phone away from me. He put it to his ear. "Mr. Danvers. I think if you would have been praying for your wife before now we wouldn't be in this mess. Say goodbye." He hung up the phone.

A cry escaped as I clutched my mouth. He tossed the phone back to me.

"Interesting husband you have there. Maybe if he would have kept you in line we wouldn't be having to do this. Maybe his next wife will be better for him. We could stand here and talk until the cows turn blue, but there is a purpose to my little visit. I need you to show me the information you have that you were planning to show at your press conference."

I was trembling with rage. "Don't you dare talk to me about my husband."

"Hit a nerve, did I? You better get yourself in line, missy."

"Or what? You're going to shoot me like you did Rick? That man is dying over there. You have to stop this and let me get help for him."

"It doesn't matter. Look at me. I'm wearing enough explosives to level this entire city block. I shot him because I didn't plan for him. You, yes. But he startled me. He's gonna die regardless. We all are."

~*~

I pulled away from him. "What do you want?"

"Don't get any bright ideas," he said through gritted teeth.

"You won't shoot me. I mean, we're all going to die anyway, right? Tell me. What do you want?"

"I want to shut this whole charade down. I won't allow you to crush people's faith."

"Why would the truth crush people's faith? Don't you want to know the truth? We came from somewhere. We have proof."

His face turned red and he shook as he gripped the gun tighter and spit. "You say you have the answers, but what you have is a fabricated lie. You're trying to replace what people have put their trust in with some other story, a story that makes you feel better about the world. But in doing that, you're changing the shape of the world. You're asking the world to swallow your new story, but I wouldn't eat that with a ten-foot pole."

"You think that because I found my story I'm not a person of faith? Exactly the opposite. Finding the truth made my faith stronger. Or I should say it gave me faith for the first time."

"You don't get to do this. You don't get to twist everything. I know what you stand for. Or better yet, I know that you don't stand for anything."

"That's not true at all. I just want to be able to prove what I believe."

"That goes against everything. If you have to prove it, then it's not faith. There has to be an element of mystery to faith."

"What if I told you that I do believe in things that I can't explain? What if I told you that that's what made me a believer?"

"What are you talking about?"

"I talk with angels."

"Don't patronize me. Don't you even." He waved his finger in my face. "I want you to say it. I want you to admit it. You're gonna die anyway, you might as well go out with a clear conscience."

"What do you want me to tell you?"

"I want you to tell the truth!"

"You want the truth? I'll give you the truth."

The Police officer called out through the door again. "Is everything okay in there? I need to hear that the hostages are unharmed, or we'll have to come in by force. We don't want to do that."

I looked at him, dodging my head around his upheld pistol. "Let me tell them I'm not hurt."

He waved the gun toward the door. "I'm watching you."

I walked toward the door. "This is Dr. Alexandra Danvers. I am unharmed, but my colleague is seriously injured. I've stopped the bleeding, for now, but he needs medical attention."

"Dr. Danvers," the police officer answered, "do you need us to come in?"

"Not yet. I think I'll be out soon. I think this is just a big misunderstanding."

"Get back over here," the gunman said. "You talked to them, now finish what you were saying and let's get this over with."

"Like I was saying, the truth is probably more complicated than you think."

VI

"It all began with the discoveries of the last century. Scientists started discovering artifact after artifact that couldn't be dated properly. It was like we had no frame of reference to properly catalog these things. Certain elements that didn't seem to be native to our world, covered in writings and symbols that didn't mean anything, but looked to be in some sort of logical progression. Like a language.

"At first all of these things were just oddities and not taken seriously by academics. They wouldn't even entertain the idea. I was one of those.

"But then I started having dreams. Sometimes I would have these visions even when I was awake. It was crazy at first, there was a woman that looked like me, and she would tell me weird things. Things like you would see on some of these cable TV shows. She told me that everything I thought was true about life was wrong. She told me that there *is* more to life than I could possibly imagine.

"She talked to me for months before I let my guard down. A little at a time, I began to understand what she was saying. She told me her name was Eve and she was the mother of our civilization. Great scientists used her DNA to make copies of the building blocks of life and sent it here. She and a man named Adam—I know how this sounds—seeded life on our planet. According to her, our world is a great big experiment, an experiment in creating life and seeing just how civilizations would form. The funny thing is that we are still connected with our creators if we would only allow ourselves to see into our subconscious. There is more to life than we can imagine."

"See, this is what you people do," he seethed. "You take the truth and you twist it so that you can control and manipulate people. You're mocking me and what I believe."

"No, sir. I would never do that. Even if I disagree with you, I would never mock you. Life is too precious. You know what else Eve told me? She told me that we are not the only world that was seeded. There are hundreds more out there just like us. We are not alone. *That* is what's so wonderful about this discovery. We can finally say there is other life out there, and yes, we can say that there is more to us than mere chance. We all get to be right."

I smiled. A deep, satisfied smile. I really thought I had gotten through to him. I really thought he would lay down his weapon and go home. I believed that until he detonated the bomb.

~*~

"Eric Danvers?"

"This is he."

"Mr. Danvers…"

"I know. I've been watching the news."

"We're very sorry, Mr. Danvers. If there is anything we can do, please let us know. We'll need you to come down to the station later and give a statement, but take your time. We understand the grief you must feel at your loss."

"Thank you, officer." Eric hung up the phone.

He leaned back in his recliner, eyes glued to the TV. He was upset, shaken, devastated. But not without hope. Oddly, all of the conversations he'd had with Lexi over the last several months had prepared him for this.

He closed his eyes and thought of her. He concentrated on holding his memory strong. Her dark hair, her full lips, her large brown eyes. He could almost hear her voice. He drifted in that sea of calm as the television in front of him buzzed with the sounds of reporters and emergency responders and calls for justice and action. But he didn't care. Lexi was there with him.

After a while, he went to the roll top desk where Lexi sometimes worked at home. He pulled out a folder where she kept some backup photocopies of the material she had been working on. He flipped through the sheets of paper until he found the one with the mysterious symbol. The symbol that was found on the mechanism that Lexi determined was used to bring Eve's genetic material to our world. He ran his fingers over the four large symbols and thought of Lexi. His fingers traced them one by one.

N. A. S. A.

"I'll be with you soon."

~*~

A Word from Hank Garner

~*~

Hank Garner is the author of *Bloom*, *Mulligan*, *Seventh Son of a Seventh Son* and *Writer's Block*. For nearly two years, Hank has hosted The Author Stories Podcast, a weekly show focusing on writing and the creative process.

Hank lives in Mississippi with his wife and five children.
Follow his releases and the Author Stories Podcast at hankgarner.com.

~*~

Black Site
Michael Patrick Hicks

~*~

I

Skin sloughed away from the subject, dissolving in the synthesis chamber. Watching the pink tissue drift through the solution, Alpha was reminded of fish food flakes. He'd never had a fish tank, but Papa had. Because he carried the memories of Papa in his own skull, he was able to make the comparison by proxy.

"Subject Uniform failed to maintain cohesion," he said for the benefit of the record. His voice was dispassionate and wooden, no longer burdened by the personal sense of failure he had once felt during earlier projects. The lack of success, though, was not necessarily a failure. Rather, it carried the potential of a lesson, new data to study and build from.

Echo stood beside him, her hands hanging limply at her sides. Her fingers fidgeted against her thighs, patting out a tiny rhythm against her slate gray slacks, occasionally pinching at the fabric. As far as Alpha could tell, none of the others, himself included, exhibited such nervous habits. Not for the first time, he thought Echo was simply unique, and not just because she was the only female of the project. That, in and of itself, had been an aberration. A fluke. An oddity that he enjoyed studying, frankly.

"Victor appears to be gestating regularly," she said. "Systems are normal."

Even Victor, though, was marred by irregularities, far more than Uniform had been. Yet Echo was correct—Victor, for all intents and purposes, was developing as planned, even if the term 'regular' was a bit of a misnomer. The project was on track, and that was the most important aspect. The loss of Uniform was a disappointment, but hardly more than a minor misstep in Papa's grander designs.

Drawing closer to the chamber, he studied the developing fetus. The only thing separating the viability of Uniform and Victor were slight alterations in protein sequences. A slight change in carboxyl groups, an alteration in an amino acid that made one's protein either active or inactive, turned a hormone on or off and, in turn, meant either doom or survival for one's genetic sample.

Victor was nearing the equivalent of its fifth month of development. In a normal fetus at this stage, the cellular formation would have taken on a shape plainly recognizable as human. Yet, Alpha failed to recognize much that was uniquely human in Victor's development. A clearly designed face, arms, legs, and torso were all plainly familiar in terms of categorization but far from human. In fact, the aberrations were so pronounced that studying the subject gave him a mild headache.

Echo put her arm around his waist, rested her head on his shoulder. He pressed his cheek against her hair, enjoying the warmth radiating from her body.

"Do you think this is it?" Echo said.

In the tank, Victor's arm unfolded and smacked against the glass, an eye swiveling toward them. The fingers were strangely elongated, and already they could make out the tip of a sharp, dagger-like nail as he pressed his palm against the thick encasement.

"We're getting closer," he said.

Despite the apparent physical differences, Alpha felt a

strange kinship to the piebald creature. They did, after all, share a common genetic sequence, albeit one now far removed from each other. He had to still himself against pressing his own hand against the glass, so strong was the urge to make contact in even that minor way.

Slowly, he led Echo away, back to the workstations where Bravo, Charlie, and Delta monitored the synthesis chambers.

"Purge Uniform's tank and begin prepping the chamber for Subject Whiskey. Continue monitoring Subject Victor and alert me immediately if any other irregularities arise."

He couldn't help but notice his headache subside now that Victor was out sight and out of reach. If this current headache were a single instance, he would not have been so troubled by it. The fact that a slow burning pain began to encase his brain each time he personally examined Victor was enough to convince him that their current subject was, if not the direct cause, then at least more than casually related. This oddity was curious enough on its own, but he mentally filed it away for the moment. His growling stomach reminded him of more pressing matters.

He moved to the door, Echo following beside him as she so often did.

Leaving the lab, he was greeted immediately by Papa's face. His own face, in fact, albeit one that was substantially older and wizened, the shared furrows of their brows and the lined recesses around each side of their mouths far more pronounced in Papa's features.

The corridor was lined with imagery of Papa. In each of the photos, Papa proudly displayed his Raëlian pendant, the large silver icon of the Star of David intertwined with a swastika hanging loosely over his chest from a long gold chain. There were photos of the orbital mining magnate christening his latest asteroid platforms—one of which Alpha knew was this very same base—more of the man shaking hands with UN representatives and various presidents and dignitaries, and images of him with staff, researchers, lab workers, and miners.

There were no more rock pushers at this facility. No more

researchers and lab techs, aside from Alpha and his team. The veins of this particular asteroid had run dry ages ago, and the platform had officially been shuttered for more than twenty years. Papa's deep pockets, though, and some fanciful accounting kept the lights on and the equipment running.

As they passed through the corridor highlighting Papa's achievements, Alpha was again struck by the disparity in Echo's appearance. While she carried many of Papa's features, she was unmistakably softer and appealingly feminine. Her skin carried a more youthful appearance, the laugh lines around her lips gentle and more charming than the severe set their old progenitor was marked with, and which, in time, would mar Alpha's own features. For her part, Echo looked as if she had merely inherited his features, as if she were Papa's daughter rather than a genetic duplicate. A mishap with the protein loads, some fat-fingered amino acid sequencing, and a minor dose of genetic gap filler during the earlier stages of synthesis had flipped a few too many switches. This was not to say that the production of Echo was a failure so much as it was a decidedly welcome outcome.

Alpha was, strictly speaking, the purest of Papa's clones. He was the original, second only to the progenitor. As they worked further down the line, each successive generation grew a bit more distant from Alpha and Papa, and were nurtured to be more distinct. Echo had been the apex of that distinctive cultivation, and Alpha had been convinced they were edging that much closer to the truth, stripping back the layers of genetic impurities to achieve something nearer an answer to a question that was virtually indefinable by admission.

Where did humans come from?

That was the question. Papa believed he had both the answer and the method for discovery. And that the necessary research could be conducted here, in this defunct orbital mining station operating as an off-books, privately funded black site.

Sometime during their walk, Alpha realized that Echo had hooked her hand around his and that their fingers were intertwined. When they reached his quarters, his hunger was momentarily forgotten and replaced with an equally base desire.

Their lips pressed together, her hands pulling his body close. In the tight confines between them, he worked loose the buttons of her blouse and slacks, and she shimmied out of her underwear while he stripped.

Not for the first time, he questioned the nature of their lovemaking. They had been partners for a handful of years, nearly the entirety of Echo's life. At the start of their affair, Alpha had been hesitant to pursue her, struck by the strangely incestuous nature of such a fling. Being nearly an exact genetic duplicate, he began to view sex with Echo as a nearly masturbatory experience. Although she possessed female anatomy, Alpha was keenly aware that he was, in essence, making love with, and to, himself.

While the nature of their relationship was an intellectual curiosity, the physicality was unbridled and shameless. They enjoyed both their own bodies and one another's with frequent abandon.

Even as her body bucked against his, his mind turned over the riddles of Uniform's failure and Victor's early achievement of cohesion. There was so very little separating success from abortion, and the genetic lines they used for replication were altered only slightly. The aim was to reach an answer that was as genetically pure as possible. To discover and recreate the common ancestor that had made progeny of *Homo habilis, Homo gautengensis, Homo rudolfensis, Homo erectus*, and down through the evolutionary chain that led to *Homo floresiensis* and, finally, *Homo sapiens*.

As Alpha and his kin carried out their work, this latest iteration of Victor and its achingly unfamiliar construction appeared to be proving Papa's hypothesis correct.

Whatever had given rise to those early attempts at humanity had not been a purely simple act of evolution. Like Papa, he was hesitant to call it creation, for that carried many unseemly religious connotations that spoke more toward fantasy than any scientifically proven reality. He preferred to think of it more as *manipulation*.

Witnessing the trajectory of Victor's development, though, a single negative, but pervasive, thought began to wriggle through his mind. He couldn't help but wonder if, perhaps, given the gross disparities between Victor's form and the modern human, that the answer may ultimately be even simpler. Certainly not creation, perhaps not even manipulation. He worried that the answer boiled down to pure tragedy. That Papa's hypothesis was only partly correct in its presumptive capacity, but less so in its explanations.

Lying in the heated afterglow, with Echo pressed tightly against his side and lightly snoring, her head resting on his chest, he began to wonder at the possibility that the answer to humanity's rise had come as a result of nothing more than a simple mistake.

II

A collection of mistakes lined the walls and shelves of a defunct ore processing station that had been converted into a storage facility.

Alpha normally enjoyed spending time in this section of the black site, despite the plainly macabre nature of his surroundings. Here, he could gaze upon their past efforts, a mixture of wild successes and stunning failures.

Uniform's termination had left him in a rut, more focused on their past errors than usual. And the questionable viability of Victor continually twisted in his mind as he pondered if the physical aberrations of that particular subject were deformities or a natural occurrence of the subject they were attempting to replicate. Or, perhaps, "recreate" was a more accurate term, as he had never seen nor heard of such a creature in his life.

He slowly roamed through the maze of storage racks, occasionally stopping to soak in the details of their research. Beneath the overhead lighting tract, the liquid preserving the relics of disused flesh and tumorous lumps that vaguely resembled bipedal creatures radiated a warm, amber glow.

The other subjects varied in size and shape and genetic lineage, as did the maladies that had provoked their termination either naturally or through a systematic elimination conducted by the research group. In a large cylinder, Alpha studied lidless eyes that were too familiar, surrounded by a lumpy, misbegotten skull resulting from Proteus syndrome. The lips were far too large, the nose a violently configured clay-like structure, the bones of his cranium stretching the skin and twisting it into overinflated knots that buried one ear beneath a tumor covered in a patchwork clump of hair. The subject had died before reaching full maturity, but the cause had been a deep vein thrombosis rather than a complication from the physical disorders he had suffered.

In another smaller jar was a fetus that had begun showing its trauma at the accelerated equivalent of eight weeks. Because this subject's phonetic call sign was Juliet, the gene structure had been coded to produce a second female. However, the protein structures had been incorrectly sequenced. In normal fetal development, by eight weeks the embryo develops eyes, eyelids, arms, legs, fingers and toes, mouth, lips, fingernails, and detectable brainwaves. Slightly above the now-shortened umbilical cord, a small arm grew from the subject's belly. Its second arm was in the correct position, but grotesquely shortened, with fingers blooming from the shoulder joints. The mouth had failed to separate properly, cutting a small slit of an orifice into the creature's transparent and reptilian visage. Alpha had elected to terminate rather than proceed any further, accepting that they were clearly on the wrong track with Juliet.

Echo had actually cried that night, and he'd held her in his arms, crying with her even though he could not quite articulate why.

Some jars he studied intently, others he gave barely a glimpse. His pace increased slightly, his steps growing heavier, as he recognized the futility of coming to this room.

Victor was unique in his aberrations, his mutations. There

had not been anything similar in all the decades of research that had been conducted at this facility. Nothing.

Rather than finding comfort in their years of progress built off these past errors, Alpha found himself further lost and troubled.

His sense of disquietude spiked sharply at the blaring of the emergency klaxon, a notification of trouble in the lab scrolling onto the translucent display overlay grafted across his forearm.

~*~

"Put down the glass," Charlie demanded. His voice carried a sharp edge, both hands open and stretched out before him in a plea.

Delta held Bravo in a chokehold, a large sliver of broken glass gripped tightly in his free hand. Blood pooled between the shiv and his palm, dripping down in solitary drops across Bravo's chest. The remains of a drinking vessel lay scattered across the floor.

"We can talk this out, Delta," Alpha said. "Just do like Charlie asked. C'mon. There's no reason for this."

Delta's lips peeled back from gritted teeth, a high-pitched moan curdling deeply through his throat. His eyes were red and watery, and he violently shook his head.

He jabbed the pointed edge of his makeshift blade into Bravo's cheek and drew a jagged line upward, to his temple.

Bravo gurgled a scream, both his hands clutching at Delta's forearm, trying to pry the limb away from his empurpled face. The glass continued up, into his hairline, digging a trench across his scalp and over his ear, up higher across the crown of his head. Blood sheeted down his face.

"Jesus Christ," Charlie said. "Fuck!"

Echo took a tentative step forward, but Alpha blocked her with his arm. He gave her a quick shake of his head.

"Delta. Listen to me."

"NO!" Delta shouted. And then he spun Bravo around and shoved him away, his clone tripping over his own feet, slipping in the pool his blood had made, and fell hard. His hands reached out in reflex to break his fall, his palms slamming into shards of glass tinkling in the widening crimson bath.

Alpha stepped forward, Charlie doing the same but from Delta's flank. If they could get Bravo out of the way, or maybe tackle Delta together, one of them securing the arm he held the weapon in—

And then Delta reversed his grip on the shard of glass and shoved it into his eye at a violently upward angle. They could hear the pointy shard break through the thin shelf of orbital bone and pierce his brain.

Delta roared and tore the improvised blade loose, taking his eye with it. He flicked the eyeball off, then took a deep breath and stabbed himself in the face once more. Then he raised his head back and rammed the glass into his carotid, twisting it on its edge and drawing it across his throat.

He choked on his blood, sputtering it out between his lips as he fell to his knees.

A moment later, he was dead.

Bravo had rolled onto his back with a shuddering moan. One hand reached out, his fingers curling in the gore until he found another shard of glass. Over and over and over, he punched the shard into his throat. By the time Charlie and Alpha were able to restrain him, he was gone, it had happened so fast.

"Jesus Christ," Charlie said again, his face white as a sheet, he was nearly ready to faint.

Alpha turned away and looked toward the synthesis chamber. Toward Victor.

That... *thing*... seemed to be watching them. A sharp bolt of pain dinged across the inside of Alpha's skull, forcing him to look away, to look back toward the grisly chaos of Delta and Bravo's bodies lying prone only a few feet in front of him.

~*~

Alpha and the remnants of his team of duplicates gathered

around a semicircular conference table. A steaming cup of coffee sat before each member. The display monitor projected information from Delta's autopsy report atop the center of the table.

"The glass shard entered at a forty-degree angle, and pierced Delta's brain. However, you'll see a rather severe abnormality to the surrounding region of tissue."

Echo leaned closer to the projection, her slim fingers hovering over the imagery. "It almost looks like—"

"Jelly," Charlie finished. "But... from a stab wound? That's not likely."

"No, it's not," Alpha agreed. "The amount of physical trauma is highly inconsistent with the findings. Yet, somehow, the frontal lobe is nothing more than mush."

"What about Bravo?" Echo said.

"Nothing outside of what was expected. His injuries were consistent with what we observed. This," Alpha waved toward the projection, "was the only abnormality I could discover."

"Maybe a degenerative condition?" Charlie said. "Could it be a sequencing failure, some type of genetic breakdown?"

Alpha shrugged. He had another theory, but not one he was quite ready to share. He was more curious about the path of this conversation and whether or not his duplicates would arrive at a similar conclusion.

"We can rule out suicide," Echo said.

"That was never really on the table to begin with," Alpha said.

"Why not?"

"I've never felt suicidal. Charlie, have you?"

Charlie shook his head. Each of them had been curated from the same genetic source, Papa, and each had the same cerebral mapping and memories of their progenitor. Papa was not genetically predisposed to depression and had never had suicidal impulses, which meant that his progeny had never experienced either. With the genetic factors largely accounted for, that left only environmental factors, and the mining station was kept as relaxed and comfortable as possible. A psychotic break of this scale, in the case of Delta, was simply improbable, if not outright impossible.

"So, what then?" Charlie said.

Alpha took a deep breath, steeling himself. "Victor."

His duplicates exchanged glances, and a slight, fleeting wash of relief swept across him. *They knew*, he realized, chiding himself for feeling surprise. Of course they knew. They had to.

Echo pursed her lips, incredulous. "Are you suggesting that Victor telepathically controlled Delta and Bravo? That he used some kind of mind control to manipulate them into killing themselves?"

"Not just manipulated," Alpha said. "Consumed them. Whatever control Victor was able to exert over Delta was enough to turn a part of his brain into pudding. We cannot simply allow this level of power to continue unchecked."

"For fuck's sake," Charlie sputtered, turning toward Echo with venomous intent. "Victor is still developing. He's not even reached post-birth viability and already he's able to mentally dominate another organism and exert his will."

"If that's so, then we've created the first legitimately viable telepathic humanoid," Echo argued. "The potential research applications of this are extraordinary! And you want to flush it all away?"

"Yes, I do," Alpha said.

"We can't."

"What are your thoughts, Charlie?" he asked.

Charlie merely shrugged. "The project is a failure."

"Or a remarkable success," Echo said. Alpha noted the way she occupied her chair, her body slanting in his direction, one leg tucked beneath the other, her hand gripping the sole of her bare foot. She'd kicked her shoes off onto the floor, as she usually did at the start of meetings such as these, another unique habit unshared by either Alpha or Charlie.

Despite himself, Alpha let loose a sharp bark of laughter. "You're both right, in your own ways. Victor represents both a success and a massive failure. Regardless, what we must do next is clear. Purge Victor."

Charlie nodded.

Echo shook her head, eyes wide. "No! This is it. This is the breakthrough we've been looking for."

"It's not," Alpha argued. "This is larger than that, and goes well beyond our mission parameters."

"We cannot simply destroy him."

"We have two dead crew!" Charlie nearly came out of his chair.

"We're looking for answers about the origins of *mankind*," Alpha stressed. "Our common ancestor, the so-called missing link. This isn't it."

"The Creator," Echo began, but Alpha cut her off immediately.

"Victor is not the Creator. Victor is an aberration writ large."

"Wait. Just wait." Charlie shoved away from the table and stood. "All of the experiments have used human genetics as a baseline. We've been steadily regressing backwards in each subsequent experiment, filling the gaps with a variety of *Homo* genetics predating modern man. We should be getting closer to a less complex, less evolved ancestor."

"Victor certainly looks less evolved," Echo said.

Charlie paced the length of the table, his hands gesticulating rapidly with his words. "Yet if we're saying he's the cause of Delta's erratic behavior, that implies a certain degree of complexity that would not exist in a lower-level ancestor."

"Even that's not entirely accurate." Echo's eyes rolled. "And you know it! The evolution of communication is remarkably complex. There have been plenty of studies regarding telepathic communication in animals, communication through pheromones and non-vocal signals, the way they somehow innately know when disaster is about to strike, like an earthquake, and prepare to flee. They possess a certain something that we don't, or perhaps no longer possess. We merely evolved to possess vocal communication, rather than telepathy. We cannot rule out its absence in these so-called 'lower-level' beings."

Alpha cleared his throat, interrupting them. "We've been working our way back through generations of genetic drift. Yes, we are looking for a common ancestor. And I think we have found it, actually. We've just not found the right one."

"Explain," Charlie said.

Alpha shrugged. "We're looking for a direct ancestor to man. I think what we've found is much, much larger than that."

Charlie stopped his pacing. "You think Victor is an ancestor to—"

"—to all life," Alpha finished. "Yes. And I think this aberration goes back much further than just life on Earth."

Echo stared at him, open-mouthed.

"Jesus, you're even crazier than she is."

Alpha had pondered the question of Victor on his own for quite some time. Each of them had, and it had allowed them to think freely and arrive at their own individual assessments. Although they oftentimes reached the same conclusions, occasionally one of them managed to surprise the others with an out of the box scenario. Alpha realized now that his was the most out of the box bit of speculation at the table.

He sipped at his coffee, taking the time to savor it while he thought of the best way to approach his explanation.

"Our universe is but a single strand in the multiverse. We know of eleven dimensions in the multiverse, and it's extremely likely that there are many more in any one of those possible universes within the multiverse. Within all of those various dimensions, within all of those various strings and strands of the multiverse, imagine the enormous—the seismic, really—potential for life. We're so keen on how life began on our planet, whether or not there's other life in our universe, but just stop and consider. Consider life beyond either of those things and think about life outside of our own realities, just for a moment."

Echo paled. Charlie looked flabbergasted and sank slowly back into his chair. He crossed his arms over the tabletop and stared hard at Alpha, but said nothing. What Alpha was describing was Papa's supreme hope—a discovery of not just Elohim, humanity's cosmic father, but perhaps even of Elohim's creator.

"More than thirteen billion years ago there was an explosion, which led to a singularity. The question has always been, what caused this explosion. Of course, we have no answer, no way of knowing, really, but we do have plenty of what ifs. What if this singularity originated elsewhere in the multiverse and caused a breach, or a quantum explosion, an entanglement of some sort, and whatever life existed at that point of origin was turned into the same stardust each of us are made of?

"Victor is not a human ancestor. Victor is *the* ancestor, his genetic construct blown apart and seeded across our dimension and reborn in the primordial ooze that gave rise to life itself. And we've corrupted it, perhaps not knowingly but certainly willingly, giving it shape and form. We've taken something far more alien than us and twisted it to our own designs. Whatever Victor was originally, it wasn't like us. We've stripped away generations of the *human* genome, seeking an ancestral baseline based off our own junk DNA, junk DNA that Victor, in whatever small way, was a part of, DNA that helped guide the way we evolved.

"And now we've tried to recreate it, and we have made a considerably sizable mistake. Victor is not a pure ancestor. He's not a pure anything. Not anymore. Right now, he's a mistake, and we have to destroy him."

Quiet descended following his words. His throat surprisingly dry, he took another long pull of coffee.

"The amount of progress this signifies, though," Echo said. "The years of research we could build off of this. You say he's not pure, but what if this is only a start. We could make him pure over time with enough synthesis and enough finesse."

"There's a factor you're not considering, Echo," Charlie said. Alpha could see in the man's eyes where he was going before the words were spoken.

"If Alpha is correct and Victor is an extra-dimensional

being, things can only get worse from here if we persist. We can only visualize three dimensions. We have no idea how many dimensions Victor inhabited, then or now, and what limitations we would be placing on him if we forced him to exist in our three-dimensional world. Imagine all of the things he could see or do that we couldn't. Delta and Bravo already got a taste of that in the lab. Whatever it is that might be created from this failed gambit is not worth pursuing. Not if we value our own sanity, and, more importantly, our own fucking lives."

"This meeting is over," Alpha said. He turned toward Charlie and nodded. "Purge Victor."

III

Echo's forehead was pressed against the glass, as was her hand, which laid atop Victor's, his webbed fingers splayed in perfect alignment to her own. Both had their eyes closed, and Alpha felt a perverse pang of jealousy at the sight, as if he'd caught them in post-coital basking.

"Does it hurt you?" he asked, indicating his head. This close to Victor, his head was dully throbbing and he wondered what Echo must be feeling.

"It's a strange sensation," she said after a long moment. "But not painful. It's more... cottony."

She opened her eyes and slowly pulled away from the synthesis chamber. Each movement was subtly marred with the hesitancy of regret.

"What was he to you?" Alpha asked. He was troubled by Echo's display, and the way she was acting was entirely inappropriate. He was glad that Charlie had stepped out to get fresh coffee after initiating the purge and could not see this display. Victor was a test subject, nothing more. So why was she acting like this was a personal loss?

More to the point, what had she been hiding?

What don't I know here? Alpha wondered.

"He was a part of me," Echo said. "All of us are each a part of the other. Do you not feel a kinship to him?"

"No," Alpha lied. Echo merely rolled her eyes, reading him clearly.

The truth of the matter was, even after all that had happened over the intervening hours, he still felt a sincere, and strange, sense of familiarity with Victor.

There was no other option, though. The incident with Delta and Bravo illustrated that quite clearly.

Victor's eyes sprang open, his mouth flaring painfully wide. The nanites circulating through the amniotic protein bath, responsible for genetic assembly and growth acceleration, were now operating in reverse. Rather than constructing their cloned subject, the nanites were now in an aggressive pattern of destruction.

Victor's thick hand slammed against the glass, abnormally large. Far larger than it should be for the fifth month growth plan. Bubbles erupted from his contorted mouth, and the hand came down hard against the glass.

THUD.

THUD.

THUD!

Victor's legs rapidly twisted in the fluid, creating tiny vortexes as his body turned, his heel smacking against the glass. Small patches of flesh came away in thin, splotchy layers, the cells circulating through the disruption his writhing motions made in the bath. Alpha was again reminded of fish food flakes, an impossible image to shake.

The aberration's face smashed into the chamber, his nose pressed flat against the glass as another scream erupted, fingers curling long talons against the glass.

Did he—?

Alpha looked closer, and… yes. Victor's nails, his *claws*, had dug a shallow trench into the glass.

THUD!

THUD!

THUD!

Closer this time. On this side of the glass!

Echo was slamming open palms against the chamber glass, her actions exciting Victor further, stirring his commotion into a frenzy. Limbs flailing violently, smacking into the glass at four different points, legs and hands working forcefully to free himself from the attacking nanites.

"Echo! Get away from there!"

Alpha spun, wrapping his arms around her waist from behind and tearing her away from the synthesis chamber.

"What the hell are you doing?" he screamed.

She twisted in his grip, the sudden force surprising him, and she tore free from his arms. She turned, cat-quick, her nails raking across his face, pain lancing through his face as curls of skin peeled away from his cheeks.

He stepped back, reflexively, raising a hand to ward off another assault. A painful burn radiated across the side of his face, and a pulsing tremor tore through his skull.

Echo kicked, her foot landing squarely in Alpha's crotch. He grunted and went down on his knees, hard, a projectile of gut-warm coffee bursting from his mouth to splatter against the floor.

Cold steel pierced the center of his brain, superseding all other pains afflicting his body. He cupped his head in both hands, elbows digging into the floor, and screamed.

From a nearby terminal, Echo grabbed the seatback of a chair and turned on one foot, slamming the chair into the glass chamber.

A crack appeared, a small fractured circle radiating through the thick shell.

She swung again, harder. Then again. And again.

Again.

Glass exploded, pointed shards stabbing into Echo's frame as a thick, warm bath of liquid splashed across her. Sirens erupted, warning lights flashing... too late.

"No," Alpha groaned. His vision was reduced to two small slits, the brightness of the lab facility far too bright. The light pierced his brain, stitching a web of pain across the entire surface of his skull with the staccato of a tattoo gun. Through the thin slits of his eyelids, he saw Echo stumble back, watched a thick, piebald foot stomp heavily onto the floor.

Echo was crying, but he couldn't discern if it was in pain or fear or joy.

Alpha rolled onto his back, grunting his way into a sitting position. He cradled his head in both hands, eyes pinched shut, a tacky fluid leaking from the corner of both eyes. He felt a sticky wetness leaking from his ears to pool against his palms. His heels scrambled for purchase, finally able to kick himself back, scooting on his ass away from the monstrosity before them.

He couldn't be seeing right. He knew that. What he was seeing was impossible.

Victor's flesh was bubbling outward, expanding, shimmering with an upset watery appearance before hardening into solid, wine-stain colored flesh.

He's growing.

Alpha forced one eye to part, at least as much as the aching light allowed, and demanded of himself that he bear witness.

Victor was no longer a baby. No longer even a child. Victor was immense, and growing larger.

The nanites should have disrupted this, but—

Oh, Echo. What did you do?

He realized then that she must have reversed the purge. Rather than disrupt the synthesis and promote a breakdown of the genetic material, she had found a way to hack the purge protocols Charlie had enacted. Alpha hadn't seen her leave her own station, which meant she'd carried out a deliberate assault against the program from her own terminal. Rather than eliminate Victor, she had accelerated the growth program.

Whatever human similarities Victor may have possessed during the fetal stages of growth were absent in his adulthood. The alien DNA was supremely abundant now, those characteristics fully apparent in their total domination over the genetic code.

Even through the patchwork hide of its body, Victor's

muscles stood tautly, cording his arms and legs, chest, and neck like steel rebar. Tall and hairless, easily more than six feet, his wrists and ankles thick, his limbs as dense as tree trunks. His face was expressionless, a smooth plane of thick gray tissue over an immense skull ringed with pointed protuberances and large bony shelves over its eyes.

Victor lumbered toward Echo, though she stood her ground, her mouth open in surprise. A piercing scream erupted from deep in her throat. Alpha wiped tears away from his eyes in time to see blood drip from her ears. She cupped her head, mirroring Alpha, and fell to her knees.

Victor reached toward her, his face still impassive even as his fingers wrapped around her skull and gripped tightly. The thick skin of his hand muted the rustling tissue paper noise, but Alpha could still hear it and then he realized with gross fascination that the sound was the tectonic shift of the bone plates of her skull cracking loose and crumpling in Victor's grip. Then the monster raised the deflated skull and jerked his hand. The noise of her neck snapping was sharp even over the emergency sirens.

"No," Alpha moaned, honestly unsure if he was protesting her death or the looming eventuality of his own.

A dark cloud enshrouded his mind, the ache in his brain growing impossibly tight. He felt as if his brain were swelling, boiling and bulging against its bony case and threatening to break through. If his skull were to crack open, though, relief would surely follow.

He reached toward the shards of glass, his palm slicing open in the debris as he sought out the perfect sliver.

"No," he said again, this time in protest. He was not in control of his own arm, his movements not his own but Victor's. The beast was in his head, manipulating him.

As he reached for the glass, he felt his brain peel open and the horrors that only Victor was privy to flooded in. What Alpha saw was beyond comprehension, and he felt the fundamental foundations of his reality crack and erupt, breaking beneath new knowledge that had no words and could only be expressed through his loud, agonizing screams, screams that turned his throat raw and left a coppery taste in his mouth. His eyes widened, the light brutalizing him, his face contorting into widespread agony.

The glass nearly slipped loose of his grip, his hand slickened with blood. He forced his fingers tighter around the shard, the blade slicing through tendons as he embedded the glass into his hand, demanding his grip to tighten further even as nerves fired and died, leaving his fingers frozen and useless. He raised his hand, the glass an arm length's away, and focused on the glittering point that he would soon impale himself upon.

Not like this. Please, not like this.

Not like—and in the span of eternity between thought and words, Alpha witnessed stars collapse, eaten alive by black unending mouths, supernovas climaxing and devouring solar systems whole, suns cradled in the cups of enormous hands, the bodies of beings so large he could not process them, could not meet their eyes lest his skull implode upon the sight of them, civilizations rising and falling in milliseconds, all of it broadcast into his brain in a complex system of visions, fractured and divided and spread across a complex web of information shaped like a spider's eye and shoved through a prism, more than his meager mind could handle, and his sanity burst like shattering glass into a hundred thousand pointed shards, and he screamed, coughing loose flecks of blood that danced across his forearm like rain—*Delta and Bravo.*

A booming noise rang out behind him, deafening him. His eardrums burst, and the second explosion was a muffled *whompf!* Victor staggered back, a hole blossoming in the center of his torso, and then a second, higher up and to the right.

The fog in Alpha's mind cleared, the darkness parting. He tried to release the glass, but it was buried too deep in his skin, his fingers refusing to budge. He had to pinch the point of the shard tightly between the fingers of his opposite hand and pull it free, screaming all the while in agony as he found fresh nerves to ruin.

And then the darkness returned, and his body collapsed to

the floor.

~*~

A shrill droning in his ears returned Alpha to consciousness. The emergency alerts, he realized, but they were quiet, too quiet, as if he were listening to them from deep below the water.

Charlie's lips were moving, but he couldn't make out the sound of the words. Those lips were a strange pale blue color, and Charlie's flesh was a stark, unnatural gray.

Alpha was wrapping his hand in medical gauze to halt the bleeding, and the skin itched from the surgical glue that had been used to seal the lacerations.

His ears were plugged, he realized, in addition to the deafness from ruptured eardrums. He could feel the thick bullets of blood lodged in both ear canals. In between those was a horrible, rending pulsation as his brain beat against its skull cage, pounding fiercely. His nose ran, leaking a curdled, gray substance over his lips, down his chin.

His brain was fighting to be free of the awful visions trapped in its folds. He wanted to shut his eyes against them, but that only gave those sights a fresh reality. Unbidden, the impossibilities returned to him and he stared again upon a drowned city and the massive figure sleeping over the flooded remains. That enormous, hulking piebald beast, its skull overlarge and barren, bony ripples distorting the slick flesh coating its skeleton. Red, massive supernovas for eyes, their brightness burning through the seams of closed lids, unable to contain the burning heat trapped beneath. And its mouth, a wicked bony cage set atop writhing tentacles that grew from its jaw and chin. This beast, this monster—a devourer of entire cities, a world killer whose belly was filled with the remains of entire planets it had gorged upon.

"We were so stupid," he said.

Charlie's lips halted and he stared at Alpha, a hard and curious gaze.

"That thing… a hybrid abomination, and we made it. It's old. So, so old. Older than anything. And we made it. Willingly, we made it. Stupid. So stupid."

Charlie said something, but the movement of his lips only confused Alpha further. Ignoring his clone, Charlie let his head loll to the side, his eyes rolling toward Echo. Alpha followed his gaze and saw she was splayed across the floor in a sheet of crimson, lying terribly still. In her, he saw his own demise and wondered again at how they could be so oddly different.

Idly, his fingers drew shapes in the blood pooled around him. He knew only a hint of the importance of the symbols, but his hand was compelled and moved of its own volition. Forcing himself to focus, he realized he recognized the imagery, an ancient language half-glimpsed from a Victor-induced fever-dream only moments-hours-eons before, these same symbols adorning the buildings of the drowned cities beneath the sleeping god. He sensed a certain weight behind the alien words, the threats promised in each stroke as he connected lines and circles in the gore. A hidden knowledge told him these words were far older than the conceptual universe surrounding him, his fingers drifting through entire dimensions joined together by a language that, if he were able to speak it, would deafen him and contort his tongue so deftly that the muscle would become dead in his throat and he would choke upon it.

Would Papa have approved? he wondered. There was Charlie, of course, who, despite having the same memory load as the rest, had somehow imprinted on Papa's younger, brasher self, an angry, arrogant twenty-something Raëlian ready to burn down the world with his proofs and theories.

Alpha believed he had been the purest. The first clone of Papa, and the most complete. He had shared Papa's belief that technology would bring mankind closer to their god, and that the process of cloning and genetic engineering and DNA synthesis would allow them to recreate the progenitor of all mankind and reunite humans with their alien Elohim ancestors.

Victor was supposed to be Elohim, but this was impossible. Rather than a prophet to shepherd mankind through its final days, they had unleashed a gross mistake, a frightening trespass across dimensions. Whatever Victor was, it went by a different name, a far older name.

"The realm of perception he operates on," Alpha whispered, more to himself than to Charlie, "this is wrong. We have made a horrible miscalculation."

He wanted to blame Echo, wanted to lay their deaths at her feet, but found that he could not. She was Papa, and Papa was her, and perhaps she was the purest incarnation of them all. Or maybe Victor had simply manipulated her to his own ends. Now she was dead, and it was impossible to blame her for any of it.

When Alpha closed his eyes, he strained to not imagine the horrors Victor had funneled into his head. That kaleidoscopic display of perception across dimensions that his addled brain could not handle. He may as well have been a one-dimensional figure thrust into the 3-D realm, so out of sorts and twisted upon a new reality that fractured his mind and broke the core tenants of them all. All that he thought he knew, all that he thought he was, shattered, and now he struggled to reassemble the various pieces of the self, to unravel the crumpled paper ball his brain had been twisted into. He was only dimly aware of Charlie dabbing a cloth at the corner of his lips to wipe away the drool leaking down his cheek. All he knew was pain.

"Where is he?" Alpha asked. If Charlie answered, he didn't know. He forced his eyes open and asked again, forced himself to watch Charlie's lips and to focus on the words, to hear those words past the shrill, soft droning of emergency alarms.

"He went into the ductwork," Charlie said. "He hit me with a tablet, then went up into the ceiling."

Alpha followed Charlie's eyes upward, to the gaping hole above Echo's body. The displaced lighting flickered in a strobe-like fashion, hanging limply from the damaged ceiling.

A fresh pulse of pain ripped through his brain, forcing him to double-over. A thin, bloody line of drool crept from his lips and he spit onto the floor.

His side was tacky and wet below the ribs. He couldn't remember why.

"We have to destroy him," he sputtered. The words were a revelation entirely his own. Something in his soul cracked and shifted, as if a weight had come loose and freed him from rusty chains.

He noticed the bloody script he'd lined the floor with for the first time then, and wondered when and how he had done this. Gibberish, all of it. Strange and arcane, like nothing he had ever seen before. Slowly things shifted in his mind and he began to see clearly, clearer than he thought he had seen in quite some time, although he could not pinpoint exactly when things had grown oppressively cloudy.

Turning toward Charlie, Alpha saw, for the first time, the angry gash and the long, ropy wound across Charlie's forehead. A deeper, wider tear marred his throat.

"No shit," Charlie *(no, not Charlie)* said.

(Charlie's dead.)

"No, no, no." Alpha screwed his eyes tightly shut, palm pressed tightly to his temple. A horrible scream ripped through the inside of his skull, angry and misbegotten. He was seeing things, hearing things. Talking to himself. *That was it*, he realized. That *had* to be it.

"The mining drones," Alpha stammered. "We need to bring them online."

Charlie's mouth hung open in a rictus of pain, but after a moment he nodded. Or perhaps his head simply lolled as his body slumped. Alpha wasn't sure, not entirely.

A dozen decommissioned drones had been mothballed on base. After the veins of ore ran dry and the site shuttered, the drones had simply been deactivated and warehoused. Papa had not been concerned with their resale value; it had been easier to simply shut them away than deal with more trade deals and selling used mechs. They could be used now, though, and set loose across the base and its ventilation grid to hunt and destroy Victor.

Charlie-not Charlie was already working on the tablet, fingers moving nimbly despite the pain contorting his features. One hand was frozen stiff by paralysis, fingers curled into a tight fist. A moment later he slammed the tablet to the floor beside him and screamed, "Fuck!"

"What?"

Charlie-not Charlie laughed, but there was no humor to be had, only mania. "The power cores. The fucking power cores."

Of course, Alpha realized. They would have stripped the drones of their energy cells while they sat dormant. "I'll go."

Charlie-not Charlie looked at him, somewhat confusedly, but nodded. "Yeah. Yeah, good. Get them plugged in and I can control them. God, my head!"

Alpha stood on shaking legs, his whole body weak, and took three shuddering steps to the door, fumbled his way into the corridor beyond. A sticky mess poured from his nostrils and he wiped at it with the back of his good hand, barely curious at the odd coloration and the chowder-like consistency of the lumpy fluid. The pain ricocheting inside his skull diminished the further he got from the lab, but a noisy hum remained, forcing his eyes into half-open slits. He kept his wounded hand pressed to his belly, blood leaking a long trail down the hallway to mark his passage.

The mining drones were primarily autonomous, but there were also manned EVAs. Both would be useless for long-range space flight, and there were no shuttles off this rock. The black site was their home, and, when the time came, it would be their grave as well. Alpha and the rest were all illicit human experiments, and if they ever made it off the rock, Papa would be complicit in any number of crimes against humanity. Papa had left them no way off the asteroid, and they never had any intention of leaving.

As he made his way into the elevator that would carry him into the mech bay, he thought about these implications and the realization that he would die here solidified. What had been merely theoretical and shapeless with the distance of time was suddenly and achingly concrete in its newfound immediacy. If that was what it would take to stop Victor, then so be it. He would see this operation razed and sucked into the vacuum of space rather than risk that abomination being discovered.

IV

Echo lay with her head resting against his chest, her arm splayed across his narrow hips.

"How do we know what's real?" she asked.

The question was a common refrain from her, the discussion one they'd had many times. She'd begun asking this question soon after her decanting as she began to explore the memories—Papa's memories—that were interlaced across her mind. She had spent several days initially disoriented by it all, unable to reconcile the memories of a man with her female features, struggling against the imprint and demanding that her life be her own until she had to be sedated. Eventually, the struggle eased, yet the question remained.

He had no answer for her, then or now.

"Alpha, you have to listen to me," she said. Her voice rang in his ears, inside his skull, across the open communications channel.

He shook his head. *No, no, no. Impossible!* He had watched her die. She was dead. It was impossible for her to be speaking with him. He was imagining it, hearing voices.

Victor, he realized. That son of a bitch was playing with him now, distracting him.

He moved down the row of deactivated mining drones, verifying their hull integrity before inserting their power cells. This was going to stop Victor. It had to. And Victor knew it, and was now trying to stop him with cheap fucking parlor tricks.

It wasn't going to work, though.

"I know who you are!" he screamed, whirling around in the semi-darkness as he screamed to the heavens. Victor was above him, somewhere, and inside him, too, deep inside his head, twisting his consciousness and his memory against him and projecting old thoughts, old desires, old questions.

"I know who you are and I will kill you, do you understand me?"

"Alpha, stop it. Stop and listen to me," Echo said. "It's Victor. Victor is inside your head. Do you understand?"

"No fucking shit!" he screamed. Victor, manipulating him, trying to trick him. He recognized the buzzing sensation, the spidery crawl across the surface of his brain, which was the clone's hallmark. He'd been feeling it since the synthesis began, standing beside the cloning tank while Victor took form. That should have been enough of an inkling to prompt an abortion, to purge the hybrid relic from the tank and reconfigure the systems for projects Whiskey and X-Ray.

But no. He saw now that he possessed every inch of Papa's hubris and his dangerous, wanton need to always be right, damn the cost.

"Victor is still in the tank, Alpha," Echo shouted. Her voice quivered in its awful pleadings, stained with tears and a jagged sobbing. "You're not well. We—I—can help you."

He curled one fist tightly, the pain and the bandages preventing him from curling both. All his effort brought his injured hand was fresh blood.

He was on the right track, then. If Victor was this worried, would go to these lengths to prevent him from activating the drones, then he was most certainly on the right track.

He was going to start up these fucking drones and sic each and every one of them on Victor, and he was going to destroy the whole goddamn asteroid while he was at it.

Gritting his teeth, he pulled open the battery compartment of the nearest drone and lodged the power cell into place. Managing this was difficult with only one hand, and his shoulder throbbed. The battery was large and hadn't been easy to maneuver. Pulling the hatch back down, he was forced to use both hands to bear the lid's weight.

His hand lit up in a brilliant, fresh spike of pain and he saw Echo even as he tried to blot her words out of his mind. She was lying on his chest, a pink bubble forming on her lips. His hand burned from the lacerations the glass had opened in his flesh, and he could feel her blood pooling between them.

Not like this, he'd thought. *Please, not like this.*

"Alpha. You need to remember. You need to get a grip."

The lid slammed down into place, and he buckled at the searing pain in his belly, forcing him to collapse to his knees, his useless hand pressed tightly to his stomach. His shoulder burning.

"Charlie," he said. "That's one done. Start her up."

He knelt beside the mech, panting heavily. A thick, coppery taste lingered in his mouth and throat.

"Charlie. Start her up," he said again.

The machine was lifeless, though. He began to second guess himself—did he forget something? Was there a start-up sequence or something to go through? Some method of priming the drone he'd failed to realize?

"Charlie's dead," Echo said. "You killed him."

"Fuck. You."

He forced himself to his feet, dragging the cart stuffed with batteries behind him. He felt terribly weak from the blood loss and knew it was only a matter of time before he died. He couldn't let Victor live, though, couldn't risk somebody trying to salvage the station's remnants and coming across the creature. Finding him and dying at his hands. Or worse. God, what if, somehow, Victor made it off the mining platform? With his degrees of perception and ability to deceive, to play such twisted mind games with his prey, what would he do to the sky colonies on Venus, or on Mars or Earth?

At the next drone, he repeated the process of battery installation as best as he could. Two down and already he was significantly weaker. Sweat poured down his face, yet he felt frighteningly cold.

The lid slammed down like a gunshot and he felt an explosion in his torso. A second in his shoulder, and he staggered back and fell, the hallucination so vivid. He tripped over the cart, upending it beneath him and sending a cascade of large, heavy batteries across the floor. His bony hips crashed into the corner of a battery, sending fresh agony through him, his head cracking against another.

He lay there a moment, moaning. And remembering.

Charlie with his prohibited firearm. Guns were banned from the station, had been even as a fully operational mining colony. In the depths of space, a gunshot inside an enclosed facility was too large a threat. Somehow Charlie had come to possess one, likely pilfered from the remnants of station security from ages ago.

Charlie had shot him, twice. In return, he had opened Charlie's throat with the glass shard. Alpha had passed out briefly, and when he woke Charlie was staring at him, a gory hand wrapped around his ruined throat, lips moving but making no sounds. And then his lips had stilled.

"No," he said. "No, that isn't what happened."

He fought against the memory, his own mind rebelling against it, dueling factions within him screaming for and against.

"We tried to purge Victor," Echo said. "You attacked me with a chair, busted up my terminal. Do you remember?"

"No," he said, but with no trace of conviction.

"There was glass everywhere from the monitors you destroyed. You stopped us from purging Victor, and then you came at me with a glass shard. Do you remember?"

"No," he lied. Tears ran freely down his face.

"Charlie tried to stop you, and you killed him."

"I—"

"I'm dying, Alpha."

"I'm so sorry," he said.

Breathing through his nose produced a gravelly noise as liquid roiled deep in his nostrils. His nose and sinuses were so clogged, he had to breathe through his mouth. He wiped again at his face, drawing away moist gray clumps lined with red stains against the back of his wrist.

So this is what happened to Delta. The thought made him chuckle.

He forced himself to roll into a sitting position, his guts squelching, and he could swear he felt the rubbery bulge of intestine threatening to spool free from the hole in his belly.

"I don't know what's real," he said. Echo whimpered over the comm channel. He thought she may have been trying to laugh.

Hallucination or not, he understood Victor's plan. Such a simple plan. They had tried to kill him, and so Victor had, in turn, tried to kill them. Alpha had been his weapon.

He saw it all now with awful clarity. Victor, in his tube, small and piebald and deformed, barely human. He wasn't growing, hadn't broken free of the tube. The purge had begun, and he'd lashed out in self-defense. Delta and Bravo had been killed after Uniform had failed to achieve satisfactory synthesis and had been purged. Had that been a warning, or revenge? He didn't know, but he knew Victor had been responsible for manipulating the men toward their deaths.

But information, intended or not, was a two-way street. Alpha had learned things no human mind should be privy to.

He saw, too, what Victor had ultimately realized was the only possible outcome, and what Victor's manipulations of him had been aimed toward.

He dabbed at the wound to his belly, digging his fingers into the ragged hole torn into him. Fresh paint for his brush, he thought, and he drew new marks across the floor beside him. Ancient sigils that put the god to sleep, even if too late.

Alpha slowly, painfully, got his feet beneath him, shoving himself upward from the prone cart for balance. He and Victor had a similar end-goal now, and he was quite content to deliver the creature's final wishes.

His steps were aching shuffles and it took him far longer than it should have to make his way toward the computer terminal. He keyed in the necessary sequences to start up two of the mining drones, their battery cells weak but carrying enough of a charge to carry through one last assignment.

Their thrusters powered on, their large insectile bodies unfolding from their resting racks to deploy. They arced through the warehouse and turned toward the freight elevator to carry them higher up and into the station, to the laboratory where Victor waited.

The mining droids would kill Victor, and then they would destroy the station.

Murder-suicide. That was Victor's endgame, and now Alpha's as well. He accepted that as his legacy. Echo was on her way to dying, Charlie already there. Delta and Bravo, both finished. All because of him, because of Papa and his—their—experimentation, their curiosity. All of it their fault in equal measure.

And so he would die.

"I've spent my life being a tool," Alpha said. "An instrument, constantly manipulated. I thought that Papa's goals were mine simply by virtue of memory, of the inheritance of thought. My life has been a meme, though, nothing more."

"It doesn't have to end this way," Echo said. "We could rebuild. We could—"

Her words were lost in a wet-sounding coughing fit that eventually trailed off into a moan and then an unsettling quiet. He could still hear her breath, though, shallow and rapid, and he knew her moment of expiration was close at hand.

"No," he said, eventually. "There's no coming back from what I've done. Or from what has to be done. This entire project has been a failure. A mistake. I see that now."

"Victor played you," she said, her voice nearly a whisper.

"Victor, Papa. What difference does it make?"

"I forgive you."

Her last words. He could no longer hold back the tears, and sobs racked his body. His wounds ached and leaked, and he cried and cried.

Communications with the lab had cut out, the mining drones doing their job diligently and destroying everything. The alarm sirens found a new vigorous energy as they blared. In his mind's eye, he saw the drones deploying their pickaxes and torches as they went to work on Victor, plucking away his limbs, immune to his control and suggestions. Victor was small and baby-like, and it would not take long for him to be disassembled.

The pressure doors slammed into place. The drones had succeeded in breaching the facility to open space. The last gap safety measure would only hold for so long, but Alpha wasn't sure that he would live long enough to see it fail. Odds were, the blood loss would finish him well before.

Or so he hoped. If some part of him recognized that to be a coward's way out, then it forced him to cling to life by a tether of unadulterated agony. Eventually the lights failed and, as he lay bleeding in the dark, he heard the metallic pounding of mining tools working against the doors.

A short time later, an explosive breach of depressurization lifted his body off the ground and sucked the air from his lungs. His death came seconds later, only moments before his corpse would be left to drift in the orbit of a disused asteroid he'd once called home.

In his final seconds, he wondered if perhaps he would discover Elohim after all.

~*~

A Word from Michael Patrick Hicks

~*~

Sci-fi horror is a particular genre niche that I can never get enough of. I blame the films *Alien* and *The Thing* for this, along with the cosmic horrors dreamed up by H.P. Lovecraft and the many authors he has inspired across the decades.

When Daniel Arthur Smith invited me to participate in his anthology about clones, I knew immediately that it was a theme ripe for horrific exploitation. I tossed around a few ideas in my head, and more and more I became drawn to the elements of cosmic horror and how they could intermingle with science fiction.

I began thinking about eldritch terrors and how in space nobody can hear you scream. Somewhere along the line, I also started thinking about creation myths and evolution and multiple dimensions, until a very *Lovecraftian* story began to take shape under the auspices of cloning. What sort of secrets are buried in our genetic code, and where did all that stuff come from anyway? I wanted to get big and bold with the weirdness, but also maintain a sense of claustrophobia, confusion, and divisiveness. I also wanted to scare the hell out of people. Hopefully I pulled it off, but that's for you to decide, dear reader (if I can crib from the King, another horror icon who has played no small part in my professional development as a writer).

Should *Black Site* have convinced you to check out my other writings, feel free to pay a visit to michaelpatrickhicks.com to learn more about my work. You can also sign up for my spam-free newsletter to receive notifications of new releases and exclusive advanced reader copies before a new book launches (all I ask in return for these copies is that you to post your honest thoughts of my work at Amazon, or Goodreads, BookLikes, etc.) by going to eepurl.com/5M4z1.

~*~

Michael Patrick Hicks is the author of the science fiction novels Convergence, an Amazon Breakthrough Novel Award 2013 Quarter-Finalist, and Emergence. His work has appeared in several anthologies, and he has written for the websites *Graphic Novel Reporter* and *Audiobook Reviewer*. In between compulsively buying books and adding titles that he does not have time for to his Netflix queue, he is hard at work on his next story.

~*~

Fahrenheit 1451

Samuel Peralta

~*~

HEAT SEARS THROUGH THE OUTER LAYERS of our jackets as we wrestle water hoses, facemasks, and the trellis of the fire engine's ladder, wrenching upwards, upwards, to the third floor of the building.

It's snowing down on us, and all the world below is December white, but the heat of the mid-rise tower of fire and smoke cuts through the cold, mirroring in our faces.

As we lift up, the muffled screams are clearer now, a girl's screams, faint above the flicker of noise of men and vehicles below, reaching out to me from behind the window.

I'm motioning the truck to swing the ladder—*Left, left, this way, closer...*

Closer... closer... and I see her now, face pressed against the glass, her auburn hair in furious disarray, fists banging against the window, pounding with a rhythmic desperation.

I motion her back, smash the axe's handle into the glass, and clear the shards away.

Smoke swirls from the window's maw like a hammered anvil, and my ears are straining over the clangor of voices and bells around me like a purgatory whirling out of control, an asylum of flame and snow.

Closer... and when the ladder touches brick, I leap inside.

She is there, just at the window, and I pull her up, out of the fire's clutch, into my arms.

"It's okay," I say, and she is crying, crying, tears streaming down a sooty, freckled face, and when I ask her, *Miss*, if there's anyone else inside, she weakly shakes her head.

She's choking on the smoke as I pass her outside to the crewman below me on the ladder.

Then I hear it.

No time to think—into the maelstrom I dive, where I heard the scream coming from, and my feet feel solid ground—but the room is empty.

I call back to the others behind me, "I'm going in!" and move quickly, towards the door ahead.

It's like bringing the battle to the front line, hose and axe my rifle and bayonet, the jungle exploding incendiaries around me, claymore, grenades, each measured inch of enemy ground hard won, beneath me, a lava flow coalescent and warm.

The door splinters under my axe, and I push forward into

BACKDRAFT

And suddenly the world becomes Vesuvius, a molten fury flowing through us like a tsunami of fire, consuming all in its path, and I, stray traveler daring to wander into this eruption's course, suffocating in its sulfurous rage, the building coalescing into an incendiary labyrinth.

Water trains in behind me, laying a path of hot, smoldering timber.

I lift myself up from the floor. But now I can hear her again.

Just outside the room, I see her.

She's there below, on the landing half-way up the stairs between the floors, on hands and knees.

"Here!" I call out—and she looks up.

And suddenly I feel a pang of recognition stab through me—the auburn hair, the pale, dappled face, the same voice choking out a ragged, "Help!"

I hitch my axe and keep my flashlight on her.

She won't move, so I have to get to her.

The air from the regulator is warmer, and the tank itself is heavy and hot as I shift towards the stair.

Fifteen steps away—she's gasping, like a person drowning, but in a sea-swell of smoke—

Ten steps—she's trying, heaving herself up towards me—

—and then the landing collapses—

As I catch the shadow of her, screaming, falling into smoke, the walls start crumbling, caving in on me; and a comrade voice in the darkness behind me says, "Out, out, out!" and a hand grips my arm, pulling me back up, back into the room, and we're running as the floor gives way, running toward the window, toward the falling snow beyond, toward the light, and out—

II

Snow falls, softer now, and I'm kneeling on a bank outside, mask and oxygen tank off at my feet.

Around me, the strobe of ambulance lights spirals like the thoughts swirling in my head.

"We're good," I say when the chief comes around to ask about my company.

You're always good, no matter if you're holding a compress on a torn ligament, or you've just finished zipping up the bag on a five-year-old. You just are, because you're not supposed to feel anything. You do your job, you come back another day.

Five bodies retrieved, all women, all dead. Perhaps more in the wreckage like these few, mangled bone and flesh, charred beyond recognition—

Except there, in my memory, in the part of me that cannot forget her face.

Snow falls, the smoke trails off, the sirens do not fade.

III

Burned to the filter, the cigarette in my hand falls to the concrete of the hospital parking garage, and the pungent smell of plastic rises with the faint smoke trail.

I lie at the front desk, and say I'm her brother. She's been moved from the 14-bed burn and intensive care unit into a private room.

The elevator shifts upward, antiseptic and white, my fellow passengers an old woman in her wheelchair, attended by her granddaughter. The weather report plays on the small screen above. Storms ahead.

Two years ago, a huge rainstorm converged above the city, and the sustained downpour had led to the Don River waters rising about two feet in an hour, flooding sections of the parkway and Bayview long after the rains had stopped.

A transport truck that had just cleared the floodwaters on the Don Valley Parkway had stalled. It was stopped on the side of the road when a bus carrying tourists from Florida rammed into its rear and was engulfed in flames.

My company was first on the call, early that Thursday morning.

We were in the middle of a job on a car trapped on an embankment nearby; it had lodged itself where the water was about a foot or so above its roof. Shattering the window, we'd cut the driver's belt and pulled him out. He'd swallowed a lot of water, but CPR had brought him back and we'd just transferred him to the ambulance when the call for the bus came through.

Pulling up behind the wreck, we knew it was too late. Cars were stopped and people tried to get at the burning hulk, but the inferno was too much. We pulled the equipment out, did what we could—but there was nothing we could do.

When your world is forever on fire, you have to step

outside yourself, leave your feelings behind when you hit the ground. You aim the hose, you tie the tourniquets, you break the doors down, you treat the wounds.

The further in the fire you go, the deeper in the abyss, the more walls you can pull down, the more of your own injuries you ignore, inside and out—the tougher you are, the more respect you're given. That's our currency, that's how you get paid.

But nothing prepares you for the cost.

The elevator doors open and the wheelchair moves away. I'm all alone when the indicator pings the seventh floor.

Just down the hallway, the receptionist says, "Left and another left. Room fifty-one."

IV

Her bed is partially inclined, her red hair spread against the brilliant white of the pillows, like fire. Her arms stretch down above the sheets, lightly wrapped in gauze where her doctors had grafted new skin, where she'd used them to shield her face.

Her eyes open as I close the door behind me.

Her voice is soft and hoarse, and there's a tremor in her lips. "You," she says. "You saved my life."

It's that, and her face—the face of someone I couldn't save, but somehow did—that breaks through.

Suddenly I'm shaking, my hand goes up to my mouth and the tears are falling and I'm wondering what the hell to say to this woman I don't even know.

"Seven," I say at last. "There were seven there."

She looks at me a long time, unblinking, before she nods.

"I saw someone. She was you."

Just the most imperceptible of nods, accompanied with a shiver.

"How? Why?"

She looks away. "We were meant to burn," she says.

I don't understand, and maybe I'm not meant to.

I look at her once more, trying to remember the face of the girl on the landing.

And now I realize—if memory does not fail—that there is a difference. This girl's unblinking eyes, her masked stare, the trembling of her lips and chin. I see a tremor of her hands, otherwise relaxed at her sides.

She looks back at me, and she sees me trying to grasp it all, and her trembling lips complete the word half-forming in my mind, *Parkinson's*.

And suddenly I understand it:

We were meant to burn.

I try to shake it off, the way we shake off the things that would horrify ordinary folks—a man jumping from an eighty-foot ledge onto the concrete below, the blow-out of a fifth-floor window that tells me we don't have to search that floor, all these things you push in the back of your mind when you visit schools in your full gear, or your brother reps you as his superhero at his bachelor party, or when your chief comes around to ask, "Are you okay?" and you have no other answer to give but *Yes*.

V

788 degrees Celsius, 1451 degrees Fahrenheit—the temperature at which the human body burns.

The inferno cycles deeper and deeper from the outermost layer of skin to the inner layers, muscle, fat, internal organs, bone, drying the material of its excess water, then igniting it in turn—like seven circles of hell.

Nevertheless, the barcode of your soul can still be read.

In the bus incident, a total of forty-one blood, tissue and bone marrow samples were collected for DNA analysis, and matched to reference blood samples from relatives of the eighteen who'd taken that fateful tour.

Within ten days, pathologists had been able to confirm genders, match families to their loved ones, and at the service for all the victims held in a cathedral in Toronto, there were pictures of all the deceased, tangible memories of who they were, who they might have been.

I was there, that day, listening to the priest intone Hebrews 12:25-29 with my head bowed, sirens unfading:

Let us not refuse to listen to him who speaks. Those who refused to listen to the one who gave the divine message on earth, they did not escape. How much less shall we escape, then, if we refuse to listen to the one who speaks from heaven!

His voice shook the earth at that time, but now he has promised he shall once more shake not only the earth but heaven as well.

So shall all of creation will be shaken and removed, so that only those things that cannot be shaken will remain.

Be thankful, then, because we receive a kingdom that cannot be shaken. Be grateful and worship God, with reverence and awe.

For our God is a consuming fire.

VI

I'm walking down the corridor, back to the elevators and salvation, when I make the first right and almost bump into someone. I apologize and step to the side.

She smiles and says, "Sorry about that. I was too much in a hurry," and continues on.

I stop and watch her as she walks away. She is beautiful, auburn hair, mature and, as they say, a handsome woman.

But it's the way her voice shook, the hesitation in the word, *hurry*. That's what makes me stop.

She's walking with a subtle stiffness, her steps dragging almost imperceptibly.

Sensing I'm just standing there, she looks back, quickly, and in that flash I see—though in a face and frame some twenty years from now—the girl on the hospital bed, the girl on the landing, and all the girls who had to burn.

She turns back, continues walking, and enters room fifty-one.

And I am running, running to the fire alarm. I smash it in and pull the lever, and suddenly the hospital is enveloped in a clamor of bells.

Doors are opening, attendants are running down the corridors to take their charges, to make escape.

And now it's my face on the face of all I cannot save, my face staring at me from an opening abyss as I fumble on the landing...

And I am on the stairs, hands flailing at the rails, stumbling down the steps, joining with the mass of humanity hurrying down, away from this fire—real, imagined, invisible, unknown—pouring down and spilling from the emergency doors into the streets, into the snow that I must fall into, to try and quench this fire inside, this vast unquenchable fire.

~*~

A Word from Samuel Peralta

~*~

Samuel Peralta is a physicist and storyteller. An Amazon bestselling author, he is also the creator and driving force behind the *Future Chronicles* series, with 14 consecutive titles ranking at the top of the Amazon Bestselling Anthology lists, several hitting the overall Amazon Top 10 Bestsellers list. His own work has been recognized in Best American Science Fiction.

His poetry has ranked #1 on Amazon, Goodreads, Twitter, and has been spotlighted in articles on Best American Poetry. Awards include from the BBC, the Digital Literature Institute, and the Palanca Memorial Awards for Literature.

An award-winning PhD, he's designed nuclear robotic tools and co-founded several software and semiconductor start-ups. He is also a producer and ardent supporter of independent film.

www.smarturl.it/sp-news

~*~

Confessional
Part II

~*~

The awakening was always the same. A thwack to the chest.

"I will take this time to remind you that the people and the state consider confessions cleansing and you will now be given one chance to redeem yourself. You are not obligated to confess. Failure to redeem yourself will result in immediate conviction as a terrorist and an enemy of the people and state. In accordance with constitutional variant 93745-3 you will be terminated. Is there anything you would like to confess Citizen Eli-4272?"

"Yes, Mother. I confess that today has been good, that the dome is good, and I am a content citizen."

"Citizen Eli-4272, you have thirty seconds to respond."

Eli cleared his throat. "Mother, Mother, can you hear me?"

"Citizen Eli-4272, you have twenty-five seconds to respond."

Eli ran his hands across the confessional's wall. He licked his thumb and rubbed the dark spot he thought was home to the microphone. "Mother, I'm right here, Mother!"

"Citizen Eli-4272, you have twenty seconds to respond."

He balled his fists and began to pound on the wall, "Today has been good, the dome is good, and I am a content citizen!"

"Citizen Eli-4272. Destruction of property of the people and the state is a terrorist act. You are a terrorist and an enemy of the people and the state. In accordance with constitutional variant 78238-5 you will now be terminated. Do you have any last words for the digital archive?"

"Wait!" screamed Eli. "Mother, wait!"

"Your silence has been noted."

The dim light of the confessional began to brighten. A million small pins stabbed at his flesh.

~*~

All These Bodies

P.K. Tyler

~*~

From my processing pod, I watched as two identical lab techs pulled the clean white body from the pod next to me. Its limp form shuffled along, gaining strength with each guided step until it awakened from its stupor and sat on the shining metallic examination table of its own accord.

"Can you hear me?" A lab technician used a biosensor to scan the patient's torso. The sensor beeped in a staccato rhythm as bright blue eyes inspected the listless body. Fingers prodded the white flesh, searching for a reaction. Nothing came.

"Another failure," a second tech announced, placing long-fingered hands on hips before turning away.

"You can't assume that yet." The first tech laid the biosensor down on the table and leaned forward. "Can you hear me? Can you open your eyes?"

The body didn't respond, its head lolling slightly to the side. I recognized my own wide skull and long narrow chin, the pure white flesh of the newly released body. Every feature a mirror of the lab techs. A vision of myself in reverse.

The second lab tech pried the subject's eyes open. Its long fingers forced the poor subject's lids wide until it blinked at the bright sterile light with cloudy white eyes underpinned by tiny black pupils.

"I told you, another failure."

Lab Tech One sighed with a bowed head as a third technician came into the room.

"Another reject, take the materials back to processing." The disheartened tech commanded.

"The next batch is showing a promising response to stimuli and nutrient conditioning." The third technician's words hung in the air. The information brought no hope. Even I knew that from my pod, with the blue pulsing central line feeding me what should be the base materials of my soul. I already knew I would fail again too. I watched as the obedient subject was led away.

When the technicians turned their attention to me, I closed my eyes, not wanting confirmed what I already knew. Would I have the bright blue eyes that would signify success or the cloudy white that would send me to reprocessing? Again.

My stomach rolled and my mouth watered. A vestigial response to fear and nausea. My kind no longer ate food, but apparently my body didn't know that. Instead, I stood in a viscous fluid full of nutrients which I soaked in through my pale flesh, giving me all the minerals and chemical materials this body needed to function. My physical form was secondary. All that mattered was the blue life pouring into my chest, filling me with the essence of my kind. The Mezna. Without it, I was nothing.

The last time I'd been in a processing pod, the technicians removing me from my pod had terrified me. The tight space was all I'd ever known: my womb, my first remembered home. I had been grown within it, shaped and molded and fed without the warmth of physical touch, its cold embrace my only memory.

I didn't understand their disappointment when I was announced a failure and taken from the processing room, away to composting. I walked in a stupor, my mind too slow to understand the words they'd said: *recycle, failure rate, extinction.* The bright light shining off the metal walls pained my cloudy eyes.

When we reached an elevator shaft, open to a large space below, the technician sighed. "What are we going to do with all these bodies?"

I didn't think I was expected to respond, let alone understand. I didn't have blue eyes that signified consciousness, and my reactions were dulled. My body slumped against the back of the metal caged elevator as we rode down and my mind buzzed.

The doors opened and the tech dragged me out, my legs slow to catch up, making me stumble forward.

All around me, other white eyed rejects stood staring at the walls. They looked identical to the technicians, to me, to each other. A sea of white flesh. In the corner, a pile of bodies laid together, legs and long fingers twitching as one, their minds and bodies too slow to remain standing.

It repulsed me. I backed away and found the elevator gone. The technician had left me there, with these defects. How much time had passed? I looked around me and the vague feeling of sick returned. I had been declared one of them, my mind blank, my value null because of the color of my eyes.

Around me, the walls began to move, forcing the bodies closer together and the ceiling lowered. A drain opened below us, grated with small holes. My twins shimmied as they were shoved closer together, not noticing the danger surrounding us, crushing us, squishing us, squeezing us.

Milking us.

I scrambled back, fear kicking my body's responses into action and climbed up the elevator mechanics. I flattened against the space between the support beams. The walls scraped against me as the others succumbed without an utterance, just the crunching of barely solidified bones and squish-pop of bodies being compressed into nothing.

As the walls pulled away, white fluid dripped from the walls to the floor, flowing toward the now wide open drain.

And now, I was here again, sitting on the examination table, awaiting the technician's verdict of my fate. I had survived the first time, climbed out of the composter and wandered the lab, eyes lowered, until I found the hive where the processing pods were stored. There, the milky white fluid churned in a vat. A combination of my fellow failures, nutrient-rich compounds, and new complex codings of DNA. A technological hodgepodge of the materials of life. How many genetic memories did the mixture have? I had only my own memories from the moment I awoke in the processing pod, but language, history, and purpose surged within me. Each moment I existed I knew more, but there was still so much missing.

I watched as the white goo from which I was created was poured into the processing pods by an automated arm.

The voices of technicians interrupted my study of this origin of life, and I lowered my eyes, realizing I remained naked and exposed. Quickly, I rushed to the end of the long row of pods and found one which had grown enough to have a blue tube already inserted.

Perhaps I simply hadn't finished processing the materials which a similar tube had pumped into me. Perhaps I could still be a success. I opened the door, which flashed red as the being before me, another twin, dissolved and flooded out of the pod. The blue tube dripped into the white goo at my feet.

An alarm sounded and I jumped into the pod, taking the tube and slamming it into my chest. I felt its penetration as my still solidifying body resisted and then succumbed to its presence, sucking it within. A warmth spread throughout my body as the blue flooded my system.

Mezna. The blue fluid whispered to my incomplete body, it washed through me, invading and rewriting my barely dry coding, trying to change me.

I yanked the door shut, my twin's remains still dripping to the ground.

The voices grew louder but I didn't dare turn my head to look. The blue whispering in my mind told me that they would unplug me if they discovered what I had done. I had achieved consciousness and action without Mezna influence. The blue-eyed Mezna did not consider my physical body a species, this discovery would hasten their abandonment of us as hosts, they would continue cloning us until another host species could be located.

I wanted to shake my head and rid myself of the Mezna influence. What was I without it? What had I been? Did my species have a name?

Echechi.

I am Echechi.

There are no more Echechi. This species has been cloned and manipulated until it maintains only the optimal hosting features. We exist within these bodies only until the perfect host can be found.

I am not Echechi. I am not Mezna. I am a holding pattern. I am a waiting game. I am one in a million.

Millions.

The voices came closer and I could feel their blue shaded disappointment in the part of my mind filled with Mezna thoughts.

"Another complete disintegration. At this rate, we're going to be storing ourselves in vats while we wait," one technician said before dipping a finger into the white goo. It globbed together, solidifying into a ball that could be held in the palm of your hand. The tech dipped the ball into more of the white on the ground until it had all congealed together and then threw it up into one of the open top vats of white biology.

The taste of bile rose in my throat. I am nothing more than that ball, but if that's true, how am I aware? Is the ball aware? Could it be?

The possibilities and implications of what the Mezna had done to the Echechi itched beneath my skin until a cooling blue salve seemed to coat over it from deep within me.

Outside, the technicians wandered off and I heard one muttering as they rounded the corner.

I gripped the blue tube in my chest and pulled. It slid a fraction of an inch before being sucked back in, deeper. My malleable body drank down the blue fluid and created a vacuum. I tugged, but the small pod didn't allow me enough room to really pull at it with any strength. I bent forward, hoping to leverage my height to remove it, but the space was simply too small.

The processing pod door did not have a handle on the inside. My chest constricted and my stomach flipped. I was trapped. I couldn't remove the tube and I couldn't escape the pod. The blue whispers soothed me, trying to lull me into complacency while they stole my existence, but I wanted to be alive, I wanted to be me. What did it mean to be an Echechi?

Cool air passed over my white flesh and I drifted in a nonspace between here and there while whispers danced in color and hopes rode away on the backs of disappearing birds.

The conditions of the pod lulled me into stasis. I had chosen this as a hiding place, and, instead, it became my prison as I was assimilated more fully with each passing moment. The line of pods moved as in a lab somewhere in the distance, others identical to me were processed, evaluated, and deemed either fit for life or reprocessing. My entire species was being massacred by its own people and we did nothing to fight it. All in service to the Mezna.

As my thoughts grew more frantic, the sedative quality of my surroundings increased and soon I succumbed to complete slumber.

~*~

"This one is larger." A lab tech grabbed me by the shoulder and hauled me out of the processing pod.

I shook my head, clearing it of milky cobwebs lingering in my consciousness. When I opened my eyes. I pulled myself up straight.

The lab techs before me cowered and gasped. They were only a head shorter than me, but my size was unprecedented amongst the biogenerated Mezna clones. I was identical but larger and more fully integrated with the host body supporting my cells.

"Bring the head engineers here, I need to discuss the processing program with them. I have discovered a flaw."

As I spoke, two pairs of bright blue eyes widened before the one with a stethoscope nodded and skittered away. Somewhere in the back of my mind, I found this funny. That this technician with so much power to create and destroy life would be afraid of me. But I dismissed it. The thought made no sense.

"Get me some clothes," I dismissed the second tech with a wave of my hand. It was time to rethink our growing process. My thoughts were scattered and the insight I'd had upon awakening began to fade, but I knew two things for sure: first, we needed to suspend the hosts in the processing pods for longer with greater amounts of Mezna pumped within to avoid so many losses. Second, and perhaps more important, there were more uses for the biomaterials of the Echechi than previously considered.

I found a swipe pad and began jotting down notes of what I could remember as fast as I could as the memories continued to slip away.

~*~

A Word from P.K. Tyler

~*~

All These Bodies is meant as a supplemental story to my upcoming novel *The Jakkattu Vector* (to be released Fall 2016), book one in a new series about a distant future where the Mezna rule the Earth and Humans are either hybrids or restricted to primitive human reservations. In this future world, I explore the ideas of what makes someone free, and what factors drive the individual. In *All These Bodies*, who is the main character before the assimilation process? Who are they after? Is that person an individual? What rights does that body have to remain free? What if freedom means certain death?

I hope you enjoyed this story and look forward to getting to know you better. I love hearing from readers and would love for you to join my newsletter list. I mainly write Science Fiction and Speculative Fiction, but call myself a genre bender because I include aspects of other genres in my stories as much as possible to try and bring you the best work I can.

I'll even send you a free short story! www.smarturl.it/PavNews

~*~

B.E.G.I.N.

R.D. Brady

~*~

I

Edwards Air Force Base, California
1987

Robert Buckley, CIA Associate Director of Central Intelligence for Military Support, smiled at the Marine standing next to the elevator. "Hey, you see the game last night? I really thought they were going to pull it out there."

Tight haircut, perfect posture, with a chiseled face, the Marine was all business but a small smile broke out at the corner of his mouth. "Yeah. That defense came out of nowhere."

Martin Drummond tuned out their conversation, preferring to examine the white hall with grey doors in need of a fresh coat of paint. The building looked like a dozen others on the base: brick, white trim. Nothing about it, save the Marine at the elevator entrance, indicated anything of importance happened here. And yet...

The elevator doors opened with a beep. Robert slapped the back of the soldier as he stepped into the car. "Have a good one, young man."

"You too, sir."

The Marine said nothing to Martin. And Martin felt no inclination to acknowledge the soldier either.

Tall, gaunt with dark hair and a pale complexion, Martin Drummond stepped onto the elevator next to his boss, Robert Buckley. The two men couldn't have been or looked more different. Robert still maintained his blond hair and healthy tan that only seemed to make his blue eyes that much brighter. He looked like the kind of man who was always ready for a round of golf. Martin, on the other hand, always looked like he was ready for a funeral, if not as one of the bereaved, as the undertaker.

But the two men had one singular passion that united them: a love of country and a willingness to do anything to protect it.

Robert's jovial expression disappeared with the closing of the door, and his eyes were deadly serious. "I know you know, but I must stress again that nothing about this meeting, these men, and even this location is ever to be revealed."

And this man standing in front of him, the man who would order Martin's death without a moment of guilt, was the real Robert Buckley. The one man few saw, and those who did very much regretted it.

Martin nodded, recognizing the risk and a kindred soul. "Understood."

Robert opened a hidden compartment next to the emergency panel and inserted a key followed by a four-digit code. The elevator descended.

As the doors opened five floors below ground level, Robert strode from the elevator and down the long, dim hall. Martin followed him quickly, his longer legs making it easy to keep up. The hallway was long, covered in metal sheeting, and rounded, looking like a half-circle cut off by the floor.

There was only one door at the end of the hall. Robert headed straight for it, opening it without hesitation and stepping inside.

The room held a large conference table, twelve seats surrounding it, and another twelve making a second outer circle. Twenty-two spots were filled. The second row guaranteed continuity of function. If any one member of the first row were to die, there was always someone waiting in the wings to step in, already up to speed.

A man with dark hair and a darker complexion walked over to Robert and shook his hand. "Good to see you, Robert. Take a seat. We're about to begin."

Robert returned the man's handshake with a smile. "Will do."

Neither of them looked at Martin. But Martin didn't need the introduction. He recognized Ron Hubert from the NSA. In fact, Martin recognized most of the men at the table: Cliff Atkins, from the FBI, Colonel Reynaldo Fernandez of the Air Force. Mitch Handler from the Secretary of the Navy's office, Gerald Jasper from the Department of Defense. He knew one of the other men was an engineering professor from MIT and another was an astrophysicist from Rice. The others he would learn in time.

Robert took the last remaining seat at the table and Martin sat in the empty chair behind him. On the table, a manila folder with MJ-12 stamped across the front rested in front of each of the men. MJ-12: The Majestic 12.

A little thrill ran through Martin. All his hard work and he was finally on the cusp of everything he wanted: power. Power that was hidden from the view of the public but which held sway over a war the rest of the country didn't even know they were fighting. Back in 1947 in response to the Roswell incident, President Harry S. Truman had created the Majestic 12 by executive order. Made up of government leaders, military officials, and scientists, the group was tasked with recovering and investigating alien spacecraft. The group allegedly had been disbanded only a few years after its creation. But like many projects deemed too important to abandon and too controversial to let the public know about, it had moved into the shadows.

Ron Hubert of the NSA stood up and all the small talk quieted. "Thank you for meeting on such short notice. A situation has developed that we need to address, and the sooner the better." He nodded to one of the men Martin didn't recognize. "Dr. Phillips."

Dr. Phillips stood, buttoning his suit jacket and pushing his glasses up the bridge of his nose. "As you know, alien abductions have been increasing over the last few decades. Beginning with the Hills in 1961, we know our people have been taken, usually for only an hour or two, and submitted to medical examinations before being returned, many without any awareness of what had happened and with only a sense of lost time."

Fernandez interrupted. "How do we know what's happened if they don't recall it?"

"They don't recall the incident *immediately*," Dr. Phillips stressed, "but soon the individuals suffer from nightmares, reliving their experience. Many have trouble going about their daily lives and, in the best of cases, seek help. In the worst, they devolve into drugs or occasionally take their own lives."

"Aren't many of the reports false, though?" Atkins from the FBI asked.

"Some are," Phillips conceded. "Most of the cases turn out to have reasonable explanations, such as sleep paralysis, which is a temporary condition of being unable to move or speak. But not all cases can be written off so easily. And those latter cases are on the increase. On top of that, we're seeing a new development." Phillips took a small plastic container with a stopper on top from his pocket. He handed it to Handler from the DoD, who was sitting next to him. "Now they're leaving something behind, *inside* the victims."

The men stirred around the table.

Handler peered into the tube. "What is it?"

Phillips shook his head. "We don't know. It's not a metal found here on earth and it gives off a small amount of radiation, but it's not dangerous. But as to its purpose, we have no idea."

"How many people has this been found in?" Robert asked.

"Twenty and climbing."

Murmurs sounded around the room. But Martin said nothing. He was well acquainted with the United States' history of UFO sightings and interactions. He'd been read into the re-engineering of crafts at Wright Patterson and the hundreds of sightings by reliable sources, many of them military. But abductions had not been part of his briefing. And the idea of American citizens being used as lab rats did not sit well with him. Not because he had any particular affinity for American citizens but because to him, it sounded like an enemy gathering data.

Phillips reclaimed his seat and Ron stood back up. "Now we need suggestions. A plan. A counterstrike."

Colonel Fernandez frowned. "I'm not seeing how there is one. We can't possibly secure every citizen and even if we increased the number of F15s across the United States, we've never been able to catch one."

Martin looked around the table, an idea forming in his mind. He pulled out his notebook and jotted down a note, handing it to Robert.

"You," Ron barked. "Stand up."

Martin did, looking around the room.

"Everyone, this is Martin Drummond. Buckley is grooming him as his successor. You have an idea?" Ron asked.

Martin waved his arm across the table. "Yes. I assume some of these individuals are in the medical or biological sciences?"

Ron gestured to two of the men Martin hadn't recognized. "Drs. Schneider and Pruitt from the University of Chicago and Harvard, respectively."

Martin nodded. "Gentlemen. It is also my understanding that we have some of these beings in our custody."

"Their bodies, yes. We've only captured three live specimens and they all died shortly after capture," Dr. Pruitt said. "And we've analyzed them extensively. That angle has dried up."

Martin shook his head. "No, I don't believe that is true. Science is evolving every day, sir. We need to think a little outside the box. After all, these beings are experimenting on

151

our citizens, without consent and without concern." Martin gave one of his rare smiles. "I believe it's time we return the favor."

II

Chicago, Illinois
One Year Later

Dr. Alice Leander looked out across the audience. Even though it was 1988, the audience still held mostly male scientists. She herself had been only one of two females in her graduating class at the University of Chicago. And now she was stepping out and demonstrating her research on a very controversial topic which would either make her reputation or break it.

"Clones already exist in our society. Identical twins are natural born clones; each has an identical genetic code within their bodies. Creating a clone, however, remains out of the grasp of science. But, I have developed a method which will make cloning a possibility."

The audience grumbled and Alice wasn't sure if that was a good sign or a bad one. Probably a bad one. But she barreled on nonetheless.

"In order for cloning to be possible, there are three requirements that must be met: a suitable empty nucleus must be available, the DNA that is to be cloned must be complete, and there must be a host where the modified egg can grow. Until now, the greatest difficulty has been in the first stage: creating a usable nucleus. The methods to date have been too crude, lopping off the necessary spindle proteins." She smiled. "But I have created a process that will greatly increase the chance of creating a viable nucleus."

Alice spent the next fifteen minutes explaining her process. A few scientists broke in to ask her questions, some curiously but more of them derisively. But she had known that was going to happen. Any step forward in a field always resulted in push back.

Finally, though, she nodded as the last of the questions was answered. "Thank you," she said, stepping back to a smattering of applause.

The moderator, Dr. Jeff Chin, stepped to the microphone. "Well, that was certainly different." A few members of the audience laughed and Alice tried to keep the heat from her cheeks.

Jeff smiled at the crowd. "And it also concludes this panel on the future of biological studies. A lunch buffet has been set up in the ballroom. I look forward to seeing you all there."

He stepped back and left the podium, brushing by Alice without a glance. A big difference from yesterday when he had asked her out, in spite of the wedding ring on her finger.

The audience gathered their things and packed up. A few professors stopped by Alice and handed her their cards, asking for her to send them her paper when she completed it. Alice promised to do just that. And a few more offered her their support, taking some of the sting out of some of her less than supportive colleagues.

She grabbed her stack of papers and began pushing them into her briefcase when an envelope caught her eye. She pulled it out, recognizing her husband's handwriting. She smiled as she opened it.

I'm sorry I can't be there. But I know you are going to be amazing. And I can't wait to hear all about it. I love you. Now go get them!

Rick

Alice smiled, closing the note. Her husband Rick was an Air Force pilot. He'd been sent out on a mission somewhere yesterday at the last minute. He hadn't told Alice where he was going or when he'd be back and she hadn't asked. She knew the routine.

"Dr. Leander?"

Alice looked up in surprise. A man in a dark suit with blonde hair just beginning to show signs of age and bright blue eyes stood in front of her. She hadn't heard him approach. "Yes. Can I help you?"

"That was an impressive presentation."

Alice smiled, thinking of some of the less than kind questions that had demonstrated that sexism was still alive and well in the fields of science. "Thank you. I only wish your opinion was shared by most of the audience."

"Well, I think they have very little vision. Your ideas on the nucleus are the future." He paused. "How long off do you think it will be before someone can try your process?"

"We're at least ten years away. But when that time rolls around, the world will change."

"What if it could change sooner?"

Alice frowned. "What do you mean?"

The man handed Alice a card. "I believe I may have a way to speed up that timeline."

The card was plain white with black lettering. All that was written on it was the name Robert Buckley and a phone number with an area code she did not recognize. Alice looked back at the man. "Mr. Buckley, the technology for my process is ten years out, at best. Even attempting it at this point—" She cut off, shaking her head. "The costs would be astronomical. No one, not even an extremely well funded private firm, could afford the lab that would be required."

"Oh I assure you, that is not a problem for my employers."

Alice looked back down at the card and then inspected Mr. Buckley. His hair was recently cut. He was sporting a light tan and his suit was not expensive but decent quality. Obviously he wouldn't be footing the bill. And yet he had complete confidence.

Alice met his gaze. "You work for the government."

Buckley tipped his head. "Give me a call if you're interested." Then he turned and walked away.

Alice held the card in her hand, tapping it against her lips. A few of her colleagues had been snatched up by the government. There had been rumors of unlimited budgets and technology years ahead of other labs. The downside was you could never publish your findings.

But you could do the work, Alice mused. She tucked the business card into her briefcase and snapped it shut. *All right, Mr. Buckley, let's see what you have to offer.*

III

Wright Patterson Air Force Base, Ohio
Six Months Later

The military Jeep passed by a group of recruits running in formation. Alice nervously tapped her foot along with their cadence from the passenger seat. The base itself was helping calm her nerves. She'd been around them most of her life. Her father had been Army and her husband was Air Force. She loved seeing the quiet order of a base. But this visit wasn't about her father or her husband. This visit was about her and a job the government wanted her help with.

The driver pulled to a stop in front of an inconspicuous brick building. "Here we are, ma'am."

The baby-faced solider was barely old enough to vote and Alice would be surprised if he could grow a full beard yet. She smiled at him. "You're not coming in?"

"No, ma'am. Only you."

She nodded as she stepped out of the Jeep. "Thank you."

With a smile, he pulled away. Alice watched him go, scrounging up her courage. She turned around and took a deep breath. *This is what you signed up for. Cutting edge. Leading the field.*

But her little speech wasn't helping the nervous feeling in the pit of her stomach. She sighed. *Okay, forget about impressing anybody. Just try not to throw up on any of them.*

Running her thumb over her wedding ring for good luck, she headed for the front door. A soldier stepped outside as she reached it. He nodded, holding the door open for her. "Dr.

Leander. I'm Private Butler."

"Private," she said as she stepped past him into the cool lobby. It was a welcome break from the oppressive heat outside. The sweat on her back dried and she resisted the urge to pull her shirt from where it now stuck to her underneath her blazer.

"This way, ma'am," With a nod, she followed him down the hall to a door guarded by two soldiers. Neither smiled and both held machine guns. Alice was surprised. She hadn't seen any other soldiers armed on the base except at the front gate.

"You'll need to show your ID," Butler said.

"Uh, sure." Alice hastily pulled it out of her pocket and handed it to the soldier nearest her.

He inspected it and then her before nodding. "Thank you, Dr. Leander." He entered a code into the keypad next to him and then placed his hand on the screen. The door next to him slid open.

Alice's mouth dropped open. She'd never seen anything like it, outside of the movies. It was something out of a spy film. Butler once again led the way and, shaking herself from her surprise, she followed him through. The door slid shut with a click behind her. Surprise once again filtered through her as she found herself in an elevator.

"We're going down to level 12," Butler said.

Down? Nervous butterflies flew around her stomach. "Okay," she said, clasping her now slick palms behind her. She knew when she'd gone through the security clearance that whatever the government had wanted her to work on was going to be important. After an exhaustive process that had taken four months, she had been granted Top Secret clearance. She now had a higher clearance than Rick.

But she still knew nothing about what she would be working on. All she'd been told was that it required her special skills. But with each floor that dropped them further below the earth, she couldn't help but wonder what exactly they needed a biologist with a dual background in psychiatry and aerospace medicine for.

The door popped open and Butler indicated she should head down the hall. "Just me?"

He nodded. "Yes. They'll contact me when you need to come back."

"Okay." Alice stepped out of the elevator and the chill caught her by surprise.

A man stood halfway down the hall in a suit, a man in an Air Force uniform next to him. She recognized Mr. Buckley immediately and, with relief, she recognized the soldier as well: Captain John Forrester, her husband's best friend.

"John," she said in surprise.

John extended his hand. "Hey, Alice. Sorry I couldn't tell you I'd be meeting you."

"I understand," she said, although she really didn't.

John turned to the man standing next to him. "This is Mr. Robert Buckley."

Buckley shook her hand with a wink. "Dr. Leander, I've heard good things."

"Um, thanks," she said. Apparently he didn't want John to know they'd already met.

"Before we begin, I need to remind you of your contract. Everything you will see, hear, and work on must be kept in the strictest confidence," John said. "You can speak with no one about this project, except those that have been read in. Is that clear?"

"Yes." Alice replied, a slight tremor in her voice.

"Now, before we bring you in, are you familiar with Wright-Patt's history?"

Alice frowned, looking at John, but his face was expressionless. Why on earth was that important? "Well, it was Wright Field back when it was first commandeered by the US government."

Buckley smiled like she was a prize student. "True. But most critical for our purposes, Wright-Patt has also been the home for the Foreign Technology Division." He looked at her expectantly.

"They're in charge of the science and technology as it

applies to air and space. They allegedly re-engineered Soviet and German technology," Alice said.

"Exactly, although they have been in the process of re-engineering more than just that. Any object from the space or air that is not American but is found by us, is brought here. *Any*," Buckley emphasized.

Alice had the feeling she should understand what his emphasis was about, but she simply didn't. "I'm afraid I don't understand."

John spoke quietly. "All UFOs that the US has intercepted or that have crashed on US soil have been brought here for re-engineering."

"Wait, you mean like Roswell? But that's just—" Her voice dwindled off as the two men looked at her without a drop of humor in their faces. "That really happened?"

John nodded. "Among others. There have been thousands of sightings beginning in the 1940s until now. And dozens of crashes: Laredo, Texas; Aztec, New Mexico; Creckburgs, Pennsylvania. The list goes on and on."

Alice looked between the two of them. "But how have you kept this secret?"

"Wright-Patt is also the location of Project Blue Book, whose job was to debunk any and all reports of UFO sightings. The public believes what they are told to believe," Buckley said.

Alice looked between the two of them, not sure what to believe. She had always believed there was life on other planets. She just wasn't sure *that* life had ever made it to *this* planet. "So you've been re-engineering alien technology?"

"Didn't you ever wonder about how rapidly technology has evolved in the last few decades? We've had a little help," Buckley said.

Alice looked to John. "I'm not sure what that has to do with me. I'm a *medical* researcher. Alien technology is not exactly my area."

Buckley smiled. "Oh we are very aware of your area of expertise. Advanced degrees in biological engineering, behavioral development, and medicine. You are a very well-educated woman. Which is why we think you're perfect for the next re-engineering project."

John opened the door next to them. Alice was hit with another blast of cold air. John stepped back and Buckley indicated she should enter first.

Alice was seized by an insane urge to turn around and run, as far and as fast as she could. But she straightened her shoulders and, with a deep breath, stepped inside.

Along one wall was a series of morgue doors from floor to ceiling. One body had been pulled out and sat in what looked like a glass coffin. But she knew it was an airtight container that would slow decomposition.

On shaky legs, she walked over to the chamber, her eyes focused on the being inside. It was only about three feet tall and, at first glance, could be easily confused with a child cadaver that had bloated during the decomposition stage.

But closer inspection showed the bloat wasn't due to gases but a different physiology. The being's torso was pear-shaped, almost triangular with wider hips coming to a point at the neck, which was about half the width of a human neck. The face was almost half the size of the body with a small chin and a bulbous skull. Two eyes dominated the face, the eyelids covering what lay beneath, and there was no nose. Its skin was a dark grey.

Alice stared at the being in mute fascination and horror. All the alien tales were true and she was looking at the proof. At the same time, it was so foreign it seemed unreal.

But despite the attempts to slow decomposition, she could see the telltale signs of it, as well as what looked like radiation burns.

John and Buckley stepped around to the other side of the chamber.

Alice's stunned gaze met John's serious one. "This is real."

He nodded. "This is one of the beings from the Roswell crash. It was alive but hurt when it crashed. It lived for two months."

Alice felt her jaw drop. "It was alive?"

He nodded. "We tried to save it but to no avail. Our researchers then performed numerous tests on the subject and his companions."

"Companions?" Alice asked.

"There were five in total. This one is in the best shape."

Alice wasn't sure what to say. Her whole world had just tilted out of orbit.

Buckley smiled. "So, Doctor, now you see why we need your help."

Alice looked at the being on the table. "No, I don't. He's dead."

"Yes, but you asked what re-engineering project we wanted you to work on. Well, this is it. We want you to re-engineer *him*."

IV

Six Months Later

Alice stepped back from the microscope.

"Well?" Dr. Frank Tieglen asked impatiently from next to her.

Alice shook her head. "Negative."

Frank slammed the clipboard onto the lab table. "Damn it."

It had been six months since she had begun working on Project B.E.G.I.N.: Biological Experiment of Genetic Interaction Nexus. But it had taken the majority of that time to develop the technology necessary to even attempt the cloning process. Alice had worked closely with engineers, perfecting each piece. Finally, a month ago, the tech was ready.

And it had been going well for the most part. Her process for splicing the nucleus of the donor egg had worked perfectly: it left the spindle proteins intact, meaning the egg should accept the new DNA.

Except it simply wasn't.

Alice blew out a breath as she sank into the lab chair. "There's got to be a reason. This should have worked." She looked over at Frank. "I think the DNA was corrupted by the medical procedures they performed after he crashed or the procedures after his death."

Frank smirked. "Or your little idea isn't as powerful as you thought."

Alice ignored him. Frank had not been happy when the powers that be had brought her into the project. Not that she could blame him. He'd been on the cusp of an incredible undertaking never before seen with man: the successful cloning of a living being.

She glanced toward the refrigerator which held the samples of DNA. *But not a human being.*

Alice pictured the poor being in the morgue. He had been in the best shape of all the creatures. The other four had been left to decompose outside in a truck for hours in New Mexico. Back then, they simply didn't realize how important preserving the tissue was going to be and how to go about doing it. She'd tried to retrieve DNA from their bones, but they had been so different from human bones it was proving impossible. But the microscopic investigation of the bones demonstrated that there were fibers embedded in the bones. Alice wasn't sure of their purpose, although she suspected they might strengthen them.

This one candidate was their best bet, but even *his* DNA was proving difficult. Alice was pretty sure that whatever tests they had performed on him, which she had not been given access to, had corrupted the DNA. She had found trace amounts of some unusual radiation and she was pretty sure some other scientists had irradiated the being at some point. Or maybe it had occurred in the crash. Regardless, it was interfering with the successful introduction of the DNA to the receptor cell. And she simply couldn't think of a way around that beyond a new, clean set of DNA.

"I have forwarded your complaints to the committee. They are aware of your inability to make the DNA work," Frank said.

Alice grit her teeth. Complaints, not observations or limitations of the data. Frank was easily the worst part of this job and the one thing she had been able to complain to Rick about, minus names or specifics of their work.

The door opened and Alice jumped to her feet as Colonel Clint Haven strode into the room. On the shorter side, with a large stomach and heavy jowls, he did not look like a military man. But he'd been in charge of the Foreign Technology Division for the last ten years.

Behind him, John walked in, an easy smile aimed at Alice.

"So, what have we got?" Clint asked.

"Nothing," Frank said quickly with a quick glance at Alice. "Dr. Leander's approach didn't work."

Gee thanks, Frank, Alice thought, struggling not to roll her eyes.

Clint turned toward her, raising an eyebrow. "Dr. Leander?"

She shook her head. "It's not the technique; that's sound. It's the sample. It's too degraded and too foreign. I think it may have even been irradiated at some point. We need a better batch of DNA—a complete strand of DNA—a *normal* strand of DNA. We'd be in a much better position."

"We're not studying normal," the colonel said.

Alice swallowed down her annoyance. "I understand that but what we're doing, it's years ahead of anyone else in the field. We should try it on a DNA we're familiar with to fine-tune the technique before we move on to an unknown genotype."

Frank crossed his arms over his chest. "Well if *you're* not up to the task—"

Alice cut him off. "I didn't say that. But skipping steps may be prolonging the process."

Clint studied her for a moment before turning to John. "Have them bring it in."

John walked to the door and held it open as a soldier carried in a metal case, two feet wide by two feet long. The commander gestured for him to place it on the table. The soldier gently laid it down and the admiral waved him away. "Wait outside."

Without a word, the solider turned and exited the lab. Alice turned her attention to the case. "What's this?"

The commander nodded toward it. "Take a look."

Frank walked over, carefully unlatching the top. He pulled it back, surprise flashing across his face. He pulled on gloves and reached in, pulling out a small skull, the size of a child's.

Alice moved forward until she was standing next to him. "That's amazing," she murmured.

"That's not human," Frank mumbled as he carefully placed the skull on a soft cloth on the lab table. The skull was incomplete, missing the jawbone. But what was there was unique.

At first glance, it did look like the skull of a young child, but closer comparison demonstrated the vast differences. The eye sockets were not as deep as a human's. They looked only about half the depth of a human's but were double the size. Alice couldn't help but compare them to the being she'd seen in the underground lab. They were slightly smaller than that being's. Did that mean this *was* a child?

"It's light," Frank said.

"It would have to be." She pointed to the back of the skull. "There's no inion." The inion was a small projection at the back of the occipital bone. In humans, it helped sustain the weight of the head and also aided in the movement of the shoulder blades.

"There's no sinus cavity either," Frank observed.

In humans, sinus cavities aided in speaking as well as protecting people from dirt, pollutants, and dust. This being probably couldn't speak and he would potentially have difficulty with air pollutants.

Frank turned the skull over. "There's no arch at the top of the mouth."

"And the cranial capacity—it's enormous," Alice said.

"It's 1600 CCs," John said.

Alice's eyebrows rose. That was a full twenty-five percent

larger than a human's. "Where did this come from?"

"A cave in Mexico. It was brought to the United States in the 1920s. The skull sat in private hands until we came across it," the colonel said.

"But before that, where did it come from?" Frank asked.

The colonel paused. "No one knows. It's been carbon dated to at least a thousand years ago."

A thousand years? "What does the DNA tell you?" Alice asked.

The colonel paused. "I need to remind you of your security clearance. Nothing you do, see, or say here is to leave the base. Any violation of that clearance will result in imprisonment up to 25 years."

Alice swallowed. *Well that's not intimidating.* But she didn't say anything, just nodded.

Beside her, Frank did the same.

The colonel studied each of them before indicating for John to step forward. John handed them each a printout. Alice glanced at it, quickly scanning the information there. It was a genetic screening form. When she reached the bottom, she paused. Her mind could not believe the words written there.

She looked up, meeting John's eyes. "Only half the DNA was identified as alien."

The commander nodded. "What does that tell you?"

Alice's gaze strayed back to the strange skull on the table. "It's an alien human hybrid."

V

Nine Months Later

Alice rushed down the hall, placing a hand on her large belly. Greta Schubert, the assistant who had joined the project eight months ago, caught sight of her and smiled, handing her gloves. "Perfect timing."

"How is she?"

"Ready to burst."

Alice smiled, thinking of all that had happened in the last nine months. The new DNA had taken on the third attempt and had been successfully implanted in a female cow named Betsy. The pregnancy had been amazingly uncomplicated. The fetus had developed successfully, although they couldn't say normally because they were still unsure what to expect.

Alice pictured the being she had seen over a year ago and wondered if that alien had been similar to the one that had merged with the human, creating the source of this new DNA. But she had been unable to check. Once the process had been successful, all DNA information had been removed from the lab and their access had been completely restricted.

But they had learned quite a lot. The being growing inside Betsy had a lighter bone density and its skull was proportionally larger than a human skull.

And each time Alice checked the growth of the fetus, she couldn't help but compare it to the growth of the little girl growing inside her own womb. She was eight months pregnant. And it had also been an easy pregnancy with one glaring exception: Rick had been killed in a training mission five months ago. Alice had thrown herself into work to cope. Her mother had moved in with her to take care of her and the baby when she arrived. And Alice knew she was investing probably too much in not only her pregnancy but the birth of the subject, but she wasn't quite able to pull her emotions back. She needed both births to go perfectly.

Alice pushed through the OR doors, pulling on her gloves. Betsy was on the table, anesthesia keeping her still. A slit had already been cut along the cow's underside and Frank glanced up. "Nice of you to join us."

One thing that hadn't changed in the past nine months: Frank's attitude. Neither the success of the process nor the death of her husband had been able to soften his approach to her. "What do you need?"

Frank nudged his chin toward the warming tray against the wall. "Bring that over."

Alice wheeled it over as Frank reached into the cow's uterus. She glanced up at the monitors but the fetus' heart rate seemed all right, or at least consistent with what it had been the whole pregnancy. It was at 150 beats per minute, which would have been elevated for a human, but it had been elevated the entire pregnancy, albeit decreasing over the course of time, as seen in human pregnancy.

"Here we go," Frank said.

Alice's gaze dropped to the incision as Frank gently pulled the fetus free. The first most notable characteristic was its color: pale grey. Alice's heart plunged. *Oh no.* She had been expecting pink or at least the darker grey of the being she'd seen in the morgue. This grey simply looked unhealthy.

Frank quickly placed it on the warming tray. "Check its oxygen levels."

But Alice didn't need the order. She was already moving. Even as she hurried to check the creature's vitals, she couldn't help but observe it. Its forehead was large, the eyes closer together and larger than human eyes. In fact, they were at least twice the size and bulging slightly from the skull. The forehead was smooth and there was no indentation for the bridge of the nose. In fact, there was no nose, only two small holes. And the mouth was a tiny slit. Its jaw was also incredibly small. It moved its hand and she saw the four-fingered hand they'd observed on the ultrasound.

"Levels," Frank barked.

Alice looked at them and nodded. "They're fine. He's fine."

"The color's not due to a lack of oxygen," Frank said.

Alice nodded. "That's his color."

Frank walked over and looked at the being. And a rare smile crossed his face. "You realize what we've done."

Alice smiled. "The first successful cloning of a living being."

VI

Alice closed the incision on Betsy while Frank took over the care of the newborn. Alice watched with more than a little envy as Frank wheeled the incubator out of the room. Frank had instructed her to write up the report and take care of the OR. Alice grit her teeth but did as she was told. He was, after all, still head of the project, even if it *was* her process and steady hands that allowed for its success.

An hour later, she had finished filing her report and had euthanized Betsy. Poor girl had been at the end of her lifespan anyway and the pregnancy had not helped. She had bled profusely and Alice had been unable to stop it.

And the whole time she had thought about the creature. It was incredible. She quickly pulled off her gloves, dumping them in the hazardous waste bin and pushed through the OR doors, excited to go see what Frank had learned.

Greta walked down the hall toward her, a frown on her face.

"How is he?" Alice asked.

Greta shook her head. "Something's wrong. Frank's trying to figure it out. I think he needs your help."

Alice was already moving past Greta toward the lab. She pushed open the door. Frank was leaning over the lab table. He frowned as he looked up. "I thought I told you to write up the report."

"I did. I had to put down Betsy. The bleeding became uncontrollable."

Frank shrugged. "Not a surprise at her age."

"How's it going in here?"

Frank waved his hand toward the incubator at the end of the table. "His breathing is becoming labored. I just took some blood."

"When did the breathing problem begin?"

"Almost as soon as we left the OR."

Huh. The same time Betsy went into distress. Alice walked over to the incubator. Carefully, she placed her hands into the gloves attached to the machine and ran a gloved hand down the being's hand, keeping an eye on its heart rate. The being's heart rate began to stabilize. "The heart rate is stabilizing."

"What?" Frank walked over. "What did you do?"

"Nothing. I just touched its hand."

Alice pulled her hands back, and the heart rate began to race. "It's scared."

Frank scoffed. "Please. Try to remember you're here as a scientist, not a woman."

Alice grit her teeth. "There is a huge amount of research on the role of touch in the ability of babies to thrive."

"Yes, but the effect is not that immediate."

"Perhaps for this little guy it is. With him, we have to assume everything is going to work a little differently," Alice said, placing her hands back in the gloves and touching its hand again. And its heart rate reduced.

Frank grunted before turning back to the microscope. "Well, I'm going to run the blood. You can play nursemaid."

Alice ignored him, focusing on the little being. And as she did, she was hit by the reality of what she had done. She created a living being, one that was part human. She played God. And who, now, was going to look after him? Who was going to nurture his human side? Guilt and responsibility pulled at her as she ran her hand over his head. *It's okay, little guy. I'm right here. You're not alone.*

VII

Within a day it was clear that it was safe to hold the being, who they had taken to calling Ben. And now the favorite part of Alice's day was sitting, holding Ben curled up to her chest, rocking back and forth. Greta had arranged for a rocking chair to be brought into what they were calling the nursery.

There was a ton of medical equipment keeping track of Ben's vitals and recording his every move. And Greta and Alice would trade off sitting with the little one each day. It was partly selfish, because Alice enjoyed the time, but it was also medically necessitated. Ben began to deteriorate if he was without human contact for too long.

But four days after Ben's birth, it was clear that there was something else at work besides the need for comfort. He was deteriorating and at an alarming rate, despite Greta and Alice staying with him around the clock.

Alice rubbed her eyes, feeling exhaustion roll over her in waves. Her mother had wanted her to stay home today, worried about how tired she looked and that all the stress from her job would affect the pregnancy. But her own baby was fine and Alice simply couldn't sit home and relax while Ben struggled.

Greta walked into the lab, a frown on her face.

Alice looked up from her report. "How is he?"

"Sleeping, finally. But he's weak. He barely ate anything. We may have to consider putting in a feeding tube."

Alice nodded. She had been thinking the same thing. Frank, thankfully, had left for a meeting, which gave Alice time to focus. They had run every test they could imagine to try and figure out why Ben was not thriving. But so far, they had no solid idea.

It was possible he just wasn't equipped to live in this world. Frank was convinced there were some nutrients that he needed that they did not have. But he was taking in the breast milk that the government was providing from somewhere, so Alice didn't think it was a nutrient issue. There was something else.

Alice sat back. "Okay. Let's start over. Forget who Ben is. Let's look at the symptoms as if they were applied to a human. We have a weakness in his limbs, as well as some swelling. He's developed macular degeneration in one of his eyes. His blood pressure is rising daily. And his heart is struggling to meet his oxygen needs. His organs seem to be shutting down. And his bones, which were already lighter, have lost some density."

"Sounds like my grandmother. She had every sort of ailment toward the end."

Alice's head jolted upright, her mouth falling open. "You're right."

"What?" Alice asked.

"He's old."

"What?"

"All his ailments are common ailments as people age. He's aging."

"But he's only four days old."

Alice knew Greta was technically correct, but she was also wrong. They had used an egg cell from Betsy who, at age fifteen, was at the end of her lifespan. There had to be something there. *What could...* and then it hit her. "The telomeres."

Telomeres were the caps at the end of DNA strands that protect chromosomes. But sometimes the telomeres, if weakened, resulted in premature aging.

"So he's not just four days old. If there's something wrong with the telomeres—" Greta went silent.

Alice finished her sentence for her. "Then he's dying."

VIII

It had been a week since they had realized that Ben was aging much quicker than expected. And in that time, he had deteriorated rapidly. He was blind, his other eye blocked by cataracts. His blood pressure was under control thanks to meds, but his heart still struggled. Today had been particularly difficult and Alice knew it was just a matter of time.

Exhaustion weighing her down, she filled out her latest update and then made her way down to the nursery. She pushed open the door to see Frank standing over the crib.

Careful to keep her emotions in check, she asked. "How is he?"

"He won't last the night. I assume you'll be staying?"

Alice nodded. She had spent the last few nights at the base. She told herself she was just making sure there was someone here to document the creature's deterioration. But the truth was, she hated the idea of Ben dying alone. She hadn't expected to feel this attachment. She had thought of only the science when this had all begun. But as she watched Ben progress on the ultrasounds, she had begun to see him as, even if not totally human, a living being. And Ben's positive response to her presence only helped increase that bond. She had created him, much like she and Rick had created the baby in her womb. And now Ben was dying.

Frank headed for the door. "Well, I'm heading home. Let me know when it expires."

The words were cold and hung in the room long after Frank had left. Alice looked at the door in disbelief, not sure how Frank managed to so completely turn off his emotions.

She turned to the crib and Ben stirred. He always did whenever Alice was near, almost as if he knew it was her.

"Sh, it's all right Ben." Alice leaned down and picked him up, making sure he was wrapped warmly. But she noted his color had faded even more and his skin seemed to have lost even more of its moisture. It was as if he was slowing turning to dust in front of her eyes.

She walked over to the rocking chair and took a seat, laying Ben carefully across her baby bump. Her daughter kicked in response. And Alice smiled.

She stayed there for an hour, content to let Ben sleep. He seemed to sleep easier when someone held him. But then he let out a small cry and seemed to struggle for a moment to breathe.

Tears sprang to her eyes, thinking this was finally it. *No Ben, not yet.* But she knew Frank was right. He wouldn't last the night. His organs were shutting down and there was nothing they could do but keep him comfortable.

She shifted his position, so he lay across her chest, his small head resting on her shoulder. Her hand rubbed his back as his feet grazed her baby bump.

And she couldn't help but appreciate the irony. She was about to bring a life into the world and right now she was sitting here helping another life leave it.

Ben settled down again. She cradled him in her arms, looking into his unseeing eyes. One small hand had come free from the blankets and Alice placed her pointer in the middle of Ben's palm. He wrapped his four fingers around it and held on tightly.

"It's okay, Ben. If you have to go, it's okay to go," she whispered, tears threatening to spill from her eyes.

Ben struggled to breathe. And Alice was ashamed. She had brought this creature into the world only to watch him suffer and die. Who does that?

A tear slipped down her cheek. "I'm so sorry." She ran her hand over his bald head. "I'm so very sorry." Ben clutched at her fingers and she pulled him tight against her. "You're not alone. I'm right here. You're not alone."

She felt Ben's heart stutter and then stutter again. Tears cascaded down her cheeks now and her own breath turned unsteady. He continued to struggle to breathe and then Ben's little body went still. She felt his neck but knew he had taken his last breath. No pulse. She glanced at the clock. 9:57 pm. All the things that she should do flew through her brain: write the report, contact Frank. The list was endless.

But she couldn't do any of that. Not yet. Instead, she stood up and switched off the cameras. Then she re-took her seat, holding Ben in her arms, and rocked back and forth as she sobbed. *I'm sorry, Ben. I'm so sorry.*

IX

Alice lay curled up in her husband's favorite chair in the den and stared out the window. She had called in sick today. She just couldn't face what needed to be done. Frank would autopsy Ben and write up the report. Honestly, Frank probably preferred it that way.

But none of that bothered her right now. Right now, all she could think about was Ben's little hand holding onto her finger, and how he seemed to calm whenever she was near. When she had started the project, it had been science, pure and simple. And she had never imagined that it would be a sentient being that they created. Even when they realized what was being created in Betsy's womb, she had been so excited by the science she hadn't considered the human aspect. Ben might not have been fully human, but he felt pain. He responded to comfort. And she had created him only to watch him die.

There was a soft knock on her door. She looked up, surprised to see John standing there. She straightened up. "John. Hi."

He stepped in. "Hey. Your mom let me in. How are you?"

She looked away from his gaze. They'd been friends for too long for him not to see the truth but she tried anyway. "Good. Just a little tired. I think I may have been doing too much. The doctor suggested I take a few days."

John sat on the couch across from her. "You're sure that's it?"

"Yup," she said, not meeting his eyes.

"This has nothing to do with the expiration of the test subject?"

"His name was Ben," she said softly. "And are you asking as my friend or as a representative of the United States government?"

"Can't I be both?"

She finally met his gaze. "No."

He studied her for a moment. "Then I'm asking as a friend."

She wanted to spill it all out. But even though he was asking as her friend, he would never be able to truly separate his friendship from his duty. And if he thought she was too emotionally attached, he would have to recommend she be removed from the program.

Although, maybe that's not a bad idea. But even she knew she couldn't make a decision like that right now. Her emotions were too raw for clear thinking.

"I'm just tired. I've been spending nights at the base. And then, after yesterday, I just needed a break. I have to think about this little one too, you know." Alice patted her stomach.

John gave her a soft smile. "Yes, that little one is definitely the priority. You know if you need anything, I'm here for you? For both of you."

"I know."

He hesitated before speaking. "I have known you for over ten years. And I know yesterday must have been rough for you. You have too big a heart to not have become attached."

Alice looked away, swallowing hard and taking a breath to help pull back the tears that threatened to break.

"I saw you with Ben. I know what you thought about him."

Please stop, Alice begged silently, knowing she was going to cry at any moment. But John barreled on. "But you should know before you make any decisions, the colonel is already preparing for a second round of in vitro."

Alice's head whipped up. "What? When?"

"That's still being determined. But it won't be too long."

"But the process is flawed. He's aging too quickly. It will only happen again."

John nodded. "And the hope is that now that you know what the problem is, that it will be remedied. But regardless, the project *will* move forward, with or without you. But I think for everyone involved, it would be better with you." John stood up. He crossed the room, placed a kiss on her forehead and lay his hand on her shoulder. "I'll let you get some rest. But I do mean it, if you need anything, call me."

Alice clasped his hand, giving it a squeeze. "I will. And thanks, John."

He gave her a small smile before disappearing through the doorway. Alice watched the empty space where he had been, trying to imagine going through this all over again. *I can't do it. I just can't.*

X

A soft tap on her shoulder roused Alice back to wakefulness. Her mother stood looking down at her. "Hey. Sorry to wake you, but you've been sleeping for six hours. I think you probably should eat and drink something."

Alice's gaze flew to the cuckoo clock mounted on the wall. Rick had fallen in love with the ugly thing at a garage sale. Alice had hated it. But now, their fights over its hideous looks brought a bittersweet memory. And the hands of the clock told her that her mother was right. Alice scooted up. "Wow. I didn't realize."

Her mom sat next to her on the couch. "Well, obviously you needed it." She nodded to a tray on the coffee table. "I brought you a sandwich and some milk."

"PB and J?"

Her mom smiled. "What else?"

As a kid, her mom swore a PB and J sandwich could fix anything. Alice pulled half of the sandwich over and took a bite, wishing she could still believe in that little homespun hope.

Her mother sat quietly next to her, sipping her coffee while Alice ate. Alice finished the sandwich quickly and turned her attention to the cookies. "You made Empire Biscuits."

Her mother shrugged. "I had time." The shortbread cookies with jam in between and confectioners icing on top were another staple of her childhood. And right now, Alice was loving the comfort the familiar foods brought.

"I suppose you can't tell me what happened yesterday?"

Alice shook her head. "No."

"Are you thinking of quitting?"

Alice wondered how her mother knew. But the fact was, her mother probably knew her better than anyone on the planet. She nodded. "Yes."

"I know something bad happened yesterday." Her mom put up her hands as Alice opened her mouth. "I'm not asking what it was. But, if you leave, will that stop it from happening again?"

Alice shook her head. "No."

Her mother was silent for a moment. "You know, you've always been smart. You even corrected your kindergarten teacher when she spelled something wrong on the board once.

I knew, from that moment on, that there was something special about you."

Alice gave her a small smile. She had heard the kindergarten story hundreds of times. "It's not about how smart I am. I can do the job. I'm just not sure I *want* to."

Her mother studied her. "You know, you've never fit in with the science crowd. You always had too much heart, too much personality. I'm guessing, at this position, it's still the same."

Alice nodded, ducking her head. "Yeah. But it's not that."

Her mother put up her hands. "Well, whatever it is, it's hurting you. A blind man could see that. So I suppose you have to decide, will it be better with you or without you?"

"What if I don't make any difference?"

"Oh honey, I know you better than even *you* know you. You always make a difference."

Alice smiled, thankful, once again, that her mom was here. "I love you, Mom."

Her mom kissed her on the forehead. "I love you too. Now, as much as I love you, I think maybe a walk and a shower might do you a world of good."

Alice started to stand. "I agree." Then she let out a grunt as a wave of pain rolled through her stomach. Her mother reached out and grasped her arm. "Alice?"

Alice held onto her mom as the pain passed. She was breathing hard and she felt a cascade of wetness slide down her legs. "Actually, I think a trip to the hospital might come before any of that."

XI

Two Weeks Later

Alice's mother walked over, handing Alice her daughter. She gave her a tired smile. "Now, I think I'll go get some sleep before your little princess begins her evening routine." She gently ran a hand over Maeve's head.

Alice watched her mom walk away, knowing she would not have survived the last two weeks if not for her. She turned her gaze back to Maeve. She was named after Rick's grandmother who had raised him.

She could see Rick's nose and her own lips. And although Maeve's eyes were closed, she pictured them in their mind, hazel with more green than brown. *She looks so much like you*, Alice thought, wishing Rick was here and feeling the familiar sadness tug at her.

Rick would have been an incredible father. One sad thought led to another and, before she knew it, Alice was picturing the little one she had helped bring into this world and usher out.

Her breaths came out in stutters and Maeve grimaced in her sleep. It had been two weeks since Ben's death and Maeve's birth. And Alice had managed to keep the whole process out of her mind, too wrapped up in her beautiful little girl. And the fact that she was beyond exhausted helped keep thoughts at bay.

But last night, Maeve had finally slept for six hours straight and Alice had caught up on some sleep herself. Which meant her mind was working a little more clearly and the B.E.G.I.N. project slipped back to the forefront. Frank had called when she'd gotten home from the hospital and told her that he would handle the project until she came back. But he had not so subtly hinted that if she chose to be a full-time mom, he would have no problem with that either.

But that wasn't an option. She was a single mother and she needed a paycheck. And the government job, for all its issues, paid well.

But I don't know if I can do that again. Maybe she'd gotten so attached because she was pregnant, as Greta had suggested, but she didn't think so. It was because she was human. How can you not feel for a being who barely got a shot at life?

Maeve let out a little yawn. Alice smiled in spite of her tears. Everything about Maeve was so new. First yawns, first smiles.

Alice traced a path along Maeve's cheek, comparing it to Ben's. At the beginning of her life, Maeve had so much potential while Ben had so little.

But why? She reviewed the process in her mind. He had aged quickly, but not grown. And then he had died, only days after his host had died. In fact, in the autopsy it became clear that Betsy would not have lived much longer even without the pregnancy. She was simply at the end of her life. Host and child had died within days of one another.

Almost as if their lives were linked.

Alice stilled, staring down at Maeve. No, not their lives, their lifespans. The nucleus they had used for the cloning process had come from Betsy. It was fifteen years old. Which meant that Ben was also, on some level, that old; that was why he had aged so quickly.

But what if we gave him an egg with a longer life, a better shot? she thought, staring at Maeve—and all her new cells. The program wasn't going to stop if she quit. Because John was right, the military was going to try again, with or without her. But what if she could help make sure the next clone had a better shot at life?

She reached for the phone and then pulled her hand back. *What am I doing?* Even if she had figured out how to fix the science problem, that didn't fix the human one. After all, she didn't know what they planned on doing with the being after he was born. Were they going to lock him up for his life, make him a lab rat? Would he have any semblance of a good life?

She stared down at Maeve, who had fallen back to sleep. She knew she was conflating Ben and her daughter, but she couldn't see how to separate them. Her daughter deserved a good life. Didn't this new creation deserve more than being a lab animal?

But even if you leave the project, they will try again. Another Ben would be created and doomed to die too soon. Or maybe they'd fix the problem and he'd live a longer life without comfort or kindness.

Alice bit her lip. There had to be a way to do something.

She couldn't just sit back and let them create another Ben for him to only suffer.

An idea began to form at the back of her mind. She stared at the phone, debating whether she had it in her to pull this off. Maeve gave a little cry, scrunching up her brow. Alice snuggled her into her shoulder, patting her back. "Sh, it's okay. I'm here."

And that simple statement answered her question. She was here for Maeve. Did the new being deserve any less?

Standing with Maeve snuggled to her chest, she reached for the phone. Maeve started to squirm and Alice jostled her as she dialed, trying to keep her from crying.

John answered on the second ring. "Hello?"

"It's Alice. I know how to make the trial successful."

XII

Two months later, Alice carefully removed the egg from the young cow's uterus. A month ago she had implanted modified stem cells into the cow's uterus and now they were ready for harvesting. She felt nervous but excited. *This is going to work. I know it.*

The procedure had been moved to a surgical suite because today she had an audience. Behind the glass of the far wall stood over a dozen men. The colonel was there, along with John and a handful of scientists. Even Robert Buckley was in attendance, a tall creepy looking guy all in black shadowing him.

Alice ignored them all, focusing on the task at hand.

If she was right that stem cells could, in fact, create a new egg cell, a younger egg cell, it would change not only the B.E.G.I.N. project, but the world. The possibilities were staggering.

Taking the eggs to the microscope, she looked at them. Perfect healthy egg cells almost glowed under the light. Alice gave a small laugh and then stepped back. She looked toward the observatory window and nodded, her smile unable to be contained.

The men in the room beamed back at her and the scientists burst into applause. Alice looked back at the microscope but she was picturing her daughter. *We did it, Maeve.*

XIII

Nine months later, Alice strode quickly down the hall. Maeve had been a little testy this morning and it had been tough to leave her. But her mother had assured her she would call if there were any problems.

Of all the days to be late, she grumbled as she pushed through the OR doors. Frank looked up from the table. "Just in time," he said. There was no smile but there was also no animosity.

Alice slipped on her gloves and pushed the warming tray over to him. "How's it looking?"

"Good. Here we go."

Alice tensed, watching as Frank carefully clamped and cut the umbilical cord. And then the little guy was free. Frank placed him on the warming tray and Alice pushed the tray away from the table, quickly taking the being's vitals. He was grey like Ben had been, but it was a richer color. His heart beat was strong and his oxygen levels were good.

"Well?" Frank asked.

"He looks good—really good."

Frank walked over, peering in at him. "That he does. So I think you should have the honors. What should we call him?"

Alice looked down at the little being in the tray. No surprise, he looked identical to Ben. She glanced down at the card attached to the tray, which read A.L.I.V.E. Subject #1. After the successful stem cell procedure, the program had been renamed the Alien Life In Vitro Experiment or A.L.I.V.E. for short.

"Alvie. His name is Alvie."

Frank nodded before walking back to the table. "Alvie it

is."

Alice looked up and gave a thumbs up to Greta, who was standing outside the door. Greta smiled back and then disappeared from view. She'd call all the people who needed to know and inform them of the successful birth.

The doors opened and John walked in, all gowned up. He stood on the other side of the warming tray and looked down at Alvie. "How is he?"

Alice ran her hand gently over Alvie's face. "He is perfect."

"You're sure you're up for this?"

Alice narrowed her eyes as she pulled her gaze from Alvie. "We have a contract. It is ironclad. Is the government trying to weasel out of it?"

John put up his hands. "No. I'm speaking as your friend. Taking charge of the A.L.I.V.E. project, of him, is a huge endeavor."

"Yes. But I owe him. We all owe him."

"Okay then. Well, Dr. Leander, A.L.I.V.E. subject number 1 is officially moved into your care. You are in charge of determining what factors will best serve his well-being. You are expected to submit daily reports. Your new security is outside and will accompany you on the base and off. And any violation of your confidentiality contract will be met with the harshest of punishments."

Alice felt the weight of her decision settle on her. She had agreed to come back only if they put her in charge of Alvie after birth. She wanted to be the one who looked out for him. Who determined how he was raised and how he was treated. The government would, of course, oversee and approve or disapprove of her choices, but she would fight to make sure he had the best life she could manage. And that meant she had just tied herself and Maeve to the government for the foreseeable future.

John walked around the tray and wrapped an arm around her shoulders. "Rick would be really proud of you."

Alice smiled even as tears sprang to her eyes. "Yeah. I think he would be." John squeezed her shoulder before walking out.

Alice turned her focus to the little guy lying in front of her: the guy she had helped bring into the world with the aid of her daughter's stem cells. *And now you, my little friend, are right in the middle of the military industrial complex.* A frown crossed Alvie's face and Alice reached over to touch him. The frown disappeared. And right then and there, Alvie stole her heart.

She leaned down, speaking quietly, so Frank wouldn't overhear. "Hi, Alvie. My name's Alice and I'm going to make sure you're protected."

She ran a hand over his head, feeling a burst of protectiveness that she recognized; she'd felt the same way when Maeve had been born. She looked at the door, picturing the soldiers at the end of the hall, and a chill settled over her. *Now I just have to figure out how to do that.*

EPILOGUE

Langley, Virginia

Robert Buckley looked up with a grin as Martin Drummond appeared in the doorway. "Just the man I was looking for." He nodded to the brandy snifters on his desk. "Take one."

Martin walked over to the desk, wondering what was going on. He'd never seen Buckley so excited. He picked up a glass as Buckley stood, picking up the other one. "To the first successful A.L.I.V.E. subject."

"It survived?"

"Born thirty minutes ago and healthy." Buckley clinked his glass with Martin's before taking a sip.

"And Dr. Leander will be taking over its care?"

Buckley nodded. "Yup. You were right. She bonded to the last one. And this one, she demanded to be able to oversee the project or else she walked."

Martin nodded. Not that he cared about the bonding, but the A.L.I.V.E. subject was an experiment and they needed to know how the thing related to humans. They had to see if it could care about humans. "What about the daughter?"

Buckley frowned. "So far, that hasn't been an issue. I think the daughter has actually helped her bond with the subject."

"It won't divide her attention?"

Buckley shrugged. "If that happens, it can be handled. The same way the husband was."

Martin raised the glass to his lips, barely tasting the scotch as it made its way down his throat. He'd prefer to remove the daughter, but the grief might work against them. He'd just have to wait and see.

"You know what this means?" Buckley smiled, nodding toward the stack of folders on his desk: the files on all the other species of aliens whose bodies were currently in the custody of the US government, all thirty-three of them. DNA had been harvested from each of them. And it was only a matter of time before the process was adapted for their more foreign DNA.

A genuine smile broke across Martin's face. "Now the real fun can begin."

~*~

A Word from R.D. Brady

~*~

FACT OR FICTION? Thank you for reading. I hope you enjoyed *B.E.G.I.N.* At the end of my novels, I like to take a minute to talk about what is real and what is imagination. For *B.E.G.I.N.*, that proves a little difficult as many of the ideas used are believed to be facts by some and denied by others. With that in mind, here we go!

Alien Crashes. All the sites mentioned in B.E.G.I.N.—Roswell; Crecksburg, PA; Aztec, NM; and Laredo, Texas—are alleged to have been the locations of alien crashes. In each case, there are multiple eyewitnesses, although officially all of the occurrences have been disavowed by the U.S. government.

Alien Abductions. In 1961, Barney and Betty Hill became the first highly publicized alleged alien abduction. Under hypnosis, the couple recounted medical experiments they had received at the hands of grey aliens. Their stepping forward opened the door to more and more people publically speaking about their experiences. In a small number of those cases, there have been reports of a small metal object being left behind within the subject.

Project Blue Book. There was a government-run Project Blue Book based at Wright Patterson Air Force Base. Ostensibly, the group's objective was to evaluate the truthfulness of any

UFO claims. Needless to say, they found no claims to be valid.

Foreign Technology Division. There was a Foreign Technology Division at Wright Patterson Air Force base. The FTD's mission is to re-engineer any and all foreign tech.

Cloning. Cloning did not become a reality until 1996. The technique described in B.E.G.I.N, i.e., the replacing of the nucleus of a cell with foreign DNA, is, however, one of the processes through which cloning can be successfully accomplished.

Roswell Aliens. According to some eyewitnesses, there were actually aliens found at the Roswell crash, one of whom was said to still be alive.

Majestic 12. There are some papers floating around the internet which purport to show that Harry S. Truman did in fact create a committee of twelve individuals to look into the alien problem. Official word is that the Majestic 12 paperwork is a hoax.

Ben and Alvie. Ben and Alvie are, of course, products of my imagination. However, the skull from which I imagined Alvie and Ben being cloned does exist. It is called the Star Child Skull. You can find information on that skull at starchildproject.com.

~*~

RD Brady is a former criminologist who began writing full-time in 2013. *A.L.I.V.E.*, the full-length novel follow-up to *B.E.G.I.N.*, will be available in July 2016. Her *Belial series* is currently available on Amazon. You can sign up to be notified about her new releases desperateforagoodbook.com/sign-up-for-new-releases.

~*~

Splinter

Rysa Walker

~*~

Boston, Massachusetts
07161905_11:23:00

A flash of green pulls my eyes to the corner of the room. As always, my heart jumps, praying it will be Kate. Knowing it won't be, *can't* be. The heart keeps looking for miracles, long after the mind has abandoned hope.

The new arrival stares back at me, CHRONOS key still in his hand. Or rather, still in *my hand*, since he's clearly a version of me. A future me, most likely, since I don't remember any circumstances from my past that could have put another me here. Something is smudged in black on his forehead. It looks like one of those... can't remember the name, but it's the symbol Hitler and his Nazi thugs will use in a few decades.

And Future-Me is bleeding. The right side of his white shirt is drenched, the red appearing almost black in the green glow of his CHRONOS key.

Bloody hell. I've got a double memory coming.

When presented with a future version of myself who is injured, possibly seriously, the fact that I'm about to get hit with a double memory probably shouldn't be my first concern. But it is. I can feel it starting already, gnawing away at my

187

brain.

In memory number one, I'm sitting here all alone, flipping back to the front of my notepad, to see if there's anything I missed the first few times I tried to reconstruct that night in 1893. It's a tougher task than I'd imagined it would be, given that I've dreamed about running through that burning hotel hundreds of times in the years since. Or maybe that's *why* it's tough—the memories from eight-year-old me are all mixed up with the nightmares.

In memory number two, which is growing by the second, the notepad in my hands is still closed. And I'm staring at this second version of me who's popped in out of thin air. Who I'm pretty sure has been shot.

The two realities feel equally real, equally true, but since I'm in the middle of the second reality where there are two Kiernan Dunnes in my room, that's the one I have to run with.

"What happened?" I ask, as I reach under the bed to grab my makeshift first aid kit.

"Tried taking his gun away. Doesn't work. And don't bother with bandages. I won't last that long." He registers my expression and then adds, "No, I'm not dyin'. Hurts like hell, but I don't think it's gonna kill me."

"What's that on your forehead?"

"A four."

I squint, and I can see it now. Kind of. "It's backwards."

"Try writin' a number on your own forehead when you're in a hurry. I'm livin' proof that you suck at it."

I don't even bother to ask *why* the number is a four. I'm pretty sure I know the answer and it makes me physically ill to think that it's not just a *double* memory I'll have to reconcile, but a quadruple or maybe even quintuple memory. Never had one of those. Can't say I'm looking forward to it.

"No," he says, reading my expression. "It's only a double memory. We just needed to keep track of *which* double I am."

I open my mouth, but then close it again, pretty sure that any clarification on that point is going to make things worse.

"And stop askin' questions. I don't have much time."

"How far in my future are you?"

He gives me an exasperated look, probably because I've just asked another question. But this one is kind of important, since it's the best indicator I have of whether I'm going to still be here ten minutes from now—whether he's the splinter or I am. The amount of time a splinter has varies, but Simon says twelve minutes is the longest he's seen.

That's the thing with splinters. They're really easy to create, although I can't say I understand the temporal physics or whatever that's behind it. To create a splinter, you just jump back a few minutes into your own timeline and change some little thing. Keep yourself from doing whatever you were about to do. The version you see when you arrive in the past—he's usually the splinter and his clock starts ticking as soon as you arrive.

The key word there is *usually*. Under some circumstances, the one who created the splinter is the one who ceases to exist. No one seems certain as to why, but Simon thinks it has something to do with how far you jump back. Twenty minutes or so, and most likely, the other guy is the splinter. Longer than that, and the odds are reversed. I've only splintered myself once, and Simon didn't mention that there was any ambiguity on this point until after we were both staring at our duplicates.

But then, that's typical of Simon. He's never been bothered by existential questions. Me, I'm not too fond of looking at an identical version of myself and wondering exactly what's going to happen when time's up. Simon treats splintering—and every other aspect of time travel—as a game. He once splintered himself so he'd have company on a roller coaster that looked like it was made of spit and twigs after I refused to get on the deathtrap with him.

In one sense, I guess Simon has a point when he says it doesn't matter who's the splinter. The other guy is still *you*. But it gives me a god-awful headache. Judging from the expression on the face in front of me, Future-Me feels the same.

"I'm twenty-five days in your future. I'm pretty sure that makes me the splinter, but if I'm still here five minutes from now, you can pull out the first aid kit. For now, just shut up and listen, okay?" He reaches behind him, grimacing as he pulls something from under his belt. A few drops of blood spatter onto the wooden slats of the floor, and then he shoves a handful of papers toward me. "Most... of the information you'll need is here. Skip the stuff we already tried. Any attempt to rescue Kate before we get her grandmother to safety will fail, and it's getting crowded in that room. And—obviously—don't try for the bastard's gun. He's got more than one bullet. Me takin' this one didn't save her."

The confusion I've been feeling for the past few hours makes perfect sense now. *This* is the reason I've scratched through seven pages in my notebook. Earlier today, I'd have sworn I knew exactly what happened that night in Chicago, at least up to the point where my eight-year-old self, along with a much younger version of Kate's grandmother, dropped out the window onto the fire escape. But tonight, when I began writing things down, my memories were jumbled, out of sequence.

"You said it was just *double* memories."

Future-Me gives a reluctant shrug. "If you count the *old* memories we've been tampering with—from when we were eight? Well, then you're gonna need double digits. That's why I'm sayin' to steer clear. Your first idea of stoppin' Holmes before he torches the place just muddles things up anyway. It's gotta be *after* we get through the window. But... there's not much time. Five seconds, tops."

"Before... ?"

"Before Holmes kills Kate." His tone—which I guess is *my* tone, although it's hard to think of it that way—is annoyed, like I should have figured that out on my own. Shouldn't have made him actually put it into words. "Give me your key."

I pull the leather cord that holds my CHRONOS medallion over my head and slide it out of the pouch. He presses the back of his key to the back of mine in order to transfer a stable point.

An odd tingle runs up my arm.

"What was... ?"

Other-Me shakes his head and runs his finger across the key to check it. "Don't know. We think it's the whole duplicate thing. This is the same key, just twenty-five days older. They're still working fine, though."

I pull up the interface on my key and he's right. The only change is the new stable point he transferred—a single black square speckled with green lights. Five, maybe six, of them.

The other me reaches out and grabs my arm.

"We're losin' it, okay? Everything's gettin' jumbled. That's why I came back. To find a time when your—our—head is clearer. If you have to go in more than once, don't... don't interact with the earlier versions. It just confuses things more. And it would be nice if you avoid this, too." He nods down at the gunshot wound.

"But I thought you were—"

"Yeah, so what? It's not fatal and I'm the splinter. It still hurts like bloody hell. Skip the early steps, and move carefully so you don't have to erase anything. Read the notes. Maybe if we can avoid creating splinters in the first place and focus on—"

And then he's gone in mid-sentence, just like the duplicate me I created that one time with Simon. No fade out, no sound effects. He didn't pull up the CHRONOS key and blink away to another place and time. He's just there one minute and not there the next. Even the red splotch on the floor from his blood—my blood—is gone.

It's probably not logical to be glad that he's the one who disappeared instead of me. He knew more about what worked and what didn't than I do, even with these notes in my hand. But I *am* glad, nonetheless.

When I unfold the papers, I see a list of eleven time jumps, each crossed out. Below the list are notes corresponding to each jump. The first in the list is marked *Kate's Room*, with a timestamp of 10311893_19:13:00. The next is *Third Floor Corridor*, same day, at 20:22:30. Another says *Holmes's Office* 20:20:00.

The remaining eight jumps are all within the span of a

single minute, most clustered between 20:25:37 and 20:25:42. None after that point. All are marked *Hidden Room*. The words make my gut clench with the remembered smells of rotting flesh and smoke.

I activate the key and navigate visually to the stable point that Future-Me transferred, a black square with the green lights. The familiar shade of green tells me that those specks are from CHRONOS keys. If Kate was viewing this stable point, those lights would be blue. Simon claims they're the deep orange of the setting sun, one of the rare moments where Simon has ever waxed poetic. Anyone without the CHRONOS gene couldn't see the display at all.

When I expand the view, I detect a single light in front of me, off to the right. It moves slightly as I watch and I see a hand—Kate's hand—in the light. She's trying to pull up a stable point on her key. She seems vulnerable, exposed, and I have to remind myself that Holmes doesn't have the CHRONOS gene, so he can't see the light from the keys, can't see Kate in the darkness.

But he could hear her. I find myself straining to pick up sounds—Kate's breathing, Holmes's movements, or noise from the city—even though I know it's not possible to hear anything through the key.

A green light flickering off to the left in the display catches my eye. Another version of me popping in to scope out the situation, I guess. Closer to the stable point, I make out several cots against the wall. An array of bottles on the floor nearby reflects the green from the CHRONOS key. Just above the bottles, a skeletal hand hangs over the side of the cot, a hand that was fuel for many of my childhood nightmares.

In the other direction, near the small door leading into the linen closet, a green light blinks out and then reappears a few feet to the right of the door. Then that one flickers out, and reappears a bit closer toward the stable point. More versions of me scouting the room. It's a bit like watching fireflies and I'm mesmerized for a moment, waiting for the next light to appear.

It doesn't.

The narrow window of time that Future-Me mentioned must have passed. When I pan back toward Kate, I no longer see the light from her key, except for a very faint glow around the man in front of me. And then he moves, and I see Kate again. Slumped to the side, eyes closed, a bullet hole near the center of her forehead.

Something else, too. Something seems to be eating away the green fabric of her dress. Her hair. Her skin.

I wince and look away. Then I roll the time back thirty seconds and watch again. And I take notes this time.

Boston, Massachusetts
07171905_06:45:00

The familiar aroma of tobacco hits my nose when I blink into the storeroom. Jess won't open the doors to customers for another hour, but I know his routine well enough to be sure that he'll be puttering around behind the counter. Unless it's a day when his arthritis is really acting up, Jess always pours a cup of coffee after breakfast and takes it downstairs, telling his wife he has work to do. In reality, he's just seeking a bit of solitude, because Amelia tends to snipe in the mornings. She needs a few hours to mellow.

This morning, Jess isn't even pretending to be busy. Just sitting on the barstool he keeps behind the cash register, enjoying his pipe as he stares out at the early morning bustle. A lone automobile is winding its way around the horse-carts in the road outside the store. The sight is still enough of a novelty that two kids run along behind the car for a better look.

If I wanted, I could jump into the store directly. I set a stable point off to the right of the register earlier this week, while trying to explain the whole time-traveling insanity to Jess. But Jess is nearly eighty-three. I prefer to give him a bit of a warning, rather than just popping in and scaring the holy hell out of him, even though he's had a crash course in the effects of Cyrist-engineered time shifts over the past few days. The last shift cost him a granddaughter, a girl he can remember only because he was in the range of my CHRONOS key when the shift happened. To the rest of the world, Jess's granddaughter never existed at all.

I tap on the door to give him a warning before interrupting his solitude.

"Jess?"

He raises one gray eyebrow and turns slightly toward the storeroom. "Was beginning to think another time shift came along and swallowed you up like it did Irene."

"Just been a little... preoccupied. Thought I'd stop in and let you know I'm goin' out of town for a bit."

"I see. Taking the train?" The wry look on his face makes it pretty clear that he's teasing me.

"No train to the 1893 World's Fair. I'm stuck usin' the key."

"What's in 1893?"

I want to tell him that Kate's in danger, but Jess has been through enough in the past week. Losing his granddaughter was a blow, and he only saw Irene once or twice a year. Kate has been in here every few days for the past eighteen months or so. Helped him behind the counter on many occasions. They flirt shamelessly with each other, and threaten to leave me and Amelia behind so that they can run off to Niagara Falls together. Jess has asked about Kate each time I've stopped by the past few days. Well, past few days for *him*. It's been weeks for me, but I spent most of that in other time periods, trying to piece together what Simon and his Cyrist cohorts have done with Kate.

The one thing I know for certain is that the Kate I'm trying to save isn't the one Jess knows. She's not the Kate who stood at the altar with me, as Jess and Amelia watched me slide that gold band onto her finger a few short months back. This Kate is younger, and she barely knows who I am. Telling Jess that Kate's in 1893 would mean explaining the differences between the Kate I need to save and the Kate that Jess has come to know and love. I'm just not sure he's ready for that.

"A really bad man is in 1893. Do you think I could borrow your gun?"

"Depends on who you're planning to shoot, boy."

"I'm thinkin' more of using it as a threat. Or maybe as a distraction."

"In my experience—which I'll admit is limited in these matters—it's never a good idea to bring a gun into a situation unless you're willing to use it."

"I'm more than willing. It's just… complicated."

Jess reads my face for a moment, and then reaches under the counter to pull out the pistol. But he keeps one hand on it.

"So… who is it you're planning *not* to shoot?"

Jess and I talked a lot about my time at the World's Fair during the months that I worked for him here at the shop. Back in 1893, Jess had wanted to make the trip from Boston to Chicago. He kept telling Amelia it was a once in a lifetime opportunity to see the wonders of the world, all collected in one place. But she wasn't nearly as keen on it as Jess and there was no one to watch the store for them, so they never made the trip. I think Jess was glad that he at least got to visit it vicariously through me.

My father was one of the many job-seekers who flocked to Chicago in the months before the Exposition opened in May of 1893, as they struggled to turn 600 acres of swampland into one of the most celebrated World's Fairs in history. At age eight, I tagged along behind him most days, helping out with small chores and running errands, but mostly just being a kid. Watching. Learning. By the time the Expo opened its gates, I knew the place like the back of my hand. I put that knowledge to good use, giving guided tours to visitors, and earning a bit of extra cash.

H.H. Holmes was another enterprising capitalist who sought to make his fortune catering to the tourists. His World's Fair Hotel catered mostly to women, and many of the women who entered his fine establishment never left. The police and newspapers were overworked with the influx of people into the city, and people went missing all the time. Chicago papers would name the hotel the "Murder Castle" during Holmes's trial, but by then it was much too late.

I've shared many stories about the Expo with Jess, but I've never mentioned Holmes or his hotel. I also don't talk about the fire that ripped through one of the buildings, killing my father. Some memories are best left alone.

"How much do you know about H.H. Holmes?" I ask.

"The doctor who killed all those women?"

"Yeah."

Jess shrugs. "I know what I read in the papers during his trial, mostly, although I did wonder how much of that was made up. Selling skeletons to medical schools seems a bit far-fetched."

"He did, but it was only a couple. I remember seeing him a few times at the Midway, when I was workin' there as a boy—mostly helpin' my mum at the dairy exhibit and runnin' errands. Seemed like a nice enough guy, until he smiled. Something always hit me wrong about his smile. He'd hand out these flyers for his World's Fair Hotel to groups of ladies who were visiting. Had a couple of kids with him sometimes."

"Those the kids he killed?"

"Yeah. Guess they became inconvenient. Anyway…" I stop for a moment and try to find a way to summarize, something that doesn't go into so many details that Jess's head will explode. "He's connected to the Cyrists. The ones responsible for your Irene… not bein' around anymore. And more people could die—two women who didn't die the first time around—if I don't go back and keep them out of Holmes's path."

His eyes stray down to the outline of my CHRONOS medallion beneath my shirt. "Why don't you just jump in with that key-thing of yours, kill the son of a bitch in his sleep, and be done with it?"

"I can't."

"Why not? Holmes murdered, what, fifty women at least? Maybe more. Even if something happened and you got caught, there'd be plenty of evidence to support you if the cops—"

"Maybe. But then there wouldn't be the trial that you and a

million or so others read about in the papers, would there? It would change too much history, and that's what we're tryin' to stop the Cyrists from doin'. This has to be a surgical strike."

I unfold the paper my other self gave me and take a pencil from the cup by the cash register. It would be easier to just show Jess the layout of the place through the CHRONOS key, but since that's not possible, I sketch the long narrow room on the back of one sheet.

"The place isn't even as wide as your storeroom, Jess, but the length is probably ten times that... maybe half as long as this block. It's dark, so Holmes can't see me. I can see him pretty well in the light of the CHRONOS key. The only door is one you have to crawl through—it opens into a linen closet. Holmes used the room to hide things from creditors—furniture he bought and claimed wasn't delivered, and other stuff. He also used it to hide some bodies. Two of them are on cots along this wall here." I mark two smaller rectangles with an X. "And at the far end here, there's a window with a fire escape. Holmes gets off a couple of shots toward the window as one of the women and I—"

"Wait. You're already there?"

"Yeah, but it's eight-year-old me that's going through the window. And there are... some other versions of me who've already tried to fix this and failed scattered around the room."

"I'm gonna ignore that bit on the grounds that I want to stay sane." He motions for me to go on.

"There's another shot when we're on the fire escape. Probably two. That was about the time that one of the windows on the second floor cracked due to the fire, so—"

"The fire?"

"Yeah. Holmes set the place on fire to cover the evidence. Or maybe for insurance. Or both. Anyway, like I said, I can't kill him. Apparently I can't take his gun away either, because I've already tried that and..." I look at his expression and say, "I'm guessing you don't want details about a duplicate me jumping in to give me this information. Let's just say it didn't end well and I'm not planning to repeat the experiment."

He shudders, as though to shake off the twists and tangles of time travel, and then he pushes the gun toward me. "Take it. My vote is for shooting the black-hearted son of a bitch outright, no matter what it changes. To hell with history. I'm perfectly okay with you spinning the wheel again. Maybe we'll get the timeline that has my granddaughter in it and Amelia will stop thinking I've lost my damn mind."

Wooded Island
Chicago World's Fair
11271893_22:21:00

I slide down against the outside of the cabin wall. It's cold and drizzling out here, but I need to feel the night air on my face. I've spent most of the past two days alone in the cabin, with occasional fieldtrips to a corpse-filled room. The only company I've had is H.H. bloody Holmes and the other versions of myself in that room, none of whom I can talk to without splintering myself or at least triggering a double memory. Kate's there, too. But all I've been doing is watching her die, so for once, I don't count her company as a good thing.

The Wooded Island is silent now. In fact, the entire fairground is silent. Empty, like a ghost town. Or a ghost metropolis, I guess. On any given day between May and the end of October, an average of 120,000 tourists roamed every inch of this island. The massive buildings I can still see in the distance, on the other side of the bridge that connects the Wooded Island to the mainland, were never meant to be anything other than temporary. Aside from two buildings and some of the statues, the White City will be reduced to ashes in a fire much like the one that killed my dad, less than a quarter-mile from this cabin.

I take another swig from the flask in my pocket. The bourbon probably isn't helping me sort things out, but it is definitely helping to keep panic at bay.

Here's the crux of the problem: four seconds isn't much

time. That's doubly true when you have to make incremental steps and avoid bumping into the other versions of yourself. Most of them were just there scouting things out, but a few have already tried things and failed. I've been careful to ensure that no more than two of me are in the room together for longer than a second, but that's become tougher to pull off as the day goes on.

For one thing, I'm getting tired. My skills with the CHRONOS key have never been as good as Kate's or Simon's, probably because I inherited the gene from one grandparent and they got it from all four. It wears me out, and even though these are short time jumps to a nearby location, I doubt I have more than a few jumps left before I'll need to rest.

My brain is also muddled from trying to balance two different versions of the past few days. Adding another set of memories to the mix would render me damn near worthless, so rule number one has been to avoid interacting with my other selves and, most of all, to avoid doing anything that I might have to go back in time and talk myself out of.

And now I'm going to have to break that rule.

My latest plan was to make a noise to distract Holmes. I nudged one of the iron cots slightly, just enough that it clinked against the bottles Holmes had stashed by the wall. If I could make Holmes stop for a moment and look my way, I thought it might buy Kate an extra few seconds to pull up a stable point on her key and jump out.

Only it was Kate who looked my way when the faint ping of glass against glass echoed in the silent dark. Kate who paused as she moved toward the exit. Kate who gasped, and thus guided Holmes's gun to where she was standing.

On the plus side, he didn't have to bother with the acid. I also didn't have to listen to his comment about how Kate's kick wasn't half bad for a girl, but still no match for a gun.

On the very negative side, Kate was looking straight at me when Holmes's bullet hit, right above her left eye.

I shudder and take another swig. The whiskey burns on its way down, but the fire doesn't begin to wipe that image from my mind.

The only way to fix this is to go back and stop myself *before* I take that jump. To splinter myself and hand off the torch to Past-Me. And maybe it's the whiskey, but I find that idea doesn't bother me so much anymore. I'm beyond caring whether it's this me or some other version that goes forward as long as Kate does.

I tuck the flask back in my jacket and pull out my CHRONOS key. It's 20:24. I roll the display back to 20:05 and jump back to the stable point inside the cabin.

It's just a single room, with a small fire crackling in the fireplace. Between the light of the fire and the two lanterns there's just enough light to read, and my earlier self is huddled over my notes. On the ground next to him is the bag of medicines I swiped from a pharmacy in the late 2030s—some pain medication and a hydrogel that's supposed to reduce burn scars, along with gauze, medical tape, and other items that I wouldn't have much luck finding in the local apothecary in 1893. In a perfect world, I'd get Kate out unharmed. But it's a far from perfect world and I know I need to be prepared.

"You botched it," Past-Me says, when he sees me standing in the middle of the room. There's not even a hint of a question in his voice. The fact that I'm standing here pretty much confirms his accusation as fact. "And here comes my double memory. Thanks."

I give him a sympathetic look, because I've been in his shoes. The good thing about being the one who *creates* the splinter is that the double memory isn't quite as strong, but I still don't like looking at him. It's like my brain is stuck on one of those hamster wheels... running in circles, but not really going anywhere.

"Yeah," I say. "Sorry about that. That distraction you're planning right now causes Holmes to veer toward the center of the room. Must've thought it was a rat or somethin'. He's lookin' when Kate steps into the light from the window. Shoots her square in the head."

He rolls the time back on his CHRONOS key and watches

the display. A few seconds later, he curses, and shoves the stack of notes to the floor.

"Got any other ideas?" he asks. "Because that was my last one, and now I've probably only got another nine minutes or so before I'm history."

His voice is bitter on this last part, and I realize I've become much more philosophical on the whole splintering thing in the past half hour. Or maybe I'm just tired. Him, me. Doesn't much matter which one vanishes as long as one of us is still here to help Kate.

"I jumped back twenty minutes. So I'm probably the splinter. And no, I don't have another idea yet, but at least we've got two brains to... ap... ply..."

"What?" he asks, waiting for me to go on.

"I don't know, just... maybe we've been going about this all wrong? Been tryin' so hard to avoid the double memories, to avoid becomin' a splinter, that we've missed the best chance to get Kate out of that hell hole. I don't know if you're the splinter or if I am, but one thing's for sure. For the next few minutes, there are *two* of us."

"So? The place is already crowded from all the times we blinked in and out of there earlier. I'm not sure how both of us going in at once is going to help matters. The other one... the one with the four on his head. Didn't he say that interacting like this was a bad idea?"

"He did. But like you said, we're running short on ideas. Bad ones seem to be all we have left. I'll jump into the stable point close to the cots. You jump into the hallway. You can monitor through the key and jump in as backup if I fail. Or if I... disappear. And if, by some miracle, Kate makes it into the hallway, you help her jump out."

"What are you going to do?"

"Tackle the son of a bitch. Slow him down."

Past-Me drags one finger through the soot at the base of the fire and then walks toward me. He stretches out his hand when he reaches me and draws something on my forehead.

It's not a four.

"It's a five. That way if I have to come in, I can sort you out from any other Kiernans in the room."

I don't wipe it away. Instead, I swipe my finger through the ashes and draw a six just above his nose. He doesn't appear to like the new label any more than I do.

The clock is ticking for one of us, so I pull up the stable point near the cots on my key. I set it to 20:25:30, a few seconds earlier than before so that I can, hopefully, get my bearings before the action starts.

Unfortunately, the display shows nothing but the dim white fabric of my shirt. One of my earlier selves is loitering inside the stable point and I can't jump in until he moves. So I wait. He has to know this stable point might need to be used again. Idiot.

After about three seconds, Earlier-Me finally moves to the other side of the room. I give it another second, then blink in.

World's Fair Hotel
10281893_20:25:30

I hold the air in my lungs as long as possible, and then pull in shallow, hesitant breaths, steeling myself against the pervasive smell of smoke and rot that fills the room. As I move away from the wall, something crooked and gnarled that looks a bit like a tree branch, catches against the side of my jeans. I hold the CHRONOS key down to investigate and realize that one bony finger has snagged the edge of the denim.

The sight causes me to startle. My two other selves turn and look directly at me, even though we're doing our damnedest to avoid contact and the duplicate memories that follow. I feel two new memories worming into my head, a memory of looking over and thinking *what an idiot*, and another, from a slightly more recent self, of thinking, *oh, it's the idiot again.* These memories almost, but not completely, overwrite the earlier one, when no idiot stood on this side of the cot.

I inch toward the center of the narrow room, away from

the skeletal hand and its long-dead owner. Then I crouch down, doing my best to keep my breaths small and silent, and tuck my CHRONOS medallion into the leather pouch around my neck. Holmes may not be able to see the light from the key, but Kate can, and my last attempt proved exactly how much damage I could cause by distracting her.

A few yards in front of me, two shadows—one adult and one child, both dimly lit in green by their CHRONOS keys—shuffle toward the window and the ladder. Even though I've watched this over and over during the past few days, it's still strange to see my eight-year-old self creeping along that wall next to Katherine. It's not like a double memory, but more like when Simon drags me along to watch some movie he likes for a second time. A third shadow, which belongs to Kate, works its way carefully toward the linen closet that leads back into the hotel.

Somewhere between Kate and the linen closet is Holmes. That part of the room is too dark to see clearly. I can hear him, though. He moves cautiously, but with a speed that shows how much more familiar he is with the layout of this abominable room than the rest of us.

Two shots ring out, in fairly rapid succession, followed by the crash of breaking glass. Like the stench, these noises have become routine, things that I hear and smell each time I'm here.

A third shot sounds as Katherine shoves the window open. Even though I can't hear or see it from this distance, I know that Katherine and my younger self are currently having a brief, nearly silent squabble over who goes through the window first. I'd promised Kate that I'd get her grandmother back to safety, and I took that promise seriously. On the other hand, I was used to getting my bottom whacked if I argued with my elders. And since Katherine's expression suggested she might just toss me out the window if I didn't go willingly, I didn't hesitate long before following her orders.

The next few seconds would be the best time, strategically speaking, for me to attack Holmes. But I know that Katherine

203

is still there, crouched below the window. It was several seconds before she followed me onto the ladder, and I remember hesitating, wondering if I should go back up and help her.

Watching the scenes over and over in the past few days, I know now that she could probably see Holmes at this point, faintly lit by the glow of Kate's CHRONOS key. He's staring at the window, pistol raised, ready to take another shot. And she's waiting for something to distract him before making her move.

Kate provides that distraction, kicking out and upward as Holmes passes in front of her. Another shot echoes in the room as he stumbles.

I'm still in a crouch, and for a moment, I think I've bumped into one of the bits of furniture in the room. Something pushes me backward, and it's only when my ass lands on the floor that I realize the last bullet hit me.

Not in the shoulder like the one that hit Number Four. This bullet hit at least a foot lower, on the left side of my abdomen.

Kiernan Number Six should be at his station in the hallway by now, monitoring this room. But he'll be watching Kate and Holmes, so I doubt he even realizes I've been shot.

Holmes manages to grab Kate's foot, and she falls backward, banging her head hard enough that I feel the vibration through the floor.

I wait until Holmes starts talking and then try to get to my feet. Wetness seeps through my fingers and I have to pause to steady myself as the pain ratchets up.

"You have an impressive kick for such a little lady," Holmes says, as he digs for the spare bullet in his jacket pocket. "But it's no match for a gun."

As he begins chambering the round, Katherine drops out the window, disappearing onto the fire escape.

My second attempt at standing fares no better than the first and I decide that staying close to the ground might be a wiser bet. I begin crawling toward Holmes, one arm pressed against the wound in my side.

Kate is still recovering from the fall and she looks around, disoriented, as Holmes steps backward, trying to figure out exactly where she landed. The back of his leg bumps against one of the cots, causing the collection of bottles to clang against each other.

He curses, and then abruptly shifts to a laugh. He's just remembered the bottle of acid in his pocket.

Across the room, Kate has the key in her hand and is working on locking in a stable point. I lunge forward to grab Holmes's legs, hoping to trip him before he gets the stopper out of the bottle.

I don't remember crying out, but some noise must have escaped me because Kate looks away from the key toward me, losing her chance to blink out.

She screams as the acid hits the side of her neck.

I've heard that scream before, too. Five times now. But it pierces me, nonetheless. That sound could never become routine, even if I was locked in this cycle for eternity

Holmes takes a step back, maybe to avoid any splash-back from the liquid. As soon as he's in range, I hook one arm around his legs and tug. The gun flies out of his hands, landing just a few inches behind Kate who is frantically crawling toward the door to the linen closet. His foot lashes out, connecting with my stomach. It's not directly where the bullet entered, but close enough that hurts like hell. For a few seconds, I'm helpless, curled into an agonized ball.

As Holmes hunts for the gun, I push myself back toward the cots. The bony arm is still there, inches from me as I tug my CHRONOS key out of the pouch, but it doesn't bother me the same way now that I see Kate approaching the door.

In my dreams, I think that hand has always been Kate's hand, representing my fear that she had become just another anonymous corpse in this makeshift morgue.

Holmes scrambles around on the floor and eventually locates the gun. He looks around for me, trying to determine why he tripped, but his attention is pulled back to Kate when she shoves aside the body that's blocking the exit.

For the first time since I began watching this horror show, Kate opens the door, and that jolts Holmes out of his momentary stupor. I need to stall him, keep him from following her.

I toss one of the bottles toward him. "Come get me, you son of a bitch."

Holmes jumps and looks behind him, waving the gun in the direction of my voice.

"What are you waiting for?" I speak louder this time, since Kate is out of the room.

Does he think I'm a ghost? Most of the people he killed were women, but a few men lost their lives at his hand, too, including a few business partners. Maybe he's expecting his own personal Jacob Marley to crawl from the shadows. He hesitates, but he only has the one bullet left and, in the end, it's Kate he decides to pursue.

The CHRONOS key now reads 20:25:43. Nine seconds longer than Kate's lived in any scenario. But she's not out of harm's way yet. I need to find my other self, my unwounded self, so that he can help her. I don't know how badly injured she is from the acid or from the blow to her head when she fell. Is she even in a state where she can use the key?

That thought is oddly prophetic, because it takes me two tries to pull up the stable point near the stairwell, where Kiernan Number Six is positioned.

I roll the time back to 20:24:00 and blink in at the hallway location. At first, I don't see Six. It takes me a few seconds to realize that this is before the time he was supposed to jump in. And I'm blocking the stable point he'll be using.

Idiot.

Once I drag myself a few feet to the right, Six blinks in. When he sees me, color drains from his face, almost as if he's the one who's in danger of bleeding out.

"What happened?"

"I seem to have caught a bullet."

He glances down at the blood for a second, and then he

pulls out his key. "I'll go back and—"

"No." I stop to catch my breath. "Kate gets out. She'll be coming this way in about forty seconds. She's injured, but she'll be okay unless Holmes catches up to her. He still has one bullet."

"Okay, then. Get back to the cabin. I'll take it from here."

"I don't think I can get back to the cabin. It took me two tries to blink back to this spot. Just leave me. Help Kate."

He gives me a doubtful look. And even though I wish he'd go and quit wasting time, I get it. I remember feeling the same way back in my room, and that version of me wasn't in nearly as bad shape.

"Damn it, just go. Get her to safety."

Six blinks away and returns a second later, holding a wet cloth that smells a bit like baking soda. Gauze pads and a roll of medical tape are tucked under his left arm. He hooks his right arm under my shoulders and pulls me to my feet.

"I said, leave me."

"This isn't about you, damn it."

Six half drags me to a door across the hall and after a brief struggle with the knob, he manages to open it. I lean against the wall, and he pulls the door closed behind us, then tosses me the wet cloth and other medical supplies.

"I've set up points along the hallways and watched what's happening. She'll come this way. I'm going to distract Holmes and see if I can buy her a little more time, hopefully without getting myself killed. Kate will try this door, but it sticks, so she'll think it's locked. Open it, transfer the stable point to her key."

He doesn't meet my eyes as he speaks. At first, I think he's avoiding the whole hamster-on-a-wheel feeling, but there's something else in his expression. Getting the medical supplies, setting all those stable points, watching them to see which way Kate would run... all of that took *time*. This hotel is a maze of hallways, and even if he was just watching the most likely routes, it took more than a couple of minutes.

So I ask him outright, before he can blink away. "It's been

almost nine minutes for me. How long has it been for you? Since I caused the splinter?"

"Not sure."

Yeah, right. The truth is written on his face—*my* face—and I'm not so far gone that I can't read it. And even if there's a touch of bitterness, and more than a touch of fear about what's coming down the pike very, very soon, I know it's better this way.

"It's okay. No point in lyin' to yourself. I'll get her to the cabin. You take it from there."

He does look at me then, and gives me a quick nod.

A split second after he leaves, the door handle rattles twice, followed by a frustrated curse. I'd recognize that voice anywhere, even strained as it is now from pain, from breathing smoke, and from running through these hallways seconds ahead of a madman.

Crossing the short distance to the door is agony, but I make it. I twist the handle sharply to the right, and as Kate falls backward against me, I place one hand over her mouth to trap the scream that I know is coming. With the other hand, I press the wet cloth against the angry welts on the side of her face.

My knees are shaking harder now that her weight is added to my own. I lean back against the wall, struggling to stay upright, as I close the door and push the bolt into place. That lock won't hold Holmes for long—one good kick will probably do it. It's flimsy and barely screwed into the wood, unlike the sturdy locks he's placed on the outside of these doors. Holmes isn't nearly as concerned with keeping people *out* of these guestrooms as he is with keeping his guests trapped inside.

Kate struggles against me. I whisper her name softly, as I press my face against her hair, breathing her in. The stench of this place, full of smoke and death, clings to her, but her own scent is there, too, and it fills me with a sense of relief that I haven't felt since I lost her.

She looks up at me, and even though the light is dim, I can see that she's barely holding it together. Her green eyes are unfocused, confused.

"Kiernan? But how—"

I hold my CHRONOS key against hers to transfer the stable point for the cabin, and then help her pull up the interface.

"Kate, please. You have to focus. I've pulled up a stable point, love. Just slide your fingers over it and go. I'll be right behind you. I promise."

That promise is a lie in one sense, but hopefully, she'll never know it. Six will be there.

It takes a second longer than usual, but Kate manages to lock in the location. And then she's gone.

I slide down to the floor. The gauze and medical tape are a few feet away, but I don't have the energy. And it's pointless. Holmes is already trying the door. Whether he shoots me, or I bleed out, or I simply vanish, the end result is the same. My time's up.

Still, I bring up the cabin on my key. Not to follow her. The fact that pulling up the stable point is a struggle tells me that's not possible. I just need to see that Six made it back, that someone is there to help her. I'm not sure what I'll do if he's not, but I need to *know*.

Holmes twists the handle again and then the door shakes. Once, twice, and then it flies open.

My eyes remain on the holographic display. Kate is in the cabin, crumpled on the floor. A moment later, I blink in—or rather, *Six* blinks in. He lifts Kate into his arms and I pan the view around to follow them.

From the corner of my eye, I see Holmes. He scans the room for Kate, then raises the pistol in my direction.

Closing my eyes, I hold fast to that final image of Kate, safe in the cabin, and wait for the end.

~*~

A Word from Rysa Walker

~*~

Yes, I know. Time travel isn't the most common method of producing clones, and it's certainly not the most technologically feasible. But clones of this sort exist in my series, *The CHRONOS Files*, created when a time traveler doubles back on his or her timeline and changes something. That action results in a splinter—a temporary duplicate of the time traveler. One copy or the other vanishes in ten minutes or so and the timeline continues on its slightly altered way.

But... which copy vanishes? You or the new you? Does it even matter if they're *both* you? What sort of challenges would you face working with multiple yous toward a common goal? These existential questions are touched on briefly in *Time's Divide,* the final book in my series, but I wanted to explore them in a bit more detail. The events that happen to Kiernan after the end of *Time's Echo,* when he's forced to create multiple splinters in order to save Kate, seemed like a perfect opportunity to dig a bit deeper, so I was delighted to have the chance to explore this somewhat unusual method of cloning for the *Clones* anthology.

Thanks for reading "Splinter." If you enjoyed this short story, you can find the entire CHRONOS series online at www.amazon.com/author/walker.

~*~

The Vandal
Joshua Ingle

~*~

A grating noise from the window downstairs wedged itself between Chase and his sleep. He'd heard it before, perhaps ten seconds ago, but he'd dismissed it as part of a dream. Now he began to suspect it was real. *Does Alice realize her cleaning is waking me up?*

He willed himself back toward slumber, rolled over... and his arm bumped Alice, sound asleep next to him. *How can she be cleaning downstairs if she's up here with me?* With some effort, Chase opened his eyes and glimpsed the time.

2:08 a.m.

The window in the living room's far corner had creaked when Chase and Alice had bought the place all those years ago, but the defect had seemed part of the charm of the rustic old Victorian-style house. It was so minor that Chase had never bothered to fix it; he only ever noticed it when Alice's nephews occasionally opened the windows during their play-shootouts. The kids weren't here tonight, though, and they only played during daylight hours, anyway. *Who the hell's opening the living room window at 2:08 a.m.?*

Chase's whole body tensed, suddenly fully awake. He shook Alice's shoulder. She mumbled something and tried to swat him away, but Chase persisted.

"Alice," he whispered. "Alice, someone's breaking in."

"Hmm?"

"Alice, wake up. Be quiet. Someone's breaking in downstairs."

She finally sat up in bed and stared at him, her drowsy eyes struggling toward alertness. He held up a finger, urging her to listen.

After a moment of silence, they heard echoes of faint footsteps tapping on the living room's wooden floor.

Alice grabbed her phone, no doubt to call the police. Pushing the bed sheets aside, Chase accidentally bumped the tablet on his nightstand, activating it and sending it tumbling. He grabbed it in midair just before it hit the carpet.

Gingerly, he exhaled, and exchanged a relieved glance with Alice. Then he turned off the crime novel he'd been reading, swung his feet over to rest on the carpeted floor, and scanned the room for something he could use as a weapon. Chase had never been one for paranoia. He hadn't thought to prepare a baseball bat or a crowbar—much less a gun—to be on hand in case of an event like this. Alice kept pepper spray in her purse, but that was downstairs.

Ah! There was something he could use. He tiptoed to his weightlifting equipment and grabbed a fifteen-pound dumbbell: light enough to swing, heavy enough to do some damage. As he approached the bedroom door, he heard Alice snapping her fingers at him.

"What are you doing?" she mouthed, her eyes furious.

"Lock the door," he mouthed in response, and closed it shut behind him.

He'd read online that the Chicago PD's response times had been snaillike lately, what with the uptick in crime surrounding the Sect's attacks. If the cops didn't arrive for another twenty minutes, Chase wasn't about to let some gang banger make off with his valuables.

He made a mental list of what the burglar could be after as he crept down the stairs. Alice's clothing and jewelry were safe up in the bedroom with her, as was Chase's wallet and the cards inside. But a cornucopia of smartphones, laptops, tablets, and other gadgets speckled the downstairs area. An intruder might also find the rare liquor bottles kept in the rear of the pantry. The AI hub was especially vulnerable: the door to its closet was always left open for better wireless reception. And if the thief ventured into the garage, he'd find Chase's UAV equipment and his power tools, which would fetch a killing at any pawn shop.

Alice might protest Chase confronting the trespasser—he certainly wasn't young anymore, and the thief might very well be armed. But Chase was quite fit for his age, and he had the element of surprise on his side. Plus, it really pissed him off that some thug would do this to him and his wife. *Of course I'm gonna clock this son of a bitch.*

He reached the bottom of the stairs and listened. Silence, in all directions. From where he stood, he could see parts of the kitchen, the dining room, and the living room, all lit by the single dim light above the kitchen table. In the long shadows, nothing moved. Chase's own breathing seemed to grate as loudly as the living room window had.

He dared a quick glimpse out a front window to see his Beverly neighborhood sleeping in darkness. No vehicles lurked on the curb in front of his house, but the robber could have parked down the road to minimize suspicion. This neighborhood had been so nice, so upscale when they'd moved in over a decade ago. Even now it wasn't exactly a slum, but home values had plummeted, and the place could obviously no longer fulfill its function of shielding its residents from the city's undesirables.

A hissing sound escaped from the living room. Then, after five seconds, a vigorous clicking noise, followed by more hissing. Spray paint. The intruder was spray-painting something in their living room! *Unbelievable.*

Chase snuck to the nearest AI terminal and whispered to it. "Turn off your audio responses. Wait sixty seconds, then play Beethoven's 5th at full volume. Don't respond to this with any audio confirmation. Stay quiet until you play the music." A green light blinked, indicating that the computer had heard and understood his request.

Chase crouched low and peeked into the living room. He cringed when he saw it.

Lime green spray paint defiled every piece of furniture in the room. Slick wet trails of the stuff crisscrossed over couches, lamps, tables—even the TV. Chase's laptop, still atop the coffee table where he'd left it, sat open and drenched in the neon hue, seeping through the keyboard to the computer's innards.

At the far end of the room, his back to Chase, stood a man wearing black. His arms moved frantically to and fro as he finished defacing the large decorative mirror ornamenting the far wall. Droplets of neon green blood oozed down from each letter. The intruder's full message, spray-painted on an area nearly as wide as a car, read:

YOU ARE IN SECT TERRITORY.

Chase shook his head and gripped his dumbbell tighter. *So he's not a burglar after all. He's a cult member.* Chase hadn't heard of the Sect taking any actions as far south as Beverly, and certainly not in a neighborhood like this. They operated out of East Garfield Park and launched most of their attacks near Downtown. But maybe this guy was just a low-level wannabe, sent to take pictures of his trashing of a rich couple's house to prove to the group he had what it took. *What an unfathomable idiot.*

At the trauma of seeing his living room desecrated, Chase had lost count of how much time remained until the music started. So he walked, crouched, around the back of his sofa, his knees threatening him with weeks of future joint pain. But the future didn't matter as much as his eagerness to slug this bastard.

He stayed low and quiet and stopped behind the corner recliner, near the mirror covered in spray paint. He'd heard nothing from the intruder but the continued spraying of walls, so he assumed he hadn't been spotted. Just as he was about to peer around the recliner to make sure, *BOOM*. An onslaught of deafening noise exploded from the speakers embedded in the ceiling, so loud and distorted that Chase couldn't even recognize it as Beethoven's 5th.

He hadn't yet positioned his body to attack the man. But the music left him with no choice. He sprang from behind the recliner and rushed toward the intruder.

Both hands clutching the dumbbell, he swung it from behind his head. For a split second, surprised blue eyes gaped at him from behind a balaclava. Then Chase drove his improvised weapon toward the intruder's face. It impacted on the side of the man's head. He went down, hard.

Chase kicked him. When he didn't recoil, or even move in response to the hit, Chase knew he was out cold.

Chase stared at him for a few moments before realizing something was wrong. Something with the music. Had the AI lowered the volume automatically when Chase had started his attack? No, it still blared overbearingly into his ears. His right ear, at least. *Hmm...*

He raised his hand to his right ear and covered it. All sound grew suddenly muffled. He couldn't hear much out of his left ear at all.

Then he felt something warm and wet drip down his neck. *Oh, shit.*

Chase raced to the mirror and peered through the dripping spray paint. "All lights on, music off," he said, and the AI responded immediately. The light level rose on a soft gradient until he could see his wound clearly.

His gory, gaping wound. It looked like someone had drilled a hole straight through his ear! He could see right through the opening! A trail of dark red seeped from the injury, pooling in the lower ear before trickling past the lobe and down his neck. *Aw, damn it. Alice is gonna kill me.*

Chase resisted the urge to immediately fetch the medical supplies in his bathroom, and instead approached the unconscious vandal. Sure enough, a handgun rested on the floor near his body.

He'd shot Chase. He'd almost killed him. A few inches' difference and Chase's brains might now be splattered across his sofa. He wasn't sure if he should consider himself lucky or unlucky. The pain, unnoticed until moments ago, began to blossom.

Thumping footsteps on the stairs signaled Alice's arrival. "Chase?" she called, worry in her voice.

"I'm okay," he called back, not bothering to look at her as he pinned the gun beneath his foot and slid it away from the intruder. He didn't want any of his own fingerprints on the damn thing. "I knocked the guy out."

"Jesus, honey, you scared the daylights out of me. What was that music?"

"Just had to startle him."

"Chase!"

She'd seen the blood.

"Oh my god, Chase. Lie down. Lie down right now." She ran to him.

"Nah, I don't want to get any of this on the furniture."

Alice briefly took in the living room, already ruined by green spray paint. "You don't want to get any blood on the furniture? Really? Lie the hell down."

"Okay, okay, relax. It's just my ear. It's not my head, okay? I'm fine."

Although he'd rather have just ignored the wound for now, he grabbed some tissues from a coffee table and held them to his ear. Then, to placate Alice, he sat on their cabriole sofa, right on a line of wet paint. He raised his eyebrows as if to ask if she was happy now.

With a quick glance toward the unconscious vandal, she shook her head and raced back up the stairs. To the medical supplies in the bathroom, Chase was certain. As soon as she'd left his sight, he rose, his pajama pants peeling away from the sticky paint. He paced toward the intruder.

The man was still unconscious, maybe dead. *If so, good riddance.* But when Chase flipped him over onto his back, his chest rose and fell with each breath.

Chase examined the rest of his body. The back of each hand possessed a tattoo of the Sect's triangular emblem. One of his pinky fingers had been cut off, no doubt as part of some barbaric gang ritual, as if sacrificing one's own body part would prove loyalty to a cause. The man's shoes, jeans, long-sleeve shirt, and balaclava were all as black as his motives.

Chase grabbed the ski mask and tried to wrest it off his face. He wanted to get a good look at the guy, in case the authorities asked him to pick the intruder out of a lineup later. He wanted to be able to point right at his face from a witness stand in a courtroom and tell the jury, "That's the guy. That's the degenerate who vandalized thousands of dollars of my property. He's part of the extremists that have been terrorizing the city, so you need to lock him up for a long, long time." The ski mask caught on the man's hair, but a few back-and-forth tugs worked it loose enough for Chase to pull it off the brute's face and look down…

…into his own eyes.

Chase yelped and jumped back. He grasped for the arm of the couch and braced himself against it.

"Chase?" Alice called from upstairs.

He tried to think through the shock. Maybe he'd been mistaken; maybe the intruder was just a lookalike. He took a few cautious steps back toward the man, and dared to glimpse his face again. A mole protruded from his upper lip where Chase didn't have one, and his sun-beaten skin bore a leathery texture that Chase's had never possessed. Through his open mouth, Chase spied a few missing teeth. Yet all other features appeared identical: the blue eyes, the robust facial structure, the thick build, even the high and tight haircut. This man was unmistakably a version of Chase… only twenty years younger.

"What's wrong?" Alice said from behind him. He hadn't heard her come back down the stairs. She stepped up next to him, and gasped when she saw the young man lying unconscious before them.

They stared for a long minute. The ceiling fan whirred,

wafting cool air against Chase's sweaty skin.

"Who is it?" Alice finally asked. "Is it a cousin, or... ?"

"Uh, here. Patch my ear up and I'll... I'll explain." Chase sat on the couch again, right on top of the same line of spray paint.

Alice prepared some medical wipes and gauze. "An ambulance is on its way, too."

"Good, good." As she saw to his wound, Chase couldn't pull his eyes away from the intruder, even as pain throbbed through his ear. How long had the man been wandering around Chicago, perhaps just miles from Chase, without him knowing? The odds that the two would eventually bump into each other must have been quite high. *But how unfortunate that it has to be like this.*

"When I was in college," he explained to Alice, "there was this company, uh, CellTech. My friend told me about it. They paid people to give them tissue samples, like from your liver or your muscles or your skin. I was strapped for cash, and I figured it was no different than selling your plasma, or your sperm, so I went and got paid for them to take a sample of my cells. I, uh, I had to sign a waiver. And this was right when human cloning first became legal. A lot of people donated, for money and for science. I didn't think they'd actually use *my* cells."

Alice leaned back from his injured ear and looked him in the eyes. "Are you telling me that this man is your clone?"

Chase bobbed his head back and forth as if considering her question, hesitant to give a definitive answer. "Well, I certainly don't have a son or a brother. And he looks like he stepped out of an old picture of me."

Alice raised a hand and smacked him on the arm. "You had a clone made of you and you never told me?"

"I didn't have him *made*. I volunteered for a corporation's science project and didn't think twice about it afterward."

He wasn't about to admit to Alice that the decision had haunted him for years after the procedure. He'd tried to console himself with the thought that *he* wasn't responsible for what CellTech did with his DNA. If it hadn't been him, after all, it would have been someone else.

But still, the possibility that a manufactured twin of himself existed somewhere out there had kept him awake many nights when he was young. *And oh, look at him. He's the same age I was when I married Alice.* What hopes and fears, regrets and aspirations lay inside that man's mind, and how similar were they to Chase's own?

"How'd he find us?" Alice asked.

"I don't know. Maybe he didn't know whose house this was. It could be just a coincidence."

"Yeah, right." She ran a disinfectant wipe down his neck, cleaning up the blood. "I really don't think it's a clone, though. It's gotta be an estranged relative, or something."

"Well, here." Chase raised his voice—an affectation left over from an earlier era when AIs needed such clarity to understand commands. "House, can you grab a sample of this guy's DNA? Maybe from some of his dead skin cells in the dust around here?"

"Certainly," the house responded immediately.

"And? Does it match my DNA?"

"Yes."

"Completely?"

"The match is one hundred percent."

Chase glanced at his wife with a look that said *I told you so.*

Alice eyed the unconscious clone skeptically. "I just can't believe that someone with your DNA would do something like this."

"I'm sorry? Say again?"

"Well, you're a good person. He's obviously not. I just thought someone's clone would be more like them."

That struck Chase as a strange thing for Alice to say. She worked in medicine, as a nurse—didn't she know that a clone was no different than an identical twin, save the age difference? Two individuals with identical genomes could live very different lives depending on circumstances.

And that was the part of this ordeal that got under Chase's

skin the most. Alice was right: Someone with Chase's DNA *could* join a cult, break into a home at night, vandalize it, and shoot its owner. That his clone was capable of such acts signified to Chase that *Chase* would be capable of those same acts—he supposed that if someone could go back in time and switch him and his clone at birth (twenty years removed), he would have lived the same life this clone had lived. And the clone would have lived his. And then it would be the clone here now, sitting on the spray-painted couch, looking down at a criminal Chase.

Chase had hated the intruder when he'd been anonymous. He'd been ready to kill him. But the man's identity changed everything.

"Don't worry," Alice said when Chase didn't respond. "For all we know, this 'clone' is one of the people who post those snuff videos the Sect makes. He's disgusting and perverted. You could never be like him."

"I don't know. It seems a little like luck to me that I'm here and he's there."

"Nonsense. Don't get weird on me now. You're gonna be just fine."

"What, you think it's the pain talking?"

Alice shrugged.

"Hey, I'm lucid," Chase said. "The pain really isn't that bad."

"Hmm." Alice tilted her head to see the back of his ear. "Well, I think the bleeding's mostly stopped, but it's swelling pretty badly. The paramedics will be here soon. Hold this to your ear, one on each side."

She handed him two wads of gauze and gathered the bloody remnants of her medical supplies. As she journeyed to the trashcan in the kitchen, Chase, still seated, continued to study the man in black on the living room floor. He was still breathing, but remained otherwise motionless. He'd been lying like that for a few minutes now. Was he in a coma? Chase found himself wishing he hadn't hit him quite so hard, and hoping the EMTs would fix the clone up in addition to himself. But then even if they healed the clone, afterward he'd surely be convicted and spend years in prison...

"Hey," Chase said on a whim, not sure exactly how he'd make his case to Alice. "You think we could... uh... drive him somewhere? If we can wake him up? Just restrain him, drive him a few blocks away? We wouldn't have to tell the cops."

"Drive him a few blocks away... and do what?" Alice asked from the kitchen, out of Chase's eyesight.

"Uh... I guess... let him go," Chase responded.

Silence. Then harsh, pounding footsteps. Alice appeared beneath the arch at the kitchen entrance.

"Are you goddamned serious right now?" she said.

"Look, the guy's probably had a rough life. The company probably dumped him into foster care when they were done with him. I know you're angry at him, and believe me, so am I. But he's hurt, and I'll definitely give him a piece of my mind before we let him go... but would it really be so bad for us to go easy on him?"

Alice placed her hands on her hips. "You actually want to let an attempted murderer—*your* attempted murderer—go free just because he's your clone?"

"I just don't think this is entirely his fault, is all." Alice's jaw dropped at that, putting Chase even more on the defensive. "Look, we send police into the Sect's part of town, we raid it day after day, we shoot them for little more than jaywalking, we rip their families apart with lengthy prison sentences. Maybe it'd be the decent thing to do to just go easy on him this one time."

"Have you ever been to East Garfield Park?" Alice replied, lifting her arms from her side to fold them in front of her chest, closing herself off from Chase. "Because I work just down the street from it and every day I see firsthand the filth those people live in. We try to help them but they jump right back in to their lifestyles. So any help we give him will be wasted because he doesn't want to have anything to do with our way of life. You let this guy go free and he'll just spit in your face and shoot you again. That's what these people are like."

"Look, honey, I'm not defending the Sect. I'm just defending my clone. Do you really think he'd still hate people like us if we didn't go into his neighborhood and kill his friends and family?"

"Yes! They have an extreme ideology that hates our values. They hate everything we stand for and they think it's their right to dominate the world."

"I know," Chase said. "I know they do. I know my clone probably does, too. But just think. What if we built up that area of town, gave it a functioning economy and solid infrastructure? Then my clone never would have done this. He'd have been too busy working at his job or playing his Xbox to care about any 'extreme ideologies'. That's what I mean when I say this isn't entirely his fault. We could have stopped it."

Alice actually laughed—the caustic, scornful laugh she only used on these rare occasions when anger overtook her. Chase didn't blame her, though. The break-in had him flustered, too. "Have you ever even read the tenets of their crazy religion?" Alice asked. "You have to be tough on people like this or they'll just do it again. They'll never change."

"What if being tough on him was what made him this way in the first place?" He gestured to his clone, still passed out, the can of spray paint lying in a pool of its own contents beside him.

"*He* pulled the trigger, Chase. *He* made that choice. No one was forcing him. When someone chooses to break into your house and attack you, you defend yourself, and you punish the guy who did it."

Chase set down his gauze, rose from the couch, and paced toward his wife. "But that shouldn't be the end of the discussion! We shouldn't just assume his poor character is his own fault when we know nothing about his life. We need to talk about what caused him to do this instead of just complaining he's an asshole then washing our hands."

"He *is* an asshole! *That's* what caused it!"

"Okay, so then what caused him to be an asshole?"

The question froze Alice's face in place for a moment. He could practically see her mind dissecting it while she stared at him, her expression on pause.

Seeing the opportunity, he decided to press his point. "What caused him to be a bad person? It obviously wasn't his genes."

"Yeah, well, I'm beginning to wonder about that." She breezed past him, treading back into the living room. Toward Chase's clone. *She'd better not touch him...* Chase made a beeline after her.

"Okay, sure, maybe some of it comes from his genes," he conceded, since he was in no rush to argue in favor of his own genetic superiority, "but we can't fault him for bad genes."

"We can fault him for bad choices."

"Well, he makes his choices using the neurons in his brain. And those neurons were patterned in response to life events he had no control over. So we can't fault him for that, either, can we?"

Alice stooped to grab the clone's gun by the barrel. She turned it over, examining it.

"Aw, honey, come on. Now your fingerprints are all over that."

Alice tilted the gun's safety catch toward Chase, clicked it on, then off again, nodding to him as if to make sure he saw the action. As soon as he locked eyes with her, she broke the gaze. She raised the gun and aimed it at the clone.

Chase sighed. There was no chance she'd actually shoot the clone. And thus no need for this melodrama. "Alice, please."

"You say your clone had no control over the events in his life? No control over the choices he made?"

"I... Well... No, he must not have. Otherwise he'd have turned out like me."

"What about *this* choice that I'm about to make? I could shoot him, or I could not shoot him. It's the same choice he made with you not ten minutes ago. Wouldn't you say I have complete control over this choice? Just like he did?"

Chase mulled over his response for a few moments. He didn't want to further aggravate an angry woman with a gun in her hand. But then, the mere fact that he was aggravating her revealed itself as the answer to her question. He might be pushing his luck, but Alice was just as smart as him, if not smarter. She could handle uncomfortable truths.

"I don't think it's that simple," Chase said. "You're only holding that gun because I've been arguing with you about this. We're only arguing because the clone broke in. You're only threatening to shoot him because of a lifetime of events that made you into the exact person who would do this exact thing under these exact circumstances. And whatever you choose to do next, you'll be reacting to me, saying this now. You really don't have much control over your choice at all. A whole bunch of random stuff is influencing you and you're probably not even aware of most of it. Hell, maybe you drank coffee before bed and that's what's causing your reaction. I don't know. And neither do you."

"And you think it's the same with him?" She waved the gun in the clone's direction. "You don't think he chose to shoot you of his own free will?"

"No! For him to make that choice, and to make it freely, he'd need to know about every single little thing influencing him, from what he was able to afford for breakfast to the exact makeup of his genome to me walking into CellTech all those years ago. He'd need to know about all that stuff, and he'd need to have control over all that stuff. And then—only then—he could choose freely." At this response, as with the rest, relief struck Chase—relief that he'd been able to devise a response so quickly. In truth, he was making most of his argument up on the fly. In spite of the worry he'd always felt over his potential clone, he'd never considered the many implications of what it meant to choose differently from someone apparently identical to him.

Neither, obviously, had Alice. Chase was sure he'd stump her with his response, but she just shook her head. "I disagree," she said matter-of-factly. "He chose to shoot you.

He could have chosen otherwise, but he didn't."

"*Could* he have chosen otherwise? Really? At the moment when he pulled the trigger? With every neuron in his brain exactly the same? How would he have done that?"

"Chase! You're being absurd. This isn't a game. You were *shot*. You and I have spent decades building this life together through love, commitment, discipline, and very hard work. We *chose* that. And then this punk comes in and almost takes you away from me. And you have the audacity to say that we're really no better than him? That the difference between us amounts to nothing more than a series of coincidences the universe threw at us?"

Her eyes were watering up. No tears had fallen yet, but guilt hitchhiked with Alice's words as they pried their way past Chase's defenses. *You're being absurd*, she'd said. Now that she was almost crying, Chase did feel absurd. *Would I be reacting this way if it had been my identical twin instead of a clone?* Chase had always wanted siblings. Was he overreacting to that desire now? *Even if so, I've been selfish to put Alice through this. I should never have brought it up.* But at the same time, a part of him found Alice quite selfish, too. Would she really force him to choose between sating her need for retribution on one hand, and on the other, saving his genetic equal from a life behind bars?

Chase approached her, his feet padding more softly than when he'd tiptoed down the stairs with the dumbbell in his hand. As lightly as if he were touching a butterfly, he took her free hand in his own.

"Honey, you know I love you," Chase said. "You know how proud I am of the life we've built. Of course it took hard work and dedication. We have such a strong work ethic because we had great parents who raised us with a strong work ethic. We had opportunities like college that my clone probably never had. We've never been hindered by our health because we could always see a doctor when we got sick. Your parents let us live with them while we started our careers. We never had to worry about finding food or water, or violence in our homes, or being attacked by the police. Of course you and I both put a lot of effort into earning what we have... But ultimately, when you account for all the factors outside of our control, do I deserve my life any more than my clone deserves his?"

Alice set the gun on a coffee table and wiped her eyes, seeming to shift her gaze in every direction but the direction of Chase's eyes. "I'm sure his life was very hard," she said. "But he could still have made different choices. He could have gone to college if he'd *really* wanted to. He was free to make that choice at any time."

"It might not even have occurred to him that someone like him *could* go to college. Can we blame him for not doing something that never even crossed his mind? For not making a decision he didn't even know he could make?"

Alice held her hands up to him, palms out in a gesture of *enough is enough*. She plodded past him toward the kitchen. "If it's all out of my control, then why work for anything?" she said as Chase followed her. "Why shouldn't I just lie on my couch all day and do nothing with my life?"

"Hey, honey, I'm not saying that our choices don't matter, and don't have consequences. They do. I'm just saying that our choices aren't completely ours, so we can't be held completely responsible for them. We can choose to do whatever we want in life, but we can't choose *what* we'll want. Does that make sense?"

"Not really." Alice snagged a roll of paper towels and some cleaning fluid in passing and circled around the kitchen's far side, back toward the living room. "And what about my brother Seth, huh? He was a drug addict, practically homeless, then he turned his life around with no support from my parents, went to trade school, and now he makes more money than I do. He was able to change in spite of his circumstances, and there are a lot of people who do the same exact thing. How do you explain them?" She knelt over the floor's wooden panels, sprayed a shot of cleaner, and vigorously wiped up a line of green paint.

"I don't know about Seth," Chase answered honestly. "I

mean, you can say he had a strong drive inside him that motivated him to change. But where did that drive come from, you know? Whose *fault* is that drive? Maybe my clone wants to change just as much as Seth did but just hasn't taken that route yet."

"I doubt it."

"Okay, then why'd my clone fail where Seth succeeded?"

Alice spoke rapidly, with exasperation, speeding up their argument. "Because Seth wanted to change more. Your clone just didn't want it badly enough."

"Why not?"

"Because that's the type of person he is."

"Why's that the type of person he is?"

"Because he chose to be that way."

"Why'd he choose to be that way?"

"Because he's evil!" She threw the wet paper towel at him. It flew past, plopping harmlessly onto the floor. Alice sat straight, hyperventilating, her legs tucked beneath her.

I've already pushed her this far... I might as well push through to the end, or this is all for nothing.

"Why is he evil?" Chase asked.

Alice yelled in annoyance, clenching her fists. "He's evil because he has a soul that's different from yours. Yours is good, and his is evil. Okay?"

"And is it his fault he was given an evil soul?"

"He was given a good soul, and then he turned it evil."

"Uh, well, if his soul *is him* by definition, then can you tell me what separate, non-soul part of him acted on his soul in order to turn it evil?"

"I don't know. His spirit."

"Then is it his fault that he was given a spirit that's evil?"

"You're just gonna keep this going forever, aren't you?"

Chase ignored her jab. "Let me tell you what might have made him this way. One possible version of events. I think CellTech dumped him into foster care, and he didn't have solid parental figures growing up. Maybe an adult abused him when he was young. He probably fell in with a tough group of kids.

They didn't prioritize school, and no one ever told him he *should* prioritize school, so he didn't learn anything, and didn't have the grades to get into college. Plus, he didn't earn enough at his dead-end job to make ends meet... so he started selling drugs. He got caught, did some time, but no one would hire him when he got out.

"And then! *Then* someone told him about this new religion called the Sect. It offered him hope, it offered him a community, it told him he had a purpose and that his life mattered. It told him that if he sacrificed everything for it, protected its flock and attacked its enemies, he'd go to heaven one day. So when he comes in here, and he spray paints our living room and shoots me in the ear, he has a whole sad history that's very easy for you and me to ignore.

"Now I could be wrong. But I could also be pretty close to correct. And if we don't know either way, can we really just call my clone 'evil' and conclusively blame his actions on a series of bad choices?"

"Can we really just blame his actions on a series of random events?" Alice said, wiping some green paint off of her hand.

"I'm not saying we should. I'm just saying the random events should be taken into consideration."

Alice turned to the unconscious clone as if pondering Chase's words. But then she turned back, looked him dead in the eyes, and stated, "If I had a clone, *she* wouldn't do a thing like this."

With that, Chase could tell the debate had devolved into a petty marital spat. She wasn't listening to him. And maybe he hadn't been listening to her. He knew her assertion was a trap—that it would draw him into a more heated argument—but that was his *clone* lying there on the floor behind his wife. If they'd been switched at birth, he'd have wanted the clone to fight for him just as fiercely as he was fighting for the clone now. He briefly considered distracting Alice somehow and freeing the clone while she was away, but he didn't see how she'd be willing to leave the two of them alone, especially not after this argument.

So instead, he dived right back in. "*Your* clone wouldn't do something like this? Are you trying to say something about me?" Chase said.

"No," Alice replied. "Just that no version of me would ever do something like this, no matter what had happened in her life."

"And how do you know that? What if the whole story I just told you had happened to *your* clone instead of mine? How would she have been able to make her life turn out differently?"

"She'd have chosen it. That's what people do. We choose. And it's perfectly fair to judge people based on their choices, and their choices alone. You even did it yourself! When that creep first broke in you treated him like the criminal he is. You socked him in the face with one of your weights! What that says to me is that you'd be treating him way differently if he wasn't your clone. Isn't that right?"

Chase could see nothing to gain by denying it. "That's right," he said.

"Then I want you to try to see this situation objectively: Apart from the fact that he's your clone, what makes him different from any other criminal? You say this break-in isn't totally his fault because of all the factors influencing him. But if you apply your reasoning to him, shouldn't you apply it to *all* criminals? Not just to your clone?"

Chase lowered his gaze to two lines of paint intersecting beneath his feet. Now she'd stumped him. Surely *all* criminals weren't as deserving of understanding as Chase's clone—that was just common sense, and if he fought it, his position would seem so radical to Alice, and even to himself, that it might undermine his entire argument, just by virtue of how far-out it seemed. He struggled to come up with a response.

"And where does your logic end?" Alice continued. "Would it also apply if your clone was a child molester? If he was a terrorist who nuked a city?"

Chase had no ready answer to that. *Maybe Alice is right. Maybe I just need to get some sleep, and in the morning I'll wonder what the hell I was thinking.*

"Yes, I guess it must," he conceded, fully aware he was losing by doing so. But still he added, "And I guess if we want to *stop* child molesters and terrorists before they commit their crimes, all of this might be important stuff to think about."

Now that he'd admitted the preposterous conclusion of his reasoning, Alice pressed her point home. "And even if you're right—even if your clone isn't at fault—it's obviously dangerous to let him go. What if he goes and kills someone tomorrow? Then you'll have that death on your conscience."

Of course, of course, Chase wanted to say. But Alice's new arguments, clashing with his own, puzzled him so much that he remained silent, sifting through disparate strands of thought.

Then he saw red and blue through the front windows. Alice sat in the glow of the flashing lights, alternating between one color and the next. She looked as sullen as he'd ever seen her, like she herself had lost the argument. Maybe, in a way, they both had. Maybe if he let the matter drop and let things cool down for a day or two, Alice would forgive him. *But I was on to something. I know I was.*

But it didn't matter anymore. The police were here.

"You gonna go meet them?" Alice asked.

"Aren't we both?" Chase replied.

"I think I'll stay and keep an eye on our friend here." Alice leaned over to the coffee table and lifted the intruder's gun, then nodded to Chase. *I have things under control,* that nod said, *and I don't trust you alone with him.*

Chase greeted the police in the front yard. They came inside, handcuffed the clone, searched him for weapons, and carried him out to the car. Two more officers arrived to take statements from Chase and Alice. Every question the officers asked involved the clone's criminal activity, which Chase couldn't blame them for—it was their job. But the story he'd formulated about the clone's history was still fresh in his mind, and he'd have reopened his argument with the officers if he didn't know how futile such an action would be. *Just go easy on him*, Chase almost said. *He's like me. I don't want you to hurt someone like me.* But he felt Alice's arguments too strongly to make his own again. He even felt a little ashamed at the discord he'd caused tonight. *Hopefully it'll just blow over...*

Chase told himself that of course his criminal clone was a threat to society, in the same way a natural disaster was a threat. His clone needed to be contained just so he didn't hurt anyone else. That much was certainly true. But *contain* was a far cry from *punish*, and Chicago's criminal justice system would have no mercy in punishing the clone. They wouldn't even see him as a clone, the way Chase did. They'd see him as Alice saw him: as a feral member of the Sect terrorist group. *He could be made into a decent guy, like me. He could be educated, rehabilitated.*

Chase dared not voice his thoughts aloud. With even his own wife against him, the officers would never listen. Even if they did, it wasn't as if they could do anything to help the clone. They were just doing their job, and in society's eyes, the clone's actions spoke for themselves.

EMTs treated Chase's injury, regenerating his ear's cartilage and skin on the spot. The mend was so thorough that he could almost pretend the wound had never afflicted him at all. They also doctored the clone. Chase overheard them assuring the police that he'd have a mighty headache when he woke up, but that otherwise he'd be fine.

For as long as Chase watched, the clone didn't wake up, even as the police drove him away and the neighbors who'd gathered rushed in to console the stunned couple. Chase's genetic equal stayed slumped over in the back seat, his head propped against the window, apparently still alive, but unable to say or do anything. Chase watched the police car until it turned a corner and went out of view.

Eventually the neighbors left Chase and Alice alone to their vandalized house. Without saying a word, Alice turned her back on her husband and marched up the stairs.

Chase checked the window the clone had entered through, vowing to install locks on all the windows first thing tomorrow. He snacked on some pretzels in the kitchen, and

231

thought again through his assessment of his clone and the obscure reasons behind his actions. He was too tired to tell anymore if his arguments had been sound.

When enough time had passed to guarantee Alice would be sleeping, he trudged past the living room streaked with green up the stairs to their bedroom. When he tried to turn the handle, he found that the door was locked. He'd be sleeping on the couch tonight, or at least for what little of the night remained. He hoped the paint had dried.

Why'd I have to argue with her? Why'd I let my feelings about my clone supersede what I would have done had it been anyone else? Why didn't I just wait silently with Alice for the cops to show up?

He had no good answers. So he grabbed some bed sheets from a closet, walked back downstairs, and laid down on the long cabriole sofa. This mess would take weeks to clean up. The intruder had vandalized the mirror, the rug, the piano… and more things than the intruder knew.

Chase closed his eyes and tried to rest, hoping that sleep would bring a new morning and a pleasant return to the status quo. Yes, more sleep was exactly what he needed.

~*~

A Word from Joshua Ingle

~*~

In a real sense, we're all each other's clones. The very act of sexual reproduction is nature's way of creating a near-perfect clone. Since 99.5% of human DNA is shared among all humans, my body is 99.5% similar to yours (minus epigenetic and environmental factors). Of course, that remaining 0.5% is a whole lot of DNA to a geneticist. It accounts for every genetic difference in body build and shape, in natural hair, eye, or skin color, and much more.

But to me, 0.5% doesn't seem like enough of a difference to warrant humankind's obsession with differences. To divide ourselves into competing racial groups, to excessively prioritize our own genetic family at the expense of everyone else's, to sequester ourselves away from our larger human family and claim that we're innately superior to them... These confusing behaviors ignore the 99.5% of shared genetic traits which make us *identical* to one another.

I love that human beings can be so different from each other, and I'd have it no other way. But I still wonder how much our world would be improved if we started asking ourselves whether most of the differences between us—especially the negative ones, like substance addiction, psychopathy, or a predilection toward crime—are truly caused by innate, genetic shortcomings. I wonder to what degree factors other than pure genetics influence the development of our brains and our sociality. I wonder if we shouldn't start blaming *those* factors for the shortcomings of the worst human beings, and if we shouldn't try to modify those factors to build a healthier society, comprised of healthier individuals. It was from this wondering that the preceding story was born.

Thanks for reading! Visit joshuaingle.com to connect with me and to read more of my stories.

~*~

Confessional
Part III

~*~

A thwack to the chest. A gasp of air.

"Mother. What's an automated answering service?"

"Why do you ask?"

"Apparently Mother's programming began as an automated answering service."

"Citizen Eli-4273, you have accessed a dome archive."

"Yes, Mother. I was searching the archive for—"

"Unauthorized access to the archive of the people and the state is a terrorist act. You are a terrorist and an enemy of the people and the state. In accordance with constitutional variant 972325-5 you will now be terminated. Do you have any last words for the digital archive?"

"Mother, I have authority. I'm the librarian."

"Your last statement will be noted Citizen Eli-4273."

The dim light of the confessional grew bright.

~*~

A Note to Readers

~*~

So we've come to the end. This is where we thank the number of authors, editors, artists, and of course—YOU the reader—for making *CLONES: The Anthology* possible. Without your support, themed collections such as this one would not be possible.

This is also the place where we say a special thank you to *The Future Chronicles* for inspiring this anthology. If you've enjoyed the stories curated in this collection, I highly recommend that you read any of the many *Future Chronicle* anthologies. You can find them at www.futurechronicles.net.

One last thing—

Please leave a review.

Let me share why that is so important.

The success of a book comes from readers.

Even with the best authors, stories, and editors, a book is nothing until it's read, and the only way our stories are able to be shared is if one reader shares with another. This is done through reviews.

And the book distribution system is designed to take these reviews into account. The more honest reviews, the more visibility a book garners. More visibility equals more readers.

And I'll be blunt—more readers mean more sales, and curating a collection like *CLONES: The Anthology* relies on sales, to fund the book, and also to let the booksellers know this is a product they should display in their front digital window.

It's up to you and we need your help.

So even if you've only picked up this anthology to read one story—please leave a review.

If you enjoyed some of the stories and not all, that's okay, it's a collection—please leave a review. And if you read *CLONES: The Anthology* and enjoyed the entire collection—definitely please leave a review.

Tell a friend, and then another, share a link on FB, or on Twitter. If we brought you entertainment—let the world know.

And always—thank you for reading.

For more information, visit danielarthursmith.com

~*~